LADY ANNA'S FAVOR

LADY ANNA'S FAVOR

PROPER ROMANCE

KAREN TUFT

SHADOW
MOUNTAIN
PUBLISHING

Library of Congress Cataloging-in-Publication Data

Names: Tuft, Karen, author.
Title: Lady Anna's favor / Karen Tuft.
Other titles: Proper romance.
Description: [Salt Lake City] : Shadow Mountain Publishing, [2025] | Series: Proper romance | Summary: "In war-torn France, Lady Anna Clifton seeks her missing brother while battling a detestable cousin for her family's estate. The Duke of Aylesham offers his yacht for her quest, where she meets—and clashes with—James, the duke's diplomatic associate. As James learns more of Lady Anna, the two unravel her brother's mystery and find unexpected love amid perilous adventures."—Provided by publisher.
Identifiers: LCCN 2024022930 (print) | LCCN 2024022931 (ebook) | ISBN 9781639933037 (trade paperback) | ISBN 9781649333087 (ebook)
Subjects: LCSH: Man-woman relationships—Fiction. | BISAC: FICTION / Romance / Historical / Regency | FICTION / Romance / Clean & Wholesome | LCGFT: Romance fiction.
Classification: LCC PS3620.U37 L33 2025 (print) | LCC PS3620.U37 (ebook) | DDC 813/.6—dc23/eng/20240612
LC record available at https://lccn.loc.gov/2024022930
LC ebook record available at https://lccn.loc.gov/2024022931

Printed in the United States of America
Publishers Printing

10   9   8   7   6   5   4   3   2   1

To Stephen, my hero and eternal companion.

REGENCY MAIN CHARACTERS BY FAMILY

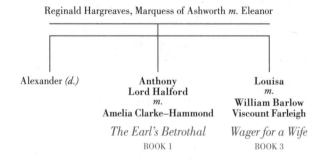

Reginald Hargreaves, Marquess of Ashworth *m.* Eleanor

Alexander *(d.)*

Anthony
Lord Halford
m.
Amelia Clarke–Hammond

The Earl's Betrothal
BOOK 1

Louisa
m.
William Barlow
Viscount Farleigh

Wager for a Wife
BOOK 3

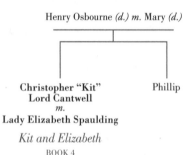

Henry Osbourne *(d.) m.* Mary *(d.)*

Christopher "Kit"
Lord Cantwell
m.
Lady Elizabeth Spaulding

Kit and Elizabeth
BOOK 4

Phillip

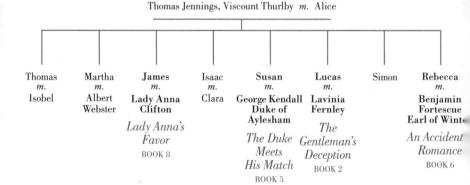

Thomas Jennings, Viscount Thurlby *m.* Alice

Thomas
m.
Isobel

Martha
m.
Albert
Webster

James
m.
Lady Anna
Clifton

Lady Anna's
Favor
BOOK 8

Isaac
m.
Clara

Susan
m.
George Kendall
Duke of
Aylesham

The Duke
Meets
His Match
BOOK 5

Lucas
m.
Lavinia
Fernley

The
Gentleman's
Deception
BOOK 2

Simon

Rebecca
m.
Benjamin
Fortescue
Earl of Wint

An Accident
Romance
BOOK 6

MAIN CHARACTERS BY BOOK

Character also appears in:

1 *The Earl's Betrothal* ✿

- ♣◆ **ANTHONY Hargreaves, Earl of Halford**
- ◆ **AMELIA Clarke-Hammond**
- ♣ Louisa Barlow, Lady Farleigh
- ♣ William Barlow, Viscount Farleigh
- ♣ Alexander Hargreaves *(d.)*
- ◆★❀✳✤ Lady Walmsley
- ♥ Lucas Jennings
- ♣◆ Lady Elizabeth Spaulding

2 *The Gentleman's Deception* ♥

- ✿ **LUCAS Jennings**
- **LAVINIA Fernley**
- ★✳✤ James Jennings
- ★✳✤ Susan Jennings
- ★✳✤ Rebecca Jennings

3 *Wager for a Wife* ♣

- ✿ **WILLIAM Barlow, Viscount Farleigh**
- ✿ **LOUISA Hargreaves**
- ✿ Anthony Hargreaves
- ✿ Alexander Hargreaves, Earl of Halford
- ◆★✳✤ George Kendall, Earl of Kerridge, heir to Duke of Aylesham
- ✿◆ Christopher "Kit" Osbourne, Lord Cantwell
- ✿◆ Lady Elizabeth Spaulding

4 *Kit and Elizabeth* ◆

- ✿♣ **CHRISTOPHER "KIT" Osbourne, Lord Cantwell**
- ✿♣ **Lady ELIZABETH Spaulding**
- ✿★✳❀✤ Lady Walmsley
- ♣★✳✤ George Kendall, Duke of Aylesham

5 *The Duke Meets His Match* ★

- ♣◆✳✤ **GEORGE Kendall, Duke of Aylesham**
- ♥✳✤ **SUSAN Jennings**
- ✿◆✳❀✤ Lady Walmsley
- ♥✳✤ James Jennings
- ♥✳✤ Rebecca Jennings

6 *An Accidental Romance* ✳

- **BEN Fortescue, Earl of Winton**
- ♥★✤ **REBECCA Jennings**
- ♣◆★✤ George Kendall, Duke of Aylesham
- ♥★✤ Susan Jennings Kendall, Duchess of Aylesham
- ✿◆★❀✤ Lady Walmsley
- ♥★✤ James Jennings

7 *Lady Walmsley's Christmas Surprise* ❀

- ✿★◆✤ **Lady WALMSLEY**
- ✿★◆✤ **Jacob FOSTER**

8 *Lady Anna's Favor* ✤

- ♥★✳ **JAMES Jennings**
- **Lady ANNA Clifton**
- ♣◆★✳ George Kendall, Duke of Aylesham
- ♥★✳ Rebecca Jennings
- ♥★✳ Susan Jennings
- Phillip Osbourne
- ✿★◆✳ Lady Walmsley

CHAPTER 1

March 1814

It had been an exceedingly difficult winter, and Lady Anna Clifton was grateful it was coming to an end. Papa's injured hip and leg had ached terribly from the cold all winter long. He also seemed to be growing weaker, especially after they'd received the terrible news that her eldest brother, John, had died of pneumonia while visiting his in-laws with his wife, Sarah, and their little daughter, Betty, for the Christmas holidays.

"I must write to Avery," Papa had said at the time. "Avery must return home immediately. I must have my heir here at Clifton Hall. Not in the military. *Here.*"

Ever since that dreadful news, Papa had spent most of each day seated in his favorite chair next to the fireplace in the parlor, a blanket over his lap and a shawl around his shoulders, napping on and off throughout the day, waiting for Anna's only other brother, Avery, to write or return.

But now it was March, and spring seemed to have arrived at last, and today's sunny weather gave Anna hope—hope that Papa's health would improve despite his not having received any word from Avery. She would try to convince Papa to take a turn about the garden with her; it would undoubtedly do them both good. She hadn't seen him since luncheon and had noticed he hadn't eaten much again today, which had become a common thing as of late and was another source of worry for her.

Anna rapped on the closed door of the parlor. "Papa?" she said softly. If he was napping, she didn't want to awaken him. "Papa?" She opened the door to peek inside when she again received no answer.

He sat quietly facing the fireplace in his chair, draped in his shawl, his hands resting on the lap blanket. His head rested against the back of the chair, and his eyes were closed.

"Papa?" Anna said again, approaching him.

He didn't move.

The mail must have arrived while she'd been in her room reading after luncheon, for there were a few letters on the small table that stood next to Papa's chair. In fact, there was a letter on Papa's lap, under one of his hands . . . and then Papa's stillness hit Anna like a bolt of lightning.

"Hastings!" she cried out. "Come quickly! Sparks! Oh, Papa!" She collapsed to her knees before her father and clutched his hands. They were cold.

"No, Papa!" she breathed. "Don't leave me!" She lowered her head into his lap, and her entire body shook with sobs.

"What is it? Oh dear!" Hastings, Papa's steward, said behind her. "I shall call for the doctor immediately, Lady Anna."

"It's too late," she cried. "It's too late."

She barely remembered the next few hours—the arrival of the doctor and the vicar, her personal maid, Mary, urging her to drink tea, the undertaker speaking with Papa's valet, Sparks. It was all a blur.

Except one notable thing was *not* a blur. The letter that had been on Papa's lap, trapped there by his hand, had apparently been the last thing he'd seen, and Anna was convinced it was the cause of his death. She read the missive once more.

> *To the Right Honorable Earl of Westbury,*
>
> *It grieves me to inform you that your son, the Honorable Lieutenant Avery Clifton of the 61st Regiment of Foot, was wounded in battle near Orthez, France, while serving his country in the war against Napoleon and is currently listed as missing. We shall inform you should any further information reach our local headquarters. Our men of the 1/61st Regiment do honor to us all. May God be with your son and with you.*
>
> *Yours, Major Jonathan Wilde, retired*

Over the next few days, Anna went through the motions as others asked for advice regarding how she wished to have Papa laid out for viewing by their neighbors and friends in the village, choosing hymns for the funeral, and what the menu for luncheon should be following his burial next to Mama in the churchyard at Clifton Cross. Meanwhile, Mary set about adding more black to the wardrobe Anna had been wearing since John's passing.

Anna's grief was a heavy dullness in her heart; she felt detached from everything and everyone around her. She had lost her entire family, except, perhaps, by the slightest of chances, her brother Avery.

She had no one.

"I'm sorry to bother you on the day of Lord Westbury's funeral," Hastings said after the last of the guests had finally left.

"What is it?" Anna said. She was so exhausted she could barely move from her seat at the table, where Mary had brought her a fresh cup of tea. Right now, she was only staring at the cup, unable to garner the strength to pick it up.

"Mr. Wheeler, your father's solicitor in Bristol, has just arrived," Hastings said. "I felt it my responsibility to inform him of Lord Westbury's death. I hope you don't feel that was presumptuous of me, but as his steward—"

"Of course I don't believe it was presumptuous," Anna said. "Please have Mr. Wheeler shown to the parlor, and see that tea is arranged."

"Certainly, but as he is your father's solicitor, perhaps meeting in your father's study may be more appropriate?"

"Whatever you think best, Hastings," she said dully.

She took a few minutes to collect herself before going to Papa's study. Both Mr. Wheeler and Hastings were already there and rose from their chairs when she entered the room.

"Lady Anna," Mr. Wheeler said, bowing over her hand. He was a sturdy man with graying temples and florid cheeks. "A pleasure to make you acquaintance, albeit under such sad circumstances."

"Thank you, Mr. Wheeler," Anna said.

Hastings then gestured that she should sit in Papa's chair across the desk from the two gentlemen. How could sitting in Papa's chair feel both soothing and agonizing at the same time?

"First, Lady Anna, I should like to offer my condolences on the passing of your esteemed father, Lord Westbury," Mr.

Wheeler said. "He was the finest of gentlemen, and we enjoyed a long association. Forgive me for not arriving in time for the services today and then imposing upon you this afternoon. I'm afraid I had urgent business to attend to before leaving Bristol, and must also leave as soon as our meeting is completed, for the same reason. I am sure you understand."

"I'm sure you are exceedingly busy," Anna managed to say.

"It is the way of things," Mr. Wheeler said. "But when Mr. Hastings wrote, informing me of Lord Westbury's death, combined with the passing of your brother John, I felt it imperative that I speak to you in person as soon as possible." He pulled his handkerchief from his pocket and dabbed at his forehead before setting a folder upon Papa's desk and opening it.

"You understand, Lady Anna, that I must consider the fact that as your brother Avery has been reported wounded and missing, I must contact the individual to whom your father's properties are next entailed, in the event of his and your brothers' passing. Neither your father nor I, for that matter, could have conceived of a situation wherein he and both of his sons would perish in such an untimely manner. Adding a third party to the entail was merely an additional precaution taken by your father when Avery purchased his commission and John had no son of his own to inherit. But as such is now the unfortunate case, I have sent word to your cousin, Mr. Ambrose Harcourt-Clifton, that the entail is passing to him. I expect he will arrive within a fortnight and will be staying as the new owner."

Anna's heart leaped into her throat. Lose Clifton Hall? To *Ambrose*, her horrid, distant cousin? But what of Avery? "Mr.

Wheeler, forgive me," Anna said, surprised she could speak at all. "But isn't it rather hasty to presume that Avery is dead? That was not what the letter from the regiment said."

"My dear girl," Mr. Wheeler said, shaking his head and looking sorrowful. "After receiving Mr. Hastings's letter, I called in at the regiment's Gloucester headquarters before traveling here, which was partly why my arrival was so poorly timed. They have no further information on your brother or his whereabouts. You cannot know, Lady Anna, at your young age, what I know about life and the ravages of war. If your brother Avery has been wounded and reported missing, it must be a foregone conclusion that he is dead. Medical aid on the battleground is meager. Death from infection to wounds and illness is rampant. I'm sorry to be so blunt, but I recommend you set your hopes aside and look to the future."

"But we can't be sure . . ." Anna trailed off, shaken by Mr. Wheeler's frank comments.

"I've dealt with several of these cases during my career," Mr. Wheeler said. "I'm as sure as I can be." He closed his folder of documents and rose from his seat, right as tea arrived. "I wish I could stay for tea, but I fear I must be on my way. Good day, Lady Anna, Mr. Hastings. I shall see my way out."

And then he was gone.

"I suppose we might as well not let the tea go to waste," Hastings said.

"Yes," was all Anna managed to say. She felt as though she'd turned to stone, but she mustered her strength and served the tea as she thought about Mr. Wheeler's words regarding looking to the future.

Whatever the future was, right now, it appeared only bleak.

"Glad to see you're in fine fettle this morning, my impetuous friend," James Jennings said when he met up with his associate Phillip Osbourne at Whitehall at ten o'clock in the morning. They had just returned from a diplomatic mission to Paris with their third colleague, the Duke of Aylesham, and were due to report at the Foreign Office to update the prime minister. Aylesham, blast him, had gotten ill on their way home and couldn't join them today.

"Naturally I'm in fine fettle," Osbourne replied. "I did not overindulge when we were out with friends last evening, and meeting with Lord Liverpool will be an easy undertaking after all we've experienced. We've met with enough of the royalty of Europe that I am well trained in decorum. You know that."

"Yes, but you do have a rather impulsive side, as you demonstrated only too well last evening," James said. "I am only looking out for the good of Britain." He grinned at his companion.

Osbourne laughed and patted James rather forcefully on the back, which made James laugh too. "Dancing with barmaids is hardly what I'd call impulsive. You could do with a bit more impetuousness in your life, Jennings," Osbourne said.

"I think not," James replied. "Especially while I'm saddled with you."

They both laughed again as they entered the eminently dignified Foreign Office building.

"The prime minister will see you now," Lord Liverpool's secretary said to them, his eyebrow raised, indicating he'd heard the lighthearted exchange between James and Osbourne. He directed them to Lord Liverpool's private office.

Osbourne cleared his throat and took on a more serious mien, which relieved James to no end. Osbourne could truly be impulsive at times, and now was not the time for that to occur.

"Gentlemen, please be seated," Lord Liverpool said. "I am most interested to learn what you have to tell me."

James removed a stack of documents from his satchel and set them on the desk in front of the prime minister. Lord Liverpool began skimming through them. "I take it you both realize how confidential these are," he said as he continued his reading.

"Absolutely, my lord," Osbourne said.

"It is a delicate balance, my lord, knowing what to say to whom and what to keep to oneself when discussing matters of war and unity among those fighting Napoleon," James said. "We err on the side of caution, always." He shot a look at Osbourne.

"Excellent," Lord Liverpool said. He remained silent as he perused the rest of the documents, so James and Osbourne stayed silent too. "This is all excellent news," Lord Liverpool said at last. "But there is still much to be done. And it appears many of the minor principalities, et cetera, et cetera, are still deciding which members of the Coalition will best see to their interests, including Great Britain."

"Precisely, my lord," James said.

"Which is why we are returning to Paris to rejoin Castlereagh as soon as possible," Osbourne said.

"Whatever information you wish us to take with us to the foreign secretary, we are your humble servants," James said.

"Excellent," Lord Liverpool said. He thumbed through some of the documents again. "I shall keep these safely stored in the Foreign Office, should they be needed further. In the meantime, I will outline my thoughts and send them in your personal care back to Castlereagh. When, precisely, do you expect to leave for Paris? I recognize that you have only just arrived."

"Within the week," Osbourne said.

"Very well," Lord Liverpool said. "I shall have my letters ready for you day after tomorrow. Will that suffice?"

"Yes, my lord," Osbourne said.

"I shall expect you in two days at this same time, then." Lord Liverpool rose to his feet, indicating that their meeting was at an end.

James and Osbourne offered bows of farewell and then left Lord Liverpool's office. They remained silent as they exited the Foreign Office and continued in silence until they were well away from Whitehall.

"You were expecting us to return to France so soon?" James said. "I promised to bring my youngest sister, Rebecca, to Town for her first come-out. And my other sister, Susan, is to be her companion."

"I shall return alone, then, as long as you follow as soon as you can," Osbourne said. "Especially with Aylesham so ill, it behooves us both to do what we can to assist Castlereagh through these initial stages of diplomacy."

"Very well," James said. "You make an excellent point. Now, how does a fine English breakfast at White's sound?"

"It sounds perfect," Osbourne said.

They hailed a hackney and headed straight to White's.

Anna awakened the morning following Papa's funeral having had a fitful night's sleep, and rang for Mary, who bustled immediately into her bedroom.

"Mary, some hot tea would be just the thing," Anna said, trying to adjust herself into a sitting position. "I've such a headache already, and the day has only begun."

Mary hurried over and assisted her and then plumped up her pillows. "I shall have Cook send up willow bark tea along with the regular," she said. "And some biscuits, which will settle nicely in the stomach."

"That would be perfect, thank you," Anna said.

After Mary left, Anna closed her eyes and, for the hundredth time, reflected on Mr. Wheeler's declarations. She could see nothing good in any of them.

Ambrose Harcourt-Clifton was next in line after Avery now, and Anna had no doubt the awful man had kept his eye upon the proceedings at Clifton Hall ever since word of John's passing had spread. He had probably watched them all like a hawk ever since Papa's accident eight years earlier, truth be told. Ambrose had made no secret of the fact that he desired the Westbury earldom and Clifton Hall and its assets, and the vile man was undoubtedly rubbing his hands together in glee that both John and Papa had passed. And now Mr. Wheeler had written to him that Avery was among the missing in France, too, and was even presumed to be dead.

"We cannot refuse him entry," Hastings had said. "Your father's entail dictates that Mr. Harcourt-Clifton inherits after John and Avery, so until proven otherwise, he is now the Earl of Westbury and owner of your father's estate."

"Cousin Ambrose," Anna said, nearly choking on his name. Their associations with this distant Clifton cousin were rare, thankfully, for her last encounter with him three summers ago had been particularly upsetting.

"What I would do with Clifton Hall, were it mine," Ambrose murmured as he intentionally walked closer to Anna as she sat reading in the dayroom. He picked up a small sculpture to inspect it before setting it back down.

"You would mortgage it to the hilt, I've no doubt, so it is a good thing it shall never be yours," Anna replied, not bothering to look up from her book. Her cousin, older than John and Avery by a handful of years, was a wastrel who had accrued great gambling debts, if what Anna had overheard Papa say to Hastings was correct.

"You're an impudent one, aren't you?" Cousin Ambrose said, sneering at her. He grabbed her face with one hand and then brought his own face close to hers, his foul breath unavoidable. "Such passion in a young lady," he purred. "And your sapphire eyes and blonde hair aren't hard on the eyes either. Perhaps I should marry you. That would at least secure your inheritance for me. I'm sure your dear papa has been generous to his only daughter."

"How flattering you are," she replied, trying to free herself from his grasp. She would have bruises along her jaw, she was sure of it. "No decent lady would have you, least of all me."

"I believe I could tame you easily enough, you little chit," he murmured. "The ladies find me pleasing, I'll have you know. I am not called Ambrosia for nothing." He pressed his lips firmly to hers in a forced kiss that felt an eternity before he released her.

Anna fled, staying as far away from him as she could throughout the remainder of his visit, not daring to tell Papa what Ambrose had done.

Anna couldn't stay in her beloved home with Ambrose taking ownership; it was abhorrent to think about. Yet leaving Clifton Hall, its memories, and its good people was also abhorrent. Mr. Wheeler was obviously not going to help, and Hastings's loyalty was to Clifton Hall's owner, not her, even if he wished it were otherwise.

She truly had no one.

"Here's yer tea," Mary said, arriving just when Anna felt beyond despair. "Hopefully this will lift yer spirits a bit, and then ye can tell me when ye wish to dress."

"I feel so alone, Mary," Anna said as Mary poured tea into a cup and added a lump of sugar before she handed the cup and saucer to Anna.

"That's understandable, me lady," Mary said. "Ye've lost yer family just like that." She snapped her fingers. "But ye're not alone, ye know. Ye've got me. Ye've got the entire staff—Sparks—"

It was true that Sparks seemed more like an uncle than a servant most days.

"And that whatsit lady in London . . . Lady . . ."

"Bledsoe. Lady Bledsoe," Anna replied, a small light dawning in her head.

"That's the one," Mary said. "The lady what sponsored yer come-out a few years back."

Lady Bledsoe. She'd been a good friend of Mama's, which was why she'd sponsored Anna. Perhaps Anna could travel to London to seek the advice of Lady Bledsoe. She set her tea aside. "Mary, I wish to dress quickly. And please tell Hastings I wish to speak with him."

She would travel to London. She had no home and no family unless she was able to discover what had happened to

Avery. It all hinged on finding Avery. Beyond making that decision, she had no idea what her plans would be—but she must do what she could for her sake, for Avery's, and for the loyal people of Clifton Hall.

She hurriedly dressed with Mary's assistance once the maid had returned from informing Hastings, and it wasn't long before Anna was in the sitting room with him. Sparks, her father's valet, stood by the doorway, looking worried. Mary must have said something to him.

That was something to address after her meeting with Hastings. She turned her attention to the steward. "I have decided to travel to London to seek the advice of Mama's friends Lord and Lady Bledsoe, who will have more current news as to the state of affairs in France and who, perhaps, can offer sources who can help me learn what has truly happened to Avery."

"Are you certain, Lady Anna?" Hastings asked, looking both concerned and a bit guilty.

"I am," she replied. "I feel this journey is imperative, after what Mr. Wheeler told us."

"I'm sorry about that, Lady Anna. Truly, I am. There are some household funds I can set aside for your travel, if you're certain about it," Hastings said.

"Thank you, Hastings," Anna said. She had pin money she'd saved over the last few years, but the additional funds from Hastings would go a long way to seeing to her needs. "I do understand your role as steward at Clifton Hall and your need to contact Mr. Wheeler. Please just pray that we find Avery."

"I certainly will do that, Lady Anna," he said.

"Thank you, Hastings," she said.

As they left the sitting room, Sparks drew her aside. "I confess, I were listening at the door, after what Mary told me. And I intend to go with ye," he said. "Yer papa would never forgive me if I let ye travel alone, a single lady such as yerself."

Anna was touched by his offer. "I'm grateful to hear you say that, Sparks," she said. Having Papa's beloved valet with her would give her the courage she needed to take this first step toward a solution to this awful set of circumstances. "Perhaps Mary might be willing to travel with us, too, for propriety's sake—and for my own personal vanity." She smiled, hoping she looked confident.

"What is that I just heard?" Mary said from behind Anna. Anna turned to see her, not realizing that Mary had been standing behind her all this time. "Ye're hoping I would travel with ye? I would have insisted on it, me lady."

It was settled, then, and Anna felt her burdens ease just a bit. They were to travel to London with the hopes that Lord and Lady Bledsoe could shed insight—or know someone who could—on where to go for information about Avery and his regiment.

Anna would add Lord and Lady Bledsoe to her prayers tonight.

CHAPTER 2

J ames had brought only one sister back to London with him after his quick visit home, as his youngest sister, Rebecca, had broken her ankle. The sister in London, Susan, was currently at the home of the elderly Lady Walmsley, who had offered to play hostess to both sisters while they were in Town.

James rapped on the door of Lady Walmsley's townhouse and then checked his pocket watch. Susan had sent him a note earlier in the day inviting him to dine with her at seven o'clock, stating she had news to share. What sort of news she could possibly be sharing, he had no idea, but then, such often seemed to be the case with sisters.

Lady Walmsley's elderly butler answered the door. "Good evening, Mr. Jennings," the man, Foster, said with a bow. "And welcome. Please, follow me."

Foster led James to the parlor.

"James!" Susan exclaimed. "I'm so glad you are here." She crossed the room and took both of his hands in hers, and he kissed her on the cheek.

That was when he realized that the two of them were not alone. Aylesham—*Aylesham?* —was standing in a corner of the room, watching him intently.

15

"I find I am not your only supper guest," James said.

"This is true," Susan said. "We are celebrating this evening."

"Celebrating," James repeated.

"Yes," Susan said. "Celebrating the fact that I am betrothed to the Duke of Aylesham."

"You are *what?*" James asked, his voice crescendoing on his last word. Certainly, he couldn't have heard her correctly.

"Betrothed to the Duke of Aylesham," Susan said.

"What have you done, Aylesham?" he asked. "You didn't even know my sister before this week. We were in France. It's incomprehensible! What are you up to?"

Susan patted James's arm. "James," she said, "is it impossible to believe that we discovered an affection for each other?"

"Quite frankly, *yes*, Susan, to put it bluntly," he said. He crossed the room and stared directly into Aylesham's eyes. "I don't know what is going on," he said, "but *by thunder*, I am going to find out. You're my *friend*, Aylesham, or at least I believed you to be. I will not have you abuse that friendship or take advantage of my sister."

"I'm not sure what should offend me more," Aylesham drawled, "that you believe I would dishonor our friendship in such a manner as you suggest, or that your low opinion of your sister's overall appeal should make me call you out in defense of her." He brushed past James to Susan, took her hand in his, and kissed it.

"You see, James?" Susan said. "You must simply accept that the Duke of Aylesham—George—and I have come to an understanding. Perhaps it seems sudden, but we are both adults who know our own minds. We wish to marry, and quickly too."

"How quickly?" James asked with a sense of foreboding.

"A week Monday," Aylesham replied.

"*What*?" James exclaimed. He began pacing the room, unable to stay in one place, trying to keep his agitation in check. "*A week Monday*? I can scarce believe what I am hearing! How are our parents and our brothers and sisters to attend on such short notice, Susan? And where will these supposed nuptials take place?"

"St. George's Hanover Square," the duke responded. "And there is nothing 'supposed' about it. As to your family, it is my understanding that your youngest sister is currently infirm, and a sister-in-law gave birth not long ago. Susan and I are in agreement that we marry now rather than later. I do not wish to go through the Season without my bride at my side, you see, nor do I wish to impose upon your family. We shall have a small ceremony, as I have no immediate family, and then we shall journey to Lincolnshire later in the Season to celebrate with one and all."

James heard Aylesham say the words, but all he could think about was the untimeliness of this sudden, suspicious betrothal. "Marry now and hold a family celebration in Lincolnshire later in the Season, you say?"

"Precisely," the duke said.

"You are in full accord with this?" James asked Susan.

His sister merely smiled. "I am. And it is my hope that you will stand in for Papa and give me away, James. I am not so girlish that I need such sentimental touches, but having you there in his place would be a comfort."

"Of course, dear sister." He opened his arms to her, and Susan stepped into them, and he wrapped his arms tightly about her. "I only want your happiness," he whispered in her ear, then added as he and Susan ended their embrace, "I am still suspicious. But as I love my sister and, more than that, I trust her intellect and her reason, I am suspending my suspicions for the time being to support her decision in this."

"Very generous of you," Aylesham said.

"Yes, it is," James retorted.

"Well, that's settled, then," Susan said. "There is much to do between now and Monday week. Now, if you both don't mind, I shall inform Lady Walmsley we are ready to dine. I myself am famished, I understand the illustrious Duke of Aylesham is in need of increased sustenance, and my brother is always hungry."

James pondered this unexpected wedding of his sister to his friend while they dined, and he somehow managed to avoid saying anything too discourteous for the remainder of the evening, for his sister's sake, if for no other reason. He respected Aylesham, even trusted his life to the duke, and vice versa, but this all seemed rushed, in James's opinion.

He couldn't imagine doing something that seemed so impulsive in nature himself.

⚬───◦◦───⚬

Anna, Sparks, and Mary arrived in London following a long coach ride from Clifton Cross after bidding farewell to Hastings and the others.

Hastings had tucked a rather large sum of money into her hands. "Keep this safe," he'd said. "We don't want brigands to see you as someone of wealth they can rob. I have informed Sparks to stay particularly vigilant, although the coach and men I hired are of good reputation. I simply wish for you to err on the side of caution." He had given her a concerned look.

"I will, I promise. Thank you, Hastings," she'd said.

And then they had entered the coach and waved farewell to the staff, who had all congregated outside.

Conversation between Anna and Sparks and Mary had been polite and a bit awkward at the beginning, but gradually, they had adjusted to being comfortable together in such a closed space for such long stretches.

Anna had learned more about Sparks's upbringing in Bristol, and Mary had shared anecdotes from her own childhood near Bath.

"I shall tell you what it was like growing up with two older brothers and no sisters," Anna said.

"I remember both as lads, me lady," Sparks said with a smile. "Lively and full of mischief. About the time I began working for yer father, it was."

"Yes," Anna replied. "I'm afraid I was no match for either of them when it came to climbing trees and such. But I learned to hold my own with them."

"That ye did," Sparks said with a nod.

"I only had sisters," Mary said. "It was marry or go into service—or both. But I weren't inclined to marry just to see to me welfare. Ye know what I mean, don't ye, me lady? Ye can't tell if a man is going to be caring to a wife or a harsh taskmaster."

Mary's remarks made Anna think of Ambrose. "One must certainly be careful," Anna said.

Sparks had been exceedingly helpful in seeing to their luggage and transport during their travels. They had stayed the first night in a coaching inn near Swindon and the second night in Reading, and had arrived in London early evening the third day.

It had been a long while since Anna had spent so much time in a coach, and she had been stiff and sore when Sparks had assisted her and Mary from the vehicle at the end of that final day. Thankfully, even though the Season had begun, she was relieved to find that the inn where they had stopped had a room available for her and lodging for Mary and Sparks in the servants' quarters.

Anna had slept better that night than she'd done since Papa had died, and first thing in the morning, she had sent a note to Lady Bledsoe, asking if she could call on her. Mary had arrived soon after with a plate of breakfast foods and hot chocolate and then had assisted Anna in washing and dressing.

They'd barely put the finishing touches on Anna's coiffure when there was a knock at the door.

"A letter for Lady Anna Clifton arrived just now," the maid at the door said to Mary when she opened the door.

"Thank ye," Mary said and then took the letter to Anna, who quickly opened it and read.

> *My dear Anna,*
>
> *I was delighted to receive your note and to learn that you are in Town. Of course you may call! I am sure there is much catching up we must do since you last stayed with Lord Bledsoe and me. I shall plan on you for a light luncheon at one, if that suits.*
>
> *With love, Lady Bledsoe*

Anna breathed a sigh of relief. She knew of no one else to whom to turn, and had Lady Bledsoe been out of town or indisposed somehow, which hadn't dawned on Anna until they had neared London, she wouldn't have known what to do next.

She arrived at the Bledsoe home at precisely one o'clock and was shown to the parlor, where she immediately found herself enveloped in Lady Bledsoe's arms and in the kind lady's familiar scent of sandalwood.

"Oh, my dear!" Lady Bledsoe said, moving Anna back from her so she could study Anna's face. "I see you are wearing mourning attire."

Anna immediately broke into tears at Lady Bledsoe's welcome. It was such a relief to have someone with whom she could share the burdens she'd been carrying. She fumbled for her handkerchief but was unsuccessful. "Papa is dead," she said at last, tears streaming down her face. "So is John. And the solicitor says we cannot keep my horrible cousin Ambrose from inheriting the title and properties while Avery is listed as wounded and missing."

She watched Lady Bledsoe frown and shake her head. "I scarcely know where to begin," Lady Bledsoe said. "Your father and your oldest brother both dead? And what is this about Avery? You must sit and start from the beginning. But before you do, with your permission, I believe I shall ask Bledsoe to join us."

Anna nodded her consent and then gratefully sat in the settee next to the fireplace while Lady Bledsoe rang for the butler and requested the presence of Lord Bledsoe.

"Ah, Lady Anna, such an unexpected surprise!" Lord Bledsoe said when he joined them in the parlor. He took her hand in his and placed a welcoming kiss upon it. Anna could see that his eyes were studying her closely. "What brings you to London?"

"She comes to us in a time of need, Bledsoe," Lady Bledsoe said. "Both her father and her eldest brother have passed away, and there appears to be a question as to whether her other brother lives or not."

"I am sorely grieved to hear of your losses, my dear. Sorely grieved," Lord Bledsoe said, shaking his head solemnly. "And what is this about the one in the military?" he asked. "Avery, wasn't it?"

"Avery, yes." Anna managed to retrieve her handkerchief from her reticule and dabbed away at her tears. "We got word that he was wounded in Orthez, France, and was missing. It was too much for Papa to take—" She wept even more.

Lady Bledsoe moved to sit next to her and placed her arm around Anna's shoulders. "Oh, my dear!"

"And the lawyer says we must presume he is dead and that Cousin Ambrose now holds the title and entail on the property. But I cannot simply let him . . ." Anna couldn't finish the sentence. It was too painful.

"What can we do, Bledsoe?" Lady Bledsoe asked.

"I can and shall make inquiries on your behalf tomorrow," Lord Bledsoe said with a firm nod of his head.

"I suggest that after luncheon, you return to your lodgings and rest," Lady Bledsoe said. "I can see how fatigued you are, my dear. And we shall all pray for good news on the morrow."

"Thank you both so much!" Anna exclaimed. She knew Lord Bledsoe would know individuals who would have military information and, more than that, would have access to these individuals that Anna would not.

She would pray even more earnestly than she had before, if such a thing were possible.

The following afternoon, Anna was invited to return to the Bledsoes' townhouse for tea. Anna was all pins and needles, wondering if they had already gotten further information about Avery or his regiment. It was odd to feel both fearful and hopeful at the same time.

"Lord Bledsoe is currently at Whitehall. He left early this morning," Lady Bledsoe said after pouring tea for Anna. "Quite early, in fact—said he wished to have whatever time the day allowed him to speak to as many people as possible on your behalf. He was greatly moved by your story, my dear, and vowed to see what he could learn."

Anna's eyes welled with tears. "Oh, Lady Bledsoe! I cannot thank you both enough for your kindness to me!" She truly was moved that Lord Bledsoe would dedicate an entire day to pursuing information for her.

"It is why I invited you over again today," Lady Bledsoe said, patting Anna's hand. "I expect he should be arriving home shortly, and I didn't wish you to wait even a moment longer than necessary for any word he received."

It was as though the mention of Lord Bledsoe conjured him up, for Lady Bledsoe had barely spoken the words when he entered the dayroom, where they were taking tea. He sat in the chair next to Lady Bledsoe and heaved a sigh.

KAREN TUFT

His sigh, coupled with his downcast appearance, didn't bode well, Anna knew, so she prepared herself for the worst.

"Tea, my dear?" Lady Bledsoe said.

"Yes, thank you," he replied.

Lady Bledsoe poured milk and tea into the remaining empty cup on the tea tray and added two sugars. "What happened, Bledsoe?" she asked. "I told our Lady Anna about your errand today, and we are eager for you to tell us everything—after you've caught your breath and had a sip of tea."

Lord Bledsoe drank the entire contents of his teacup and then set it and the saucer aside. "I'm afraid there isn't much to tell," he said. "Essentially, lists of the deceased or wounded are forwarded to the War Office, but the ones they currently have on record don't hold much, if any, additional information from what is sent to regimental headquarters and the families of the soldiers. And the last correspondence that was received regarding Avery's regiment was essentially what you told us you received from the Gloucester headquarters, except for one thing: Avery's regiment relocated to the city of Toulouse after the battle at Orthez.

"The gentleman with whom I spoke," he continued, "also informed me that since Napoleon has abdicated his throne and has been exiled to the island of Elba, everything is in a tumult right now and is affecting the timely relay of military information. The only additional news they were able to share, I'm sorry to say, was that before Napoleon's abdication, there was some communication that Wellington had taken his own troops into battle while at Toulouse. Undoubtedly, your brother's regiment was involved in that battle as well." He shook his head sadly. "I'm sorry, my dear. I'd hoped to bring you better news."

24

Avery's regiment had fought in another battle, another city, following Orthez? Lord Bledsoe's information was discouraging and made Anna's search for Avery even more daunting.

Oh, Papa, she thought, *what shall I do?* Then aloud she said, "Thank you so much for your efforts, Lord Bledsoe. I truly cannot thank you and Lady Bledsoe enough for your kindness."

"There may be more yet we can do," Lady Bledsoe said with an encouraging smile—encouraging, that was, if one disregarded her worried expression. "Perhaps you should stay with us for a while. What do you say? More news may yet be forthcoming."

It was a generous offer, and Anna was tempted to agree to it, but staying with the Bledsoes might limit her in her search for Avery. They would try to act as mother and father to her, and while she longed for Papa, gone so recently, she needed the freedom to search the way she felt she should. She was determined to stand firm in this. "That is so kind of you, but I feel I must decline for now."

"Very well," Lady Bledsoe said, although she didn't look happy about it. "But know that you are welcome here without further invitation, day or night. Do you understand me?"

Anna gave Lady Bledsoe a hug and then leaned over and kissed Lord Bledsoe on the cheek. "Thank you both from the bottom of my heart," she said.

And then she left as properly but as swiftly as she could before she succumbed to tears right there in their dayroom or was talked out of her resolve.

She also needed time to ponder Lord Bledsoe's information on her own to determine what the next step should be.

After a restless night, Anna had come to a difficult conclusion: she must continue her search for Avery, and it meant traveling to France, specifically Paris. She felt she owed it to Lord and Lady Bledsoe to inform them of her plans after all their kindness to her, which was why she called on them as early as was acceptable that morning.

"I cannot be enthusiastic about this," Lady Bledsoe said. "I cannot imagine France to be a safe place to travel at present, even with the end of the war."

"If I were your guardian, I would forbid it," Lord Bledsoe added.

Anna knew there was good reason behind their objections. But it couldn't be helped. She had made up her mind. "I understand your concerns," Anna said. "If I thought there were any other way of retaining Avery's inheritance and saving our home, I wouldn't do this. But I am resolved. I want you to know I dearly thank you both for all you have done for me the past few days."

"We are always here should you need us," Lady Bledsoe said, squeezing her hand and then pulling her in for a very long hug.

After saying farewell to the Bledsoes, Anna returned to her lodgings and asked Sparks and Mary to join her in her room.

"I intend to travel to Paris," she announced to them. "I've concluded it is my only hope of finding Avery," she further explained when Sparks frowned and Mary's eyes grew huge. "If there are any in authority who might know of Avery's whereabouts, I believe they will be in Paris at present."

"But, me lady," Mary squeaked, "what do ye even know about France? I don't speak French, and I daresay I never heard you speak no French, neither."

"I truly hadn't expected it to come to this, and I understand if you don't wish to continue with me," Anna said, hoping she sounded convincing, for she dearly wished to have Sparks and Mary at her side, bolstering her courage by their presence.

Sparks shook his head somberly. "It be like searching for a needle in a bundle of hay, me lady," he said. "But I swore to yer father many a time after his accident that I would see to yer care when he couldn't. So, if ye be going to France, I be going with ye."

Mary's huge eyes, full of fear, turned to Sparks and then back to Anna. "If Sparks be willin', me lady, then so am I, even if the idea scares me mightily," she said.

Sparks grunted, which Anna took as approval of Mary's brave words. "Thank you both for being willing to go beyond what I could have imagined," she said, relieved.

With that decision made, they each took an assignment: Sparks's task was to learn the length of time it took to reach Dover, which inns they would encounter, and the typical availability of rooms. They would then need to search for passage across the Channel when they got there.

The next day, however, Lady Bledsoe sent a note to Anna, informing her that Lord Bledsoe had spoken to their acquaintance, the Duke of Aylesham. The duke owned a yacht, *Serenity*, currently moored at Dover, and he told Lord Bledsoe that it was sailing to Calais in a few days. He offered transport for "Lord and Lady Bledsoe's friends."

It was nothing short of a miracle, as far as Anna was concerned.

Anna's and Mary's assignment, therefore, became obtaining maps of France and a book or two about speaking French, so Anna could study them while they traveled to Dover to refresh what little French she'd learned as a girl.

The first bookshop they visited, The Gilded Rose, was a lovely shop that on any other occasion Anna would have enjoyed, as the books were chosen to draw in the ladies of the *ton*. They then went to a bookstore the shopkeeper at The Gilded Rose recommended called Temple of the Muses.

"Lots of books sold cheaply," the shopkeeper had told her. "Might have precisely what you're looking for."

The Temple of the Muses certainly had a lot of books. The store was the largest collection of books Anna had ever seen. In fact, the place was rather overwhelming.

"May I assist you?"

Anna drew her gaze away from shelves of books that reached well over her head to see a young man wearing an apron, smiling at her. "I hope so," she said. "I am looking for maps—specifically of France. Also, anything you may have regarding learning to speak French."

The young clerk looked surprised at her request. He quickly changed his countenance, however, and tapped his chin in thought. "We do have a fine collection of atlases and maps. Let me see what I can find. And our collection of books regarding the French language is on shelves in a back room—not precisely what is selling the most readily at the present, you understand. I shall return as swiftly as possible." He bowed quickly, and off he went.

Anna and Mary perused the shelves together while they waited for the clerk, looking at titles and reading the first paragraphs of several stories, and after not too long, the clerk returned with books in his arms.

"I found a rather good map of France, although it's a few years old," he said as he set it on the sales counter. "Also, here are a few French primers, although I daresay they may be too simple for your needs."

The map of France was precisely what she was looking for, which was the most important thing. The French primers were rather basic, but she decided on two that seemed to cover different approaches to the language. She paid for the books, and the clerk wrapped them in paper for her.

She and Mary returned to the inn to find Sparks already there, having ordered supper for the three of them to be sent up.

"The folks around here was helpful—helpful indeed," he said while Anna and Mary removed their cloaks and bonnets. "There's a coach house not far from here what hires out for private individuals, so to speak, if ye're willing to pay the cost. It'll take us all the way to Dover. I took the liberty of arranging for one of their coaches."

"Well done, Sparks," Anna said. "That is excellent news."

"Who would have thought someone like me would be on her way to France!" Mary said in not the most enthusiastic of tones.

Anna admitted to herself that she felt much the same. If she didn't feel such an urgent need to find Avery, she would never attempt this.

CHAPTER 3

While the others in Susan's wedding party ate and drank, shared stories and laughed, and generally celebrated this highly unusual wedding, James decided he'd done all he could and that his time would be better spent returning to France with the additional documents he'd received from the Foreign Office. He needed to ensure that the documents arrived safely as soon as possible, so rather than waiting until tomorrow to leave for France, James would depart now.

After the tension of the past week, he was actually looking forward to traveling on his own. He had spent nearly the last twenty-four hours before the wedding getting a surly and somewhat drunk little brother sober . . . and bathed and shaved and dressed. Simon had sulked and complained and growled throughout the process but had ultimately cleaned up nicely and had *almost* looked like the younger brother James remembered. But James's efforts had all been worth it when he'd seen the joy on his mother's and father's faces after Simon had arrived at St. George's with him, and when the utter surprise and delight had shone on Susan's face when she'd walked up the aisle at the church and spied Simon sitting with the rest of the family who'd actually been able to attend after all.

James bid farewell to the bride and groom, kissed his mother, shook his father's and brother's hands, and then made his exit.

Once he secured a coach headed to Dover, where he would sail on the duke's yacht to Calais and, from there, onward to Paris, he allowed himself to be lulled to sleep by the jostling over well-driven roads. Such roads didn't tend to bother James; in fact, he found them rather soothing.

He intended to enjoy these brief few days alone as he traveled back to Paris, having no responsibilities except to himself and no companions to take into account either.

It was a welcome respite, and James planned to make the most of it.

Anna could smell the salty English Channel even before she could see the water. The feel of the air had changed too. Here, near the coast, the brisk air felt clean and life-giving, unlike the smoky air common in London. Their coach rumbled along until a horizon of brilliant blue sea appeared. Its beauty lifted her spirits and gave her the tiniest bit of hope.

They finally arrived in the center of town and slowed as they approached an inn that appeared welcoming and amenable.

"I shall inquire about rooms," Sparks said as they drew to a halt.

"Thank you, Sparks," Anna said, grateful for his continued assistance.

Rather than enter the inn, however, Anna was of a mood to stretch her legs and breathe in the fresh air. The sun was shining in the late afternoon, and the citizens of Dover were still bustling about, seeing to the demands of their day.

Sparks returned swiftly. "We has rooms," he said. "Our bags is being taken there straightaway."

"Thank you," Anna said. "I believe I am going to walk a bit, though, now that we're here, and try to locate the Duke of Aylesham's yacht. I shan't be long."

"Are ye sure, me lady?" Sparks said, looking concerned. "Mary can go with ye, can't ye, Mary?"

"I can, me lady, if ye like," Mary said, although her actual expression conveyed the exact opposite.

"No, thank you, Mary," Anna replied gently. "Although you are free to join me if you wish. But I do not need a chaperone. Dover looks a friendly enough town, its citizens are about, and the sun is shining. A brief stroll by myself is something I have done many times, and you both look as though you'd rather eat and rest."

Mary looked sheepish. "Very well, me lady."

"As ye wish, then, me lady," Sparks said, not sounding convinced. He shot a slightly perturbed glance at Mary.

Anna smiled reassuringly at them both and then turned and walked determinedly down the main street of Dover toward the wharf.

James had made good time traveling to Dover. Aylesham always provided him and Osbourne with one of his coaches, and the duke had this time too. The coachman knew where *Serenity* was usually anchored and took James directly there.

James jumped from the coach and strode quickly toward the yacht once they arrived, and he spied Clegg on her bow pointing at something and speaking to one of the sailors on board.

James picked up his pace. "Ahoy, Captain Clegg!" he called.

Clegg turned and saluted as James reached the yacht. "Come aboard," Clegg called back.

James deftly boarded *Serenity*, holding fast to its railing. Once on deck, he brushed off his sleeves and took a deep breath—the first *free* breath he'd had in days. He enjoyed sailing, and the time spent on *Serenity* would feel like a true respite from the demands that had been placed upon him and from the hurried pace that had accompanied his arrival here in Dover.

"You be traveling alone this time, Mr. Jennings?" Clegg asked. He pulled a pipe out of his pocket and pushed a pinch of tobacco into the bowl, then lit it.

"That I am," James said. "I presume we can leave in the morning?"

"At first light," Clegg answered after a thoughtful puff on his pipe.

"Excellent," James replied. "It appears it should be decent weather for the trip."

"P'raps," Clegg said. "P'raps not. I feel a bit of a rumble in me bones. Nothing too terrible, mind, as far as weather. But the swells, now, they may give us a bit of a ride."

James had weathered worse aboard *Serenity*. They'd been through quite a squall when Aylesham had been so ill the last time they'd returned, and somehow, they'd all managed to survive—even Aylesham.

Something drew Clegg's attention to the dock behind James. "Will you look at that," he said. "There's a sight a man don't see every day."

James turned to see what Clegg was referring to. A beautiful young woman dressed in black stood on the deck, a hand shading her eyes as she scanned the pier. Shining blonde curls escaped her bonnet and fluttered in the breeze, and her figure was delightfully slim yet also rounded in all the right places. She was quite a vision.

Clegg whistled his appreciation. "Ye're a beauty, miss, and there's no denying!" he called, then puffed on his pipe and chuckled.

"Clegg," James hissed, hiding his mild amusement. "She appears to be a gently bred lady, not one of your light-skirts!" He practically launched himself from the deck of *Serenity* onto the dock toward the lady, only realizing after he did what a spectacle he must have appeared and wondering why he'd behaved so impulsively. He straightened his neckcloth and proceeded toward her with more dignity.

Blast, but he needed to collect his wits for reacting to this young lady in such a visceral way! "Allow me to apologize for Captain Clegg's comments."

"Why must you apologize for him?" she asked.

"Why are you on the docks of Dover unaccompanied, miss? It is obvious you are not of the working class," he said, unsure why her question had made him defensive. Up close, she was even more stunning: blonde, blue-eyed, all cream and gold, and as exquisitely lustrous as a rare pearl.

"I—" she began and then stopped. She looked over at Clegg, who was smoking his pipe and watching them, and then glanced around her. "I would prefer not to address my reasons for being here in such a public place. It is of a personal matter with the captain of the *Serenity*."

"That would be me, missy," Clegg hollered from his place on board. "How can I be of service?"

The young lady strode past James along the deck and then came to a standstill, looking about her as if to determine how to board the yacht. James, his curiosity piqued, followed behind her. "Allow me to assist," he said, offering his arm to her, which, surprisingly, especially after her pert question to him in reply to his apology, she accepted.

"There ye be, missy," Clegg said. "Our Mister Jennings has got you from dock to deck, as I like to say." He chuckled at his joke. "Ye can stow yer things in yer usual spot later if yer planning to sleep aboard, Jennings; ye've done it often enough. Now, who be ye, missy? And what do ye need with old Cleggy?"

"I am Lady Anna Clifton, daughter of the Earl of Westbury, or I was until he passed away recently." She pulled a folded letter from her reticule and handed it to Clegg, who handed it to James, as Clegg couldn't read much beyond maps.

James perused the letter quickly and then let out an exasperated breath. He recognized the writing immediately—Aylesham had signed it. *When* Aylesham had had the chance to speak to Lord Bledsoe on behalf of this lady, James couldn't fathom. "It is a letter from Aylesham, stating that you are to allow Lady Anna Clifton, personal friend of Lord and Lady Bledsoe, passage aboard the *Serenity* to Calais."

"What's that you say?" Clegg said, a look of incredulity on his face. Not that James could blame him; he felt exactly the same way. He couldn't imagine Aylesham—or Lord Bledsoe, for that matter—actually *approving* of this young woman traveling to France unaccompanied, let alone assisting her in doing so.

"It says you are to provide passage for me and my two servants across the Channel," Lady Anna Clifton said firmly, staring down Clegg. Brave lady, or perhaps *reckless* was a better word to describe her.

Clegg chewed on the stem of his pipe and glared at her. James stood ready in case he were needed to help one or the other avoid throwing fists. He knew Clegg was capable of it—although never against a lady—but Lady Anna Clifton had set her jaw and looked ready to do battle, if necessary.

Eventually, Clegg removed the pipe and clucked his tongue. "We leave at first light, Lady Anna Clifton. If ye're aboard, ye have passage. If ye're late, ye don't."

She visibly relaxed. "Thank you, Captain Clegg," she said on a sigh. "We shall be here, as directed."

She nodded her head in satisfaction, and then James, feeling somewhat dumbfounded, assisted her from the yacht and back to the wharf, then watched as she walked down the street before he returned to the yacht.

"That there is trouble," Clegg said.

"More than trouble, it's foolishness," James said.

"Can't say I disagree," Clegg said. "We be in for a rougher sea tomorrow than I thought, Jennings, and I isn't talking about the weather. I'm hopin' ye're ready."

"Her concerns are not my concerns, Clegg," James said. "Once we reach Calais, we'll be good and rid of her."

"So ye say," Clegg replied. He chewed on his pipe some more. "But I wager there be more rough seas ahead fer the lass—and fer you."

"Not a chance," James said emphatically, willing himself not to think about how the shiny pearl with her sapphire eyes had been a bit jarring to his senses when he'd first seen her . . .

He shook the thought away. He'd seen plenty of attractive ladies before. There was nothing special about this one. He would cross the Channel and be done with her.

Anna hardly slept all night.

She tossed and turned and rose from her bed and gazed out the window at the sea, a rolling void of blackness occasionally glittering from the light of the moon and that of a sailor with a lantern going about his business on the pier. It seemed a metaphor for her journey. Was that what she would be facing? A rolling void of blackness with little light to direct her on her way?

Eventually, she managed to doze a bit and then awoke with a start when a hint of the first light of dawn appeared. Relieved that the long night was finally over but panicked that Captain Clegg would leave without them, she arose and quickly went about her morning ablutions before donning her sturdiest traveling gown for the voyage to France, while Mary packed her valise. Anna had barely finished dressing when there was a subtle knock at the door. It was Sparks.

"Are ye ready, Lady Anna?" he whispered through the door.

"I am," she said.

"Allow me to take yer luggage, then," Sparks said. "They're already serving breakfast in the dining room. They be used to early risers here."

"Thank you, Sparks." Anna opened the door wide for him, grabbed her cloak and reticule, and left Sparks to his task. A bit of breakfast would certainly be the best way to face the unknowns of the day.

The dining room wasn't terribly busy at this early hour, so the serving girl served Anna and Mary eggs, toast, and tea, which appeared to be the standard fare here each morning. Anna ate quickly, sipping her hot tea and dunking her toast in her egg, all the while thinking how grateful she was for Sparks's and Mary's willingness to accompany her on her search to find dear Avery.

Sparks arrived at their table. "I arranged with the inn-keeper to have the luggage taken to the *Serenity*," he said. "Ye said it was in our best interest if we arrive at the vessel early so the captain don't leave without us."

"We best go, then, if ye're finished, me lady," Mary said.

"Indeed," Anna said. She set her cup down and dabbed her mouth with her napkin before setting it aside and stand-ing.

The sun was peeking over the horizon and shooting rays of light through the misty morning air, and the walk down the main street to the pier was quiet, except for the occasional call of a gull.

When they arrived at *Serenity*, Anna saw Captain Clegg and his crew already on board, attending to the necessary tasks required before beginning the voyage, she presumed. She had no idea what those tasks might entail, as she had never been aboard a sailing vessel before. Hers had been a simple country life, even though Bristol was a port town and not far from their country estate. There had never been the need.

But there was now.

"Come aboard if ye be comin'!" the captain called out, waving at them.

Anna carefully boarded with assistance from Sparks, then Sparks returned to help Mary aboard. As Anna straightened her skirts, she saw a couple of young men she recognized from the inn bringing their luggage to the yacht.

"Good lads," the captain called out. "Ye can take those below deck. Ye know the way."

They nodded and went about their task.

"Welcome aboard," Captain Clegg said, addressing Anna this time.

"Thank you," she replied.

Mr. Jennings appeared from the opposite side of the cabin in front of them. His dark brown hair blew slightly in the wind, and he was taller than she remembered from yesterday. If she were a painter, she would paint him as he appeared right now.

What a frivolous thought! Anna shook her head to clear it.

"I wouldn't mind knowing names, me lady, if ye don't mind," Captain Clegg said. He puffed on his pipe and gestured toward Sparks and Mary with his head.

"I'm Sparks, and this here is Mary," Sparks said before Anna could reply.

It wasn't the most formal of introductions, but it seemed to satisfy the captain. "Now that we're all here and the niceties have been met, we can set sail," he said. "Ye can plan on a voyage of about three hours—or several hours, depending on the weather. But ye're not to worry—old Cleggy here has seen the *Serenity* through it all." He nodded and then turned from them and barked orders to his crew.

Three hours *minimum*—perhaps *much* longer, depending on the weather? Anna wasn't sure what she, Sparks, and Mary were supposed to do with themselves, so she looked about to see if there was anywhere to sit. She supposed she could get one of her books on speaking French from her luggage if need be.

"Perhaps we can sit there," she said to Mary, pointing to some benches alongside a cabin toward the front of the vessel, since neither the captain nor Mr. Jennings had offered an alternative.

Mary nodded, and they made their way along the deck to the benches, with Sparks following them, doing their best to avoid the sailors who raised the anchor and set the sails.

In the meantime, Mr. Jennings had moved to the front of the yacht and was staring out to sea, one hand shading his eyes from the rising sun as the crew eased the yacht away from the pier and toward the open waters of the Channel.

He was handsome, Anna thought again, with his hand shielding his face and his foot perched on a coil of rope, his expression serious. She was rather shaken that he had such an effect on her senses, and that she couldn't stop gazing at him.

She deliberately looked away and turned toward Mary, who was staring out at the sea, too, but with a grim look on her face.

Suddenly, the maid lurched toward the railing of the vessel . . . and proceeded to cast up her accounts over the side of the yacht.

"Mary!" Anna cried and dashed to her side.

CHAPTER 4

J ames wasn't the least bit surprised when Lady Anna Clifton's maid suddenly staggered to the deck railing and vomited. He had already suspected that they weren't accustomed to sea travel. The poor woman was still going at it.

He had been watching the waters of the Channel before they'd set sail. He'd traveled these waters enough now to recognize that, indeed, this wasn't going to be one of the calmer voyages, and he hadn't been referring to the other passengers. If he'd ventured a guess, not that he'd spoken to Clegg about it, he'd have predicted that this particular crossing would take at least three or four additional hours more than when the waters were at their calmest and most ideal.

Seven or eight hours of rising and falling seas, even in a heavy and sturdily made vessel such as *Serenity*, would test the resolve of many a passenger. James was exceedingly grateful that he didn't suffer from seasickness. He'd experienced only a tiny bit of queasiness on his first few crossings but had adjusted quickly and had no problem now.

The maid, however, was gripping the railing while Lady Anna stood at her side, looking rather pale herself, while the manservant ran off to beg a bucket from one of the crew.

Blast it all. James couldn't stay idly by and watch these people suffer the entire day. Begrudgingly, he walked over to the railing where the maid and Lady Anna stood. "May I be of assistance?" he asked.

Lady Anna visibly jerked at his question and spun to look at him. The shiny pearl was anything but this morning: her face was even paler up close, her large blue eyes dulled with worry and, he suspected, her own bout of seasickness. He watched her as she swallowed, undoubtedly doing her best to keep her own breakfast within her.

The maid still gripped the railing rigidly and stared out at the rolling waves. And then her entire body began to convulse as she retched once again.

Lady Anna laid a gentle hand on her back. "I don't know what to do," she whispered mostly to herself.

James took that as a "yes" in response to his question. "I'll alert Clegg," he said as the manservant returned with a bilge bucket.

"The cap'n knows already," the man said.

The maid shuddered and began to droop.

James surged forward to grab her by the arms and steady her, but the manservant beat him to the task.

"Never ye mind, sir," he said, wrapping his arm around the maid. "I've got her secure now."

"Thank you, Sparks," Lady Anna said.

Nice to meet you, Sparks; enjoy your voyage, James thought with not a small amount of irony. Then he said aloud, "The best place for your maid will be away from the sides of the yacht—being as close as possible to the true center of the vessel will minimize the movement that is upsetting her. Perhaps your man can get a bit of the fresh water stowed on board for her to sip. And I have heard that a bit of ginger root will help. I shall see if Clegg has any."

"Got that already, sir," Sparks said. "The ginger, that is." Sparks led the maid into the cabin at the center of the yacht.

Lady Anna followed behind them, as did James, both apparently wishing to be assured that the maid was settled.

"Thank ye," James heard the maid mutter. "Sparks, the bucket!" she immediately added.

"Oh dear," Lady Anna said.

Sparks placed the bucket in front of the maid, who proceeded to heave once again. "I told ye a breakfast wasn't the thing when taking a sea voyage, but ye wouldn't listen," he whispered to her in a scolding tone. "Mary always eats a hearty breakfast so she can work hard all day," he explained to Lady Anna. James doubted it would have made much difference.

Mary wiped her mouth with her handkerchief—not for the first time—and sighed deeply. "How long will this voyage last?" she asked.

"Most of the day, I'm afraid," James said. He truly felt sorry for the poor woman. Seasickness was a devil.

Mary nodded, looking utterly defeated. "Then, we shall do our best," she said, contrary to her expression.

The yacht rolled on a larger wave right then, making her moan. Sparks held the bucket up to her face just in case. She shook her head.

Now that they were in the main cabin, Sparks helped Mary onto the cot. It was Clegg's own cot, and James hoped Clegg wouldn't mind on this occasion. Once Mary was resting, she let out a groan and threw her arm across her eyes. Sparks set the bilge bucket near her face and then went to the end of the cot to remove her shoes.

"There, Mary; ye'll be more comfortable now," he said.

Mary nodded.

"Thank you, Sparks," Lady Anna said in a low voice. She perched on the side of the cot and took Mary's free hand in her own.

"Mary, here. Chew a bit o' ginger root. Apparently, eating it—just a bit," Sparks added when the maid grimaced, "can work wonders for the seasickness. I think it's worth a try, don't ye?"

She turned her face toward the cabin wall. Sparks looked at Lady Anna, who nodded reassuringly at him.

"I'm going to fetch ye some fresh water, Mary," Sparks said. "Ye need to keep drinking water. I learned that from me auntie a long time ago. But do try a bit o' the ginger first." He pulled a tiny cloth bundle from his pocket and held it out to Lady Anna.

"Sparks is right," Lady Anna said. She let go of the maid's hand to take the bundle from Sparks and unwrapped it. She broke off a piece of the ginger root and placed it in Mary's hand. "Just a tiny bit, Mary, to see if it works."

The maid sighed and shut her eyes, then put the small bit of ginger root into her mouth and slowly chewed.

"That's good, Mary," Lady Anna said in a soothing tone.

"I'll do what it takes," she murmured around the root she was slowly chewing. "Anything for ye, me lady, and for Master Avery."

"You are a dear," Lady Anna said.

"Thank you, me lady," Mary replied. And then she leaned over the cot and cast up her accounts again.

Anna broke off a bit of the ginger root and put it in her own mouth to chew. It was unexpectedly spicy and quite different in this form from when she'd tasted ginger before. Her stomach was unsettled, and although she had been spared the indignity of losing her breakfast in front of Mr. Jennings, it had been a close-run thing, especially in the company of poor Mary when she succumbed to her own bouts of seasickness. Anna swallowed down some bile along with the ginger root and put another piece in her mouth.

It was mortifying that Mr. Jennings should see them in such pathetic straits. It made her feel more vulnerable than she already felt.

"I wouldn't have you think you must spend the entire crossing playing nursemaid, Mr. Jennings," she said when her stomach settled the tiniest bit—perhaps the ginger root did work after all. "As you can see, Sparks and I are prepared to see to Mary's needs."

"Good," he replied. "I had no intention of playing nursemaid to any of you. Personally, I had expected that this voyage would be a solitary one; instead, I find myself being accompanied by novice sea travelers."

"We cannot help that we don't have your experience on the water," Anna said defensively.

Sparks returned with a flask bearing water. "Let me help ye sit up a bit, Mary," Sparks said. "A sip of water will do ye good." He crouched down and helped Mary sit up enough to sip a tiny bit of water from the flask.

"That's enough," Mary whispered. She lay back down.

"Here is more ginger," Anna said, handing her another small piece and trying to ignore the boorish man still in the cabin with them. Mary dutifully put it in her mouth.

"I daresay the ginger has helped me already," Anna added, sounding as optimistic as possible in order to give Mary hope.

"I shall be fine now that Sparks is here with water," Mary said.

It was a dismissal, if a servant could offer a dismissal to her employer.

"Come, Lady Anna," Mr. Jennings said. "I expect a bit of fresh air will do you good."

"I'll stay right here by her side, me lady," Sparks said. "Don't ye worry."

Anna sighed and stood. She broke what was left of the ginger root into two pieces and gave the larger piece to Sparks for Mary's needs.

"Come," Mr. Jennings said.

She hadn't realized how stuffy and foul-smelling the cabin had been until Mr. Jennings led her back out onto the deck. They stood facing the front of the ship, and Anna allowed the fresh sea air to fill her lungs. The yacht rolled on a particularly large swell, causing her to briefly lose her footing. Mr. Jennings put his arm around her to steady her—and lightning flashed through her, which was unexpected and incredibly alarming.

Bother. She broke off another tiny piece of ginger root and stuck it in her mouth. If there was one thing she would *not* do, it was cast up her breakfast with Mr. Jennings as her sole witness.

"Is the ginger helping?" he asked her. "I have heard that it can be a great reliever of seasickness but have never needed to use it myself."

"You're fortunate, then," she said, staring out to sea. She chewed and swallowed. He'd left his arm around her, and she could barely concentrate on anything but the feel of that arm.

"I am, yes," he replied. The yacht rolled on another largish swell, and his arm tightened around her shoulders, which only heightened her reaction to him and annoyed her further. "Perhaps we should sit awhile," he said. "If we're sitting, you might not feel as though you're being tossed to and fro."

"Very well," Anna said, suddenly feeling exhausted.

He escorted her to the benches by the main cabin and sat. He turned slightly toward her, most likely to make sure he could keep a watchful eye should he be needed to assist her across the deck so she could be sick, she thought begrudgingly. But as a result, his knee touched hers, and once again, lightning flashed through her.

It was utterly disconcerting to discover that her body could respond to him like that when she was anxious and queasy and overwhelmed and utterly provoked by him! Being attracted to Mr. Jennings was untimely and wholly inconvenient, especially when what she wanted desperately to do was dislike him.

When James had initially seen Lady Anna Clifton, with her gemlike eyes and her cream-colored hair, even while wearing mourning black, he'd seen a foolish young lady setting off on her own to mingle with the elegant elite gathering in Paris for celebrations now that Napoleon had abdicated. But right now, that same young lady was a mess. Her hair had come undone in the wind, and strands of it whipped about her cheeks, now a bright pink from the sea air rather than the ghostly pale they had been earlier. Her blue eyes were without any sparkle as she stared at the sea, and her traveling gown and cloak were the worse for wear after assisting her ill maid and were soiled in places as a result.

She continued staring at the water. James turned his face away from hers to look east, to his left. The sun had risen completely above the horizon now and shot rays of red and yellow and white across the blue of the water. "And even at our most bleak, the sun rises and gives us beauty and hope for a brighter day," he murmured mostly to himself.

"Do you consider yourself a poet?" she asked.

"Not at all, Lady Anna," James said. "But the sight of the rising sun fills me with awe and reminds me of good days in the past and better days to come."

"Better days to come," she echoed.

"Yes, better days." He took a deep breath. "I am curious as to why an unescorted lady such as yourself is attempting to travel to France in the first place," he said. "And who is this Avery person your maid mentioned?" It was an extremely personal question, and he knew it. But considering the present state of Lady Anna and her two servants, he felt an explanation was in order, especially since Aylesham had never offered the use of his yacht in such a seemingly frivolous manner before. Of course, Aylesham hadn't precisely acted as his usual self the past several days . . .

"Avery is my brother. He was reported missing and presumed dead in a battle in the south of France. I am searching for him, or for information about him, at least."

She was a lone female embarking on a fruitless quest in a strange land. James wasn't sure if he'd ever heard anything more ludicrous in his life!

"Indeed?" he replied. "You're in search of your brother who is somewhere in France. He may be dead, but he is definitely missing. Hmm. Allow me to ask: How good is your French?"

"Not very good," she admitted. "Although I have been studying it as much as possible since I've begun this journey."

James said nothing in reply, having no response fit for a lady's ears.

"After all the years of war, I presume there are many French people who are able to speak English," Lady Anna said. "I also presume the many English people who are currently in France can translate for me."

"Those are rather brave presumptions on your part," James said.

"I bought books to bring with me so I could educate myself as much as possible. I do know that I will encounter obstacles," she said, "but there is such a thing as faith, you know."

"Faith in a war," James mused aloud. "I daresay that is a rarity these days—although with Napoleon having actually abdicated, perhaps it is not a bad thing to remember. Even so, to traverse a foreign land in search of one man amongst thousands during war, or even in the aftermath of war, is essentially futile. And to expect to learn French in a few days is ambitious and not altogether sensible."

"Despite your encouraging words, Mr. Jennings, I intend on doing what I can to find my brother," she replied firmly, then turned her head again to look out to sea.

There was no point in arguing further. She was undeterred, for whatever reason. "You are chilled, Lady Anna. Perhaps we table this conversation for now and go back in the cabin so you can warm yourself."

"That is a good idea, Mr. Jennings," she replied. Then she stood and left him sitting alone on the bench.

Anna didn't think she had ever been more thankful in her life than when she realized the seas had begun to calm.

"Mary's asleep now, me lady," Sparks whispered when she quietly entered the cabin. Mr. Jennings had opted to remain outside on deck, thank goodness.

"I'm not asleep; I'm resting," Mary whispered in return. "And may God bless whoever discovered that ginger root helps," she added.

"Indeed, truer words were never spoken," Anna said while Sparks nodded his agreement. Her own stomach had mostly settled once she'd eaten some of the ginger.

She remained inside the cabin only long enough to take the chill out of her bones, as the room was still rather malodorous. "The sea is lovely now that the waves have settled," she said. "I believe I shall go outside and enjoy them."

When she left the cabin, Anna found Captain Clegg giving orders to his crew in between talking to Mr. Jennings.

She opted to stay away from them and crossed to the other side of the ship. Port? Starboard? She'd heard the words but had no idea which was which. She gripped the railing, breathing in the fresh air once again. The sun was higher in the sky now, and the light warmed her shoulders soothingly.

The yacht hit a large swell at that moment, and she lost her footing and stumbled, her arms flailing.

Strong arms wrapped around her waist, steadying and strong. "There now; you're safe," Mr. Jennings said, his low, masculine voice resonating through her entire body. His face was next to hers, and she was drawn to his intense brown eyes, his dark brows, the line of his nose, his lips . . .

He gazed at her, too, and his eyes dropped to her lips, his eyelids lowering—

"Ho, now! This be no time for romancing," Captain Clegg called from behind them, breaking the tension that had sprung up between them.

"Ridiculous," Anna muttered to herself.

Mr. Jennings moved slightly away from her, although his arms remained about her just enough to keep her steady. But she was unsteady for more than one reason now, which was utterly absurd after how dismissive he'd been about her reason for traveling to France.

"There's Calais, just on the horizon," Captain Clegg called, pointing toward the front of the boat. "It be time to let the others know we be putting to shore not long now. And ye can save all yer romancing for after ye disembark." The captain cackled after making his remarks.

"I should go tell Sparks and Mary," Anna whispered. She barely had any breath to utter the words.

"I shall accompany you," Mr. Jennings replied. "We both have belongings to collect."

"As you wish, Mr. Jennings," Anna said a little shakier than she would have liked.

He carefully removed his arms from around her and politely offered her his arm, which she reluctantly took. When she looked up into his face, she saw that the intensity of his eyes and the seriousness of his countenance remained.

And her heart, traitor that it was, raced, much against her wishes.

Having his arms around Lady Anna Clifton had sparked a fire within James that he truly had not expected. On a masculine level, the knowledge excited him. It also frustrated him.

He was not looking for a romantic entanglement of any kind, not yet anyway. Besides, while she was a beautiful lady, to be sure, she had chosen to travel through a foreign country without a proper male escort regardless of the danger she could encounter, and her foolhardiness annoyed him to no end and made him question the soundness of her mind. What sort of foolishness could possibly prompt a young lady such as her to undertake such a ludicrous journey to find her brother, as though she were more capable than the British Army?

He realized that the rolling swells they'd experienced earlier had calmed, and he breathed a sigh of relief—for all their sakes. He was tired and irritable; he'd wanted a peaceful, solitary voyage across the Channel, and it had been anything but.

She was not any of his business, he reminded himself.

But what kind of a gentleman would he be were he to abandon her right now, since he was traveling to Paris just as she was?

Blast it all. He knew what he had to do.

CHAPTER 5

Anna couldn't be more grateful to finally reach Calais and plant her feet on solid ground again. Once they had all disembarked from the yacht, Mr. Jennings offered to escort her, Sparks, and Mary to the inn where he and his associates usually stayed when traveling back and forth from France to England. She reluctantly accepted his offer.

Once he had made arrangements for them with the owner, Monsieur Blanc, Mr. Jennings took Anna aside. "Will you join me for a moment?" he asked.

Anna was tired, her clothes stank, and all she wished to do was change into something clean and then rest. "Very well," she said instead, then chided herself for not telling the irritating man no.

He began to lead her into the room reserved for meals, but then grimaced and seemed to change his mind. "Let's step outside instead, shall we?" he said.

Of course they should go back outside, Anna thought, feeling irritated. It would be awful to wear her soiled clothing anywhere near people who might be eating.

He led her away from the entrance. "I believe we are sufficiently isolated now that if you are willing, I wish for you to share your reasons for traveling to France unaccompanied. I admit to being curious, and while I realize it is not my right to know, having no connections to you, you stand before me as a lady alone in a foreign land. As such, I stand ready to offer my assistance."

Anna was tired of Mr. Jennings's obvious judgment of her. He was right; she didn't owe him any explanation, but she felt challenged and defensive. "Very well," she said, "since you asked: My mother died in an accident while riding with my father eight years ago. Papa was gravely injured, and we feared we would lose him, too, but he survived, though he never fully recovered. This winter, my eldest brother passed away, and then my only remaining brother, Avery, was reported missing and presumed dead. Papa died after receiving word about Avery. It became too much for him to endure. And now I intend to find Avery on my own."

"Lady Anna—" he began but then stopped. Wise man.

She continued her explanation. "If my only other brother is not found, and quickly, too, our family estate will pass to an unseemly relative. I cannot remain there with him in possession of my father's lands and titles; he is loathsome and not to be trusted. As a result, I will be homeless."

"Ah," Mr. Jennings said. It was all he said, thankfully.

"I realize this journey will be exceedingly challenging and may ultimately be fruitless, but I cannot allow myself to believe that Avery is dead, even though I realize that the chance that he is still alive is a meager one."

"There will surely be a plausible explanation for the lack of information," Mr. Jennings said. "Communication can be slow to arrive after a battle, and priorities are given to relocating the regiment, depending upon the strategies of the military leaders. Perhaps you merely needed to wait a few weeks more for your answers."

"Would *you* sit patiently by, waiting to learn if your loved one was dead or alive?" she asked. "When his inheritance and your entire family's legacy was at stake?"

Mr. Jennings gave her a serious look. "No, I daresay I wouldn't," he said at length.

"Trust me, I know there are hardships ahead. But I *will not* willingly see my family home left in the selfish hands of Ambrose Harcourt-Clifton. If the deed were left to others to find Avery, Ambrose would mortgage Clifton Hall to the hilt and sell all its goods to pay off his debts and support his indecorous lifestyle. *I* am the only one who can do something, who can search for Avery, and so I *must*, and I *will*."

Now that she'd started, she seemed unable to stop, so she told him about her search for information from Avery's headquarters and Lord Bledsoe's inability to learn anything at the London Foreign Office. "I did everything I could conceive of doing in England. I must now take my search to France. It may be in vain, Mr. Jennings, but I *must* do it. I owe it to my family and to Avery."

"Lady Anna," Mr. Jennings began, and then he paused. His countenance was serious, and she prepared herself for another setdown and lecture on the foolishness of undertaking such a journey with only a pair of servants in tow. "Lady Anna," he said again, his dark-brown eyes riveted on her own.

It was a look that set her aflame.

She lowered her eyes.

James was ashamed. He didn't consider himself someone who made rash judgments about people. As one of eight siblings, he'd learned long ago how to listen and see both sides of an argument, which had only helped to prepare him for his career in the legal profession. Listening, taking in all the facts, and his skill with languages had made him a useful member of Castlereagh's inner circle and the Foreign Office.

However, intrigue and political jousting between the sovereigns wishing to join the Sixth Coalition had made James suspicious of others' motives. His time spent in Paris and Vienna, among other places, had shown him how hypocritical the ruling classes could be—indulging in balls and routs, wearing jewels and the most stylish of clothing, flattering themselves, all while their citizens struggled in poverty and despair.

He'd been entirely wrong about her. While she'd looked light enough to float away on a breeze, she had faced down the blowing winds and billowing seas, determined to search for her brother. She hadn't flinched when her maid had become ill and her clothing had taken the brunt of it.

And now . . . strands of her hair, loosened by the sea winds, tempted James to wrap them around his fingers to brush against his cheek. Her lips, he'd observed, could be a straight line of defiance or full and soft and utterly tempting—

James took a deep breath to regain his composure and tried to find the words that conveyed his thoughts. "I am traveling to Paris myself, so I hope you will allow me to accompany you and your servants there. We will most likely need to spend the night here in Calais to make further travel arrangements, and once we arrive in Paris, we will need to register with the government, informing the officials that we are in the country. Did you know that?"

"No," she said, her eyes serious. "Thank you, Mr. Jennings."

Of all things, her short, quiet reply to his question only undid him further, and he realized he didn't wish to leave her side. What a dilemma he had brought upon himself! He had been determined to avoid relationships and romance while working with the foreign secretary, and now all he wished to do was help Lady Anna Clifton and, hopefully, earn her favor.

Blast, blast, blast!

James could hear Osbourne now.

"What do you mean?" Osbourne would say. *"What do you mean you plan to leave me on my own once again? All so you can play nanny to a young woman while she traipses about the French countryside looking for someone who is most likely dead?"*

Those would be nearly the exact words Osbourne would use—at a distinctively high volume—once James met up with him in Paris in the next day or two.

But what else was James to do? He knew that letting Lady Anna continue on through France unaccompanied would be impossible for him to tolerate. He would spend every waking moment concerned for her welfare were he not there to be sure of it himself.

He escorted Lady Anna back into the inn and showed her to her room and then returned to sit in the brasserie of the inn. It was a comfortable place, and James knew his three "companions," as it were, would find rest here from the travails they'd experienced while crossing the Channel.

The Duke of Aylesham kept a large suite of rooms in Paris for all of their use. James had a room, and he knew Osbourne would be there, and James intended for his three companions to stay there, too, when they arrived. The sooner he dashed off a note to Osbourne to inform him that he would be arriving within the next day or so with traveling companions in tow, the better.

He ordered tea and then stood and crossed the brasserie to where the owner was greeting customers and supervising the service they received.

"*Bonjour*, Monsieur Zhennings," Monsieur Blanc said. "'Ow may I 'elp you today?" he added in English with a thick French accent.

James knew and trusted Monsieur Blanc and his wife. The couple was not loyal to Bonaparte. "Perhaps some paper and ink?" James asked.

"*Oui*, Monsieur Zhennings, zees way," Monsieur Blanc said, gesturing toward the door that led to his private office. He then delved into his writing box and produced paper, ink, and a pen and once against gestured—this time toward his office chair—indicating that James may sit.

"*Merci*," James said. He sat and hurriedly wrote his letter to Osbourne. Once he had finished the letter, he blotted and folded it, and Monsieur Blanc produced his own sealing wax and seal for James to use.

"I need to have this delivered as quickly as possible to Monsieur Osbourne," James said. "Our rooms, as you know, are near the Paris Opera on Rue de Richelieu."

"*Bien*," Monsieur Blanc said, taking the sealed missive. "I shall see zat eet eez done."

"*Merci beaucoup*," James said, shaking Monsieur Blanc's hand before returning to his table in the brasserie.

Lady Anna walked into the brasserie in the next moment, spied James, and stopped in her tracks. She had changed out of her soiled clothes and straightened her hair, and she was utterly lovely to behold. He reminded himself that, for propriety's sake, for *her* sake, he was honor-bound to keep a respectable distance between them, despite the surprising urgings of his heart.

"Please join me, Lady Anna," he said, rising to his feet. "I imagine you may be hungry after the toils of the day. Something light, perhaps." He motioned to the serving girl, who was at a nearby table. "*Une autre tasse de thé, s'il vous plaît,*" he said to her. She nodded and left. "I asked her to bring you a cup of tea," he told Lady Anna as he assisted her into a chair. "They should be bringing it at any moment with pastries I ordered."

"Thank you," she said. She folded her hands in her lap.

What to say next? How was he to go about earning her favor after the harsh words he'd spoken before? And how was he to maintain his distance from someone he found so utterly attractive even though he had just recommitted himself to maintaining that distance?

Being near her was apparently affecting his ability to think clearly, too, blast it all.

"Perhaps after we've taken tea, you might join me for a walk around Calais," he said before his brain could stop the words from being uttered.

She didn't respond immediately but seemed to ponder his invitation at length. If she didn't wish to join him—

"Thank you," she said. "I believe I should like to stretch my legs a bit, now that they are working normally again."

"You're welcome," he said, trying not to envision what Lady Anna's legs might actually look like since she'd mentioned them.

So much for maintaining his distance.

Thankfully, the serving girl arrived with tea, two cups, and plates, and Madame Blanc herself brought out a fine assortment of pastries.

"I 'eard you ver vis us again, Monsieur Zhennings," Madame Blanc said. "Ah! I see you 'ave brought a lovely lady friend vis you zees time."

"*Oui*," he replied. "Lady Anna, may I present our hostess, Madame Blanc. Madame, Lady Anna Clifton."

"How do you do?" Lady Anna said. "I'm sorry—my French is not very good."

"Sink nossing of eet," Madame said. "Ve vill take good care of you and your servants; anysing for a friend of Monsieur Zhennings."

"*Merci beaucoup*," James replied.

"Thank you—er, *merci*," Lady Anna said. "Truly, I am so grateful."

Madame Blanc smiled and then returned to the kitchen of the brasserie.

Lady Anna poured tea into a cup. "Milk? Sugar?" she asked James politely.

"One sugar," he said, mesmerized again by the intense blue of her eyes. Then he helped himself to an eclair and stuffed half of it into his mouth in one bite. Since he didn't trust what he might say to her next, it was better to appear the graceless fool.

"*Dear Lady Anna*," he might say, for example. "*You are beginning to enthrall me.*"

Anna selected a pastry and took a small bite. It was delicious, which shouldn't have surprised her since the French were known for their baked goods—even Anna knew that much about the French. She took another bite.

"I have written to my associate, Osbourne, informing him of my—*our*—arrival in Calais," Mr. Jennings said. "The journey to Paris from here is at least two days, depending upon the horses. After a tumultuous Channel crossing, I thought you—or, more specifically, your maid—might appreciate an additional day to rest. Also, in my letter, I asked Osbourne to see what he could learn of your brother's whereabouts."

"You really needn't change your plans on our account," Anna said with a touch of bravado, though she wasn't sure she believed her own words. Watching Mr. Jennings converse in French with the serving girl had been a relief and an additional realization of the challenges to come, not that she wished Mr. Jennings to know that. "I knew we would encounter difficulties along the way and were—*and are*—willing to face them for Avery, despite your offer to escort us to Paris."

"I see," James said softly with a slight nod of his head. "May I ask you some questions, then, about some of the encounters you may face?"

"Certainly," Anna said, not really meaning it, not after the round of questions he'd asked her earlier. "Better to have you raise the questions now than encounter them later without preparation."

"True enough," he said. "First of all, how do you plan to obtain information when you don't speak the language?"

"As I said before, I'm certain many of the French citizens are skilled enough in English to be of help," she replied.

"Ah," he said, his dark eyes piercing her very core. "Very well. Which of these English-speaking French citizens you are bound to find are loyal to Bonaparte? Which are loyal to the French king? Which support a free republic, post-Revolution? Which French citizens are grateful that so many armies are currently in their homeland fighting battles and seeing their villages destroyed or their families displaced while these battles occur? How are you intending to arrange for travel? What is your destination? How will you—"

"I see your point," Anna said, relieved that he stopped speaking at her interruption. She felt utterly overwhelmed. She stared blankly at her teacup and pastry, neither of which looked the least bit tempting now. How was she really to do what needed to be done to find Avery when so many obstacles lay before her?

James gently placed his hand on her shoulder, startling her out of her worried thoughts. She turned to look at him.

"And *that* is why," he said in a low voice, his eyes burning her now, "I wrote to Osbourne. I didn't intend on telling you this, but I informed him that he may be on his own after we arrive in Paris. You see, I cannot in good conscience allow you to travel unescorted through a country I happen to know fairly well on a mission I actually find I am beginning to admire. You are putting yourselves at risk, and I can help mitigate that risk. I do not know what the outcome of your search will be, but I will assist you in getting the answers you need."

Tears Anna couldn't control welled up in her eyes and spilled over. "Oh, Mr. Jennings, I don't know what to say! But you have responsibilities of your own. Great responsibilities."

"True enough. But you have already heard me refer to my sister, whom I refused to leave on her own when she married the Duke of Aylesham," he said as he slipped his hand into his pocket and retrieved a handkerchief, which he handed to her. "I also have a brother, Lucas, who served in the military. The battles got rather fierce in Spain, and Lucas faced death there. I vividly recall the weeks my family anxiously wondered whether Lucas was alive or dead. And then, when he did return home, I witnessed the wounds to his soul. If I could have spared him that pain, I would have. And if I can help you find out what happened to your brother, it will help me atone in some way."

Anna studied James's face, seeing him in an altogether different light. His eyes were still intense from the passion he appeared to be feeling, yet there was also a gentleness there that he hadn't exhibited before.

"I don't know why I told you that last bit," James said. "I don't think I realized it myself until I spoke the words aloud." He looked rather baffled.

"Mr. Jennings," Anna said. "I am truly grateful for your words."

He looked embarrassed now. "Would you care to stroll through Calais with me now?" he said, appearing to wish to change the subject.

"I would, thank you, Mr. Jennings," she replied.

He assisted her to her feet—but not before stuffing the other half of his eclair into his mouth.

She couldn't help but smile at that.

James's stroll with Lady Anna was pleasant and frustrating.

They walked side by side—James clasped his hands behind his back—and were silent for a while. They passed a few people on the streets, he and Lady Anna nodding and greeting them along the way.

Lady Anna.

In all the times James had traveled to France with Osbourne and Aylesham, he'd never once poured out his thoughts—feelings—regarding his brother Lucas's experiences during the siege at Badajoz, Spain, to anyone. All had ended well for Lucas—he was a happily married man now, settled in his new life after leaving the military—but he had shared what he'd seen with James and only a very few others, and the scenes he'd described were horrific: death, rape, starvation. Angry, desperate men who had been turned into ravening wolves. Many enlisted men had been there only for their promised wage and had been no better than thieves when they had lived in Mother England.

He was sure Lady Anna couldn't fathom the desolation of humankind that invariably followed war.

They turned a corner and were now strolling down the Rue de la Paix toward Église *Notre-Dame*, the Church of Our Lady. James wasn't Roman Catholic—his brother Isaac was a vicar for the Church of England, for heaven's sake—but he respected the faith of those who would gather here on the Sabbath, and the building with its tall tower almost seemed to be calling to them now. It exuded a dignity and spirit that spoke of peace and strength and reverence.

"Perhaps we can go inside and sit for a moment or two," James said. "If you'd like."

"I would like that very much," Lady Anna said. "Thank you."

He opened the door for her and let her enter first and then followed her as she walked up the aisle toward the front of the chapel. About two-thirds of the way up, she sat, so he sat next to her.

She folded her hands in her lap and bowed her head.

Here was another side of Lady Anna that James hadn't anticipated. His family regularly attended the church where Isaac served. James supposed he took for granted that whomever he married would be a churchgoer too. But one didn't precisely learn that about a young lady when dancing at balls or chatting at an assembly. One didn't begin a conversation by saying, "Do you happen to be devoutly religious?" during the steps of a cotillion, for example.

Lady Anna, without meaning to, had pointed out aspects of James's character in the short time he'd known her, which, again, had taken him by surprise. At the very least, he'd learned that he was judgmental, overly proud, and impatient when he'd always considered himself to be even-tempered, intelligent, and polite.

And now he was contemplating his faith.

Lady Anna quietly reached into her reticule and removed the handkerchief he'd given her earlier, then dabbed her eyes and nose with it.

Blast, she was weeping.

James placed his hand on hers, hoping his gesture would offer some comfort. "There now," he whispered to her. "You have God with you in your cause."

He had no idea why he'd said it; the words had come to him unbidden.

His action, while intended to be reassuring, now felt forward, so he let go of her hand and patiently waited for her to regain her composure. He wanted her to have the time she needed here in the chapel, so he studied the statues and paintings in the nave and altar, he watched the sunbeams filter through the windows, and he offered more than one prayer himself. Spending this quiet time here with Lady Anna felt different from anything he'd felt before when gathered with family and neighbors in the chapel at home.

Eventually, she dabbed her nose and nodded quietly at James that she was ready to leave. He assisted her to her feet, but he couldn't resist placing a kiss—a reverent kiss, strangely enough—on her hand.

James had always been a believer, and after this afternoon's walk, he was even more so. He believed they had been led to Église *Notre-Dame*, for they had found peace and pause from their concerns here inside the church.

And James began to understand why the words *love* and *worship* were frequently spoken together.

CHAPTER 6

Anna sat next to Mary in the coach, with James and Sparks across from them, as they made their way toward Abbeville, their first evening stop on the way to Paris. There hadn't been much conversation since they'd left Calais, owing to their early departure time. Everyone had seemed to be half-asleep; certainly, Anna had felt that way.

The conveyance Mr. Jennings had been able to procure wasn't of the most recent make, nor was it luxurious; in fact, it was rather uncomfortable and small. The wheels hit a rut, and not for the first time, she was thrown against poor Mary. Anna grabbed the side of the carriage and planted her feet on the floor, trying to maintain her balance.

And not for the first time, Mr. Jennings leaned forward as though to help steady her if need be.

"I'm so sorry, Mary," Anna said, also not for the first time. She scooted as far into the corner of the seat as she could, which wasn't much.

Mary herself appeared to be holding tightly to her side of the carriage.

"The road will improve once we turn away from the coast," Mr. Jennings said.

"Ye be looking a bit peaked, Mary," Sparks said, eyeing her carefully.

"I am?" Mary said, patting her cheek as though that would remedy things.

"How *are* you feeling, Mary?" Anna asked, now concerned that the bumpy carriage ride was upsetting her stomach after her trouble aboard the yacht. "Are you well?"

"I'm fine, me lady," Mary said. "Truly, I am." These last three words were directed at Sparks.

Sparks grunted, and one of Mr. Jennings's eyebrows rose a bit.

"Lady Anna," Mr. Jennings said at length, after they'd ridden in silence for several miles. "Perhaps you might share more about Avery with me: stories of his youth that might give me a glimpse into his character."

"I don't see why—"

"We are going to be inside a carriage for the better part of three days before reaching Paris," he said. "Sharing stories such as those may help the time pass a bit swifter. I, for one, have so many siblings, I could fill your ears with stories about them to take us to the far reaches of India, and I can certainly draw on them if you would like. But as we are undertaking this journey to find The Honorable Avery Clifton, or, rather, the new Earl of Westbury, I thought . . ." His voice trailed off, obviously waiting for her to respond.

"Hmm," Anna said. "I guess I could. Sparks knows him too." She supposed she should start at the beginning. "Avery is the brother closest to me in age, two years my elder. We grew up in each other's pockets, as you might imagine, Mr. Jennings, having so many siblings of your own. My eldest brother, John, was a few years older than either of us."

She paused to look out the window and collect her emotions after mentioning John, who'd been taken much too soon. "Avery and I shared a governess and a tutor, although I also received additional training in the areas deemed lady-like—pianoforte, needlework, that sort of thing—while Avery spent time with John learning Latin and Greek, fencing and cricket, and the like. Papa sent Avery to Eton, where John was also attending." She paused. "I suppose I'm not telling this story in precise order. He wasn't learning to fence when he was four years old."

"I was raised in the country," Mr. Jennings said. "I know the general course of events children of the aristocracy take into adulthood. You needn't worry."

"I missed Avery while he was at Eton, I admit, although he and John did come home during the summer months and at Christmas. I was fortunate to have friends in the nearby village, which kept me from being too lonely. So all in all, we had a rather typical and happy childhood."

"They was good children," Sparks said, surprising Anna. "Handsome, too, the three o' them. Lady Anna always looked as though she were made of porcelain—even as a babe, there were something that caught the eye with this one. Delicate and sweet, she were." He nodded in Anna's direction. "And that Avery—" Sparks said. "Now, he were a handsome rascal—blond, like his sister, with the same blue eyes, but not delicate at all. A bit willful, he were, but only as much as a boy should be. Strong lad. Aye, a strong lad. John were a bit darker in color, with brownish hair and the like."

"I am not the delicate porcelain you make me out to be, Sparks," Anna said, embarrassed by his description. "But I thank you just the same."

"And that were the paradox o' it all, Lady Anna," Sparks said. "For, despite all appearances to the contrary, ye was as strong-willed as yer brothers."

"I've witnessed *that* aspect of her character for myself," Mr. Jennings observed.

"I don't know if I should consider that an insult or a compliment," Anna replied.

"I shall leave that for you to decide," Mr. Jennings said. "Now, I should like to know more about Avery's military service. It may, in particular, help me understand his thoughts and help determine what he might have done and where he may be."

Anna swallowed and turned to look out the window for a moment to collect herself again. The years leading up to Avery's buying his commission had been difficult, painful ones, not to mention the retelling of Papa's and John's untimely deaths. Speaking about all of it only opened hurtful wounds.

"Perhaps we can speak of something else for a while," Anna managed to say around the lump in her throat.

"Very well," Mr. Jennings said rather gently. "Sparks, perhaps you will tell me about *your* childhood."

"Ye really wish to hear about that?" Sparks said, sounding incredulous.

"Oh, yes!" Mary said, and then threw her hand over her mouth, blushing.

"Indeed," Mr. Jennings replied, chuckling. "I was great friends with the children of our servants and those in the village. I should like to hear if your experiences were anything like theirs—and mine."

So, Sparks set out to tell them details of his birth and childhood. And while Anna was interested, when added to the fact that the road was less bumpy than it had been, the swaying of the carriage and the lilting drone of Sparks's stories eventually lulled her to sleep.

"There, in the distance, you can see Paris," James said after turning in his seat to see the landmarks that lay in front of them on the third day of their journey. "And this is just the beginning."

"You needn't remind me," Lady Anna replied, shifting in her seat. "I confess to being ready for a few days of continuous sleep after three days in a coach."

James scratched at his cheek to hide a smile at her confession. It was the truth, however. The coaches he'd been able to procure since hadn't been the finest. But at least they had been small, with only room for the four of them, which had given them a modicum of privacy, if not luxury.

Surprisingly, with the close quarters, the four of them had also become cordial travelers-in-arms over the past three days. That being said, the more time he spent with Lady Anna, the stronger his attraction to her became. He would never tell her, but on that first leg of the journey from Calais, when she'd fallen asleep, he had struggled to keep his eyes off her. She'd slept thus for the better part of two hours, and they had been two heavenly hours for him.

He had tried to concentrate on his conversation with Sparks and had learned that Sparks had been—and still was—deeply loyal to Lord Westbury for allowing him to train at the manor and move up the ranks from errand boy to footman to butler and then to valet. And after the horrible carriage accident, Sparks had even become Lord Westbury's caregiver until the earl's death.

It confirmed for James a great deal about Sparks that he'd already discerned about the fellow after his assistance to Mary aboard the yacht.

Mary hadn't added much to the conversation and had been especially fearful whenever James had posed a question to her, but it had become obvious that she was a loyal servant, which James found praiseworthy.

And now the three days of travel were drawing to a conclusion. "As I mentioned before, the Duke of Aylesham has apartments for our use while in Paris, and I've already given the driver directions."

"That is good news," Lady Anna said, and then she sighed. "I confess that after three days of travel, my admiration for our military has grown exceedingly, seeing as they must march endlessly while only the officers travel on horseback or in some other conveyance. But even that for such a great length of time must be tiresome."

They were entering the city proper now, but James had been in Paris often enough that he was more interested in watching Lady Anna as she stared out the window, taking in the sights.

"What is that?" she asked, pointing to a large structure that spanned the road not long after they entered the city.

"That is the Arc du Triomphe," James said. "Bonaparte began its construction, I believe, eight years ago, after a huge victory. You'll notice, however, that a large portion of it remains uncompleted. That part there, made of wood, its original construction material, is all that is finished." He chuckled. "I hope it's incompletion is a good omen for us—the little

Corsican did not complete his victory, much like this arc, even if some future ruler decides to finish it."

Sparks was looking intently at the structure too.

"What do you have to say about the Arc du Triomphe, Sparks?" James asked, curious to get his opinion.

"I s'pose it's something to look at. I s'pose I should be impressed," he remarked. "But I never did understand the need for such a thing merely for its own sake—no offense meant."

"None taken," James said, surprised and rather impressed. "What would you do to celebrate a glorious victory instead?"

"I haven't ever given such a thing any thought," Sparks said. "I can't say as I ever experienced a victory of that sort."

"Yes, you have," Lady Anna said. "The day my father took his first steps after his bones had healed. You and I held his hands, and he walked slowly about the room. And then what did you do?"

Sparks suddenly looked sheepish, which James found interesting.

"Ye danced a jig, is what ye did," Mary said. "After Lord Westbury returned to his chair, *ye danced a jig. And sang.*"

"I didn't have the money to build something like that, now did I?" Sparks gestured toward the Arc, which was now nearly behind them.

"That was a wonderful day," Lady Anna said, and James feared the memory might upset her, but she simply smiled warmly at Sparks, which was a relief.

"I should have liked to have seen that jig," James said. "I should like to have met Lord Westbury and witnessed the miracle personally. I daresay your jig was worth more than the Arc du Triomphe can ever be, even once it's finished,"

James said with a grin. "You're as fine a gentleman as I've ever met, Sparks."

Lady Anna looked at him then with wide, incredulous eyes like brilliant blue gems, and James's heart beat so fast he could scarcely breathe. He briefly glanced at Sparks, even though he could barely tear his eyes away from Lady Anna's face. The man seemed embarrassed by James's compliment, if the rosiness on Sparks's cheeks was any indication, but he nodded his thanks to James.

"I be that humbled, sir," Sparks said.

Lady Anna leaned forward, her face nearly close enough for James to kiss. "Thank you," she said. "Thank you for truly seeing what we have always known about Sparks."

That was all Lady Anna said, and all she needed to say.

And James knew he was utterly in love. There was no turning back, in more ways than one.

CHAPTER 7

"Y ou've arrived. Excellent! Welcome," Osbourne said when he opened the door to the Paris apartments. "Come in, come in."

They filed through the door, and James set his bag down while Sparks brought the others' bags in.

"Lady Anna, please allow me to present Mr. Phillip Osbourne, my friend and colleague here in Paris," James said. "Osbourne, this is Lady Anna Clifton, daughter of the recently deceased Humphrey Clifton, Earl of Westbury. Also, two of her servants: Sparks and Mary." James was glad they'd finally arrived and he could put a bit more space between himself and Lady Anna for his own well-being. The urge to pull her into his arms had taken a toll on him.

"Lady Anna," Osbourne said, bowing over her extended hand and then nodding in recognition of Sparks and Mary. He turned back to James and gestured with his head in Lady Anna's direction. "I can see why you were so keen to assist the lovely Lady Anna, my friend. I daresay I would have been equally inclined."

"It's kind of you to say so," Lady Anna said.

"Not at all, Lady Anna," Osbourne said, his eyes gleaming, blast him. "I daresay there isn't a male around who wouldn't do your bidding if asked."

"You think so?" she replied, dropping her voice as though she were sharing the most intimate of secrets. "Mr. Jennings is, therefore, a rare male. Dare I say it? He spent a great deal of time informing me of my foolhardiness at our first meeting."

Osbourne grinned. "My friend Jennings is a hard case, Lady Anna. He has avoided the Marriage Mart for years—though I daresay there were plenty of ladies who would have fallen and did indeed fall at his feet—"

"Exaggeration, Osbourne, and you know it." James shook his head.

"As I was saying," Osbourne said with a chuckle while Sparks hid his own grin behind his hand and Mary pretended to be deaf. "Despite your claims, Lady Anna, you seem to have captured him since."

"Now, Osbourne—" James said in warning.

"For here she is, and here you are. Together," Osbourne said directly to James before returning his attention to her. "Trust me, Lady Anna, when I repeat that you are a rare beauty, and have the ability to cast a spell over every gentleman you meet. You have most certainly cast a spell on me."

"And you, my friend, are an accomplished charmer," James said.

"I believe Mr. Jennings is correct in his assessment of you," Lady Anna said with a mischievous smile. "You are indeed most charming, Mr. Osbourne. Please allow me to thank you in advance for your hospitality to us."

"My pleasure," Osbourne said with such flirtation that he practically oozed it, which irked James to no end.

"Careful, my friend. At least one man here will take you bodily apart if you are too forward with Lady Anna," James said.

"'Tis true," Sparks said, crossing his arms over his chest.

"Two gentlemen, to be precise, I presume," Osbourne added with a sly grin.

"If ye don't mind, sir, I be taking whatever room is closest to Lady Anna's and Mary's," Sparks said. "Just to keep an eagle eye on things, so to speak."

"Of course," Osbourne said with a little less flourish than he'd been using before. "Allow me to show you to your rooms. Our apartments here in Paris are ample, owing to the lofty company we keep and the fact that we are never sure how many of us will be here at any given time." He shot James an ironic glance when he said those words.

"Point taken," James said.

Osbourne then led Lady Anna and Mary to the suite of rooms usually reserved for Aylesham, and Sparks took a smaller room nearby. James's own rooms were his usual ones, at the opposite end of the hall from Lady Anna's. Ah, well. It was undoubtedly better that way.

He took a few minutes to freshen up and unpack a few things—and think. He knew Osbourne well enough to know that the cogwheels of his friend's mind had started turning the moment he'd been introduced to Lady Anna. And when the cogwheels of Osbourne's mind were turning, it was time to be on guard—in more ways than one.

Anna collapsed into the upholstered chair next to the window in her assigned room. It was an elegant room—much more ornate than any of the ones she'd stayed in along their journey and, frankly, one of the most elegant spaces in which she'd ever been. She'd heard Mr. Jennings mutter something to Mr. Osbourne about Aylesham's rooms being at the opposite end from his own and wasn't that convenient for Osbourne. So apparently, she was enjoying the luxury reserved for a duke. She wasn't of a mood to ponder what was or wasn't convenient for Mr. Osbourne.

It almost made her laugh, for all she wanted at present was a nice cup of tea and a nap to revive her spirits. She could have slept nearly anywhere; she definitely didn't need the trappings of this room, although compared to what few naps she'd gotten in the carriage the past few days, she wasn't precisely complaining.

She also wasn't of a mood to ask Mr. Osbourne about tea, so she removed her shoes and stockings and moved to the bed, which was covered in soft pillows and silky quilts, and snuggled deeply into their lushness, pulling a coverlet over the top of her . . .

The next thing she knew, there was a tap on her shoulder, startling her into sitting upright. She rubbed her eyes. Had she fallen asleep?

"Lady Anna," Mary said softly. "Ye've been asleep for three hours, and Mr. Jennings is asking after ye."

Goodness! She *had* fallen asleep, and what a sleep it had been—deep and dreamless, and for those few hours, she had been in heavenly oblivion, freed from her woes and worries about Avery. But those woes came flooding back now.

"Thank you, Mary," she replied, laying her hand across her forehead. "I just need a moment."

She eventually slid out of the lovely comfort of the pillows until she was sitting on the edge of the bed, and then she moved slowly over to the washstand and sat again so Mary could straighten her coiffure.

There was a knock at the door. "Lady Anna?" a male voice called—it must be Mr. Jennings. "Lady Anna, are you well?"

"I'm fine, Mr. Jennings; just a moment." She shot one last glance in the mirror before standing and opening the door.

"Lady Anna!" Mary hissed.

And then Anna watched as Mr. Jennings's eyes moved from the crown of her head down, down to her bare feet.

Bare feet! She'd entirely forgotten to slip her stockings and shoes back on in her haste. It was unseemly and even provocative.

"Oh dear," she heard Mary murmur behind her.

Mr. Jennings's gaze, which had been fixed on her bare feet, then meandered back up to her face, and their eyes locked. She had watched his eyes darken, and now they smoldered. She began to shiver.

"Are you cold?" he asked in a low, husky voice.

"No," she said on a breath. Quite the opposite.

"You're shivering," he said.

"I'm—"

The door to Sparks's room opened. "I hope ye had a good rest, Lady Anna," Sparks said, looking intently at Mr. Jennings.

"The guard dog arrives," Mr. Jennings replied. He took a step back and seemed to straighten.

Anna took a deep breath.

"I did, thank you, Sparks," she said even though she couldn't look away from Mr. Jennings.

"I was about to inform Lady Anna of our supper plans, Sparks," Mr. Jennings said with decidedly cooler tones than he'd used when he'd asked her if she was cold. Remembering his voice made her shiver again. "Osbourne has suggested we visit the Café de la Régence near the Palais-Royal. It is rather fine, albeit a bit quiet, considering it is known as a center for chess playing, of all things, which makes it rather unique and, perhaps, uninteresting to those looking for livelier entertainment. It will allow us some peace as we discuss the next steps toward finding your brother." He turned to Sparks. "And you and Mary are free to join us, if you like. The French are quite egalitarian in their views since their revolution thirty or so years ago. '*Liberté, égalité, fraternité*,' as they are wont to say. Or you and Mary may dine with the other servants here, if you prefer. You have been invited to do so by the landlord."

Mr. Osbourne entered the hall after that exchange and nodded in greeting to Anna. "Ah, good, you're awake, Lady Anna. I presume Jennings has informed you of our plans for the evening. If they are not to your liking, we can alter them."

"Supper at the Café de la Régence sounds lovely, Mr. Osbourne," she said. "I am quite revived from my rest this afternoon and intend to enjoy my first evening in Paris with you both."

"And perhaps you will meet some interesting characters—different from those you may have encountered at home, or even in London." Mr. Osbourne shot a glance at Mr. Jennings, and Anna wondered what that was about. "I should think that would be rather new and exciting for you. Jennings and I will be ready to translate for you, should you require it. But there are many in this fair city at present who speak excellent English, so you needn't worry exceedingly."

Now Anna shot Mr. Jennings a glance, for had he not tried to convince her that she would be at a loss not speaking French were she to travel on her own? Although, truly, despite her protestations, she was actually grateful he had agreed to join them, for the past three days had been grueling enough and would have been much worse if his knowledge of French hadn't come to bear on several occasions—not that she was going to admit it to him quite yet.

"The dress is formal," Mr. Osbourne continued, "but not overly elegant. We shall save your most elegant self for other occasions, perhaps. Come, gentlemen, let us leave Lady Anna so she may dress and ready herself"—he glanced down at her bare feet, and one of his eyebrows shot up, making Anna blush—"as we shall do ourselves."

"Thank you," Anna said.

She turned to go back inside her room, and as she closed the door behind her, she and Mary both heard Mr. Jennings speaking to the others in a low hiss. "Neither of you will say anything about her bare feet to anyone. Is that understood?"

Anna covered her face with her hands in embarrassment, not sure whether she should cry or laugh, but then felt herself shiver once again as she remembered Mr. Jennings's deep, scorching look.

———⌐Y⌐———

"Osbourne, well met. And Jennings, too, I see." Karl Philipp, the prince of Schwarzenberg and Austrian field marshal, rose to his feet and walked toward the three of them when they entered the Café de la Régence.

"Schwarzenberg, what a surprise to see you here," James said, all the while thinking that he would be speaking—firmly— to Osbourne when they had a quiet moment together. He fully suspected Osbourne had known Schwarzenberg would be here at the café tonight. Frankly, without Aylesham or Castlereagh with them, James was surprised the prince acknowledged them. But as he watched Schwarzenberg's eyes wander to Lady Anna and Osbourne and back, James began to suspect that Osbourne had an ulterior motive for bringing Lady Anna, in particular, here this evening, although James wasn't sure why.

"Allow me to introduce you to our lovely guest," Osbourne said. "May I present Lady Anna Clifton, daughter of the Right Honorable Earl of Westbury, recently deceased, sadly. She is an acquaintance of Jennings and is here in Paris for a few days. Lady Anna, may I present Karl Philipp, Prince of Schwarzenberg, one of our allies in the Coalition. In fact, Schwarzenberg was one of the generals in the final battle here in Paris that forced Napoleon to abdicate."

Lady Anna offered a deep curtsy, and then the prince bowed and pressed a kiss on her hand.

James had never noticed how charming Schwarzenberg could be, and even though the prince was married and wasn't known to be a libertine, a lot of doors tended to open for beautiful women. James's teeth—and hands—clenched. With all his might, he straightened his fingers and attempted a smile. His encounters with Schwarzenberg had been amiable ones, and the prince was an exceptional ally. It would not do to be disagreeable, even if, at the moment, he wished to take Lady Anna by the arm and march her out of the Café de la Régence.

"A great pleasure to make your acquaintance, Lady Anna," Schwarzenberg said. "My condolences on the death of your father. You are a rare beauty, if I may be so bold to say it. I imagine you gather flocks of admirers wherever you go, even while wearing the sad attire of mourning."

The prince is exceedingly elegant, with impeccable manners too, James thought, feeling even more irritated.

"Thank you; you are too kind," Lady Anna said.

"Not at all," the prince replied. "I but speak the truth."

James thought he might be ill.

"You know the Café de la Régence is well-known for its chess matches, Lady Anna," Schwarzenberg continued, showing clearly with whom he'd rather engage in conversation. "I was about to watch some excessively talented players. Do you play chess? Perhaps you may watch with me—for a while only, as matches can last, oh, so very long, and I wouldn't wish to command all of your time."

"What a generous offer. I would like nothing better," Lady Anna said, sounding to James as though she chatted with royalty frequently. "I have played chess on occasion, although I confess to being rather unschooled at it. We were about to dine, however. Perhaps you'd care to join us?" She smiled at the prince, and James saw Lady Anna in all her glory and prayed that Schwarzenberg would refuse.

"Ah, but I have already dined," Schwarzenberg replied, to James's great relief. "Perhaps afterward, then. I should delight in pointing out these masters' great skill to you." He smiled. "Adieu for now, mademoiselle," he said with a nod of his head. "Gentlemen."

Of course, Schwarzenberg would use French, the language of romance, when saying goodbye to Lady Anna, James thought as he, Osbourne, and Sparks offered their own bows to the prince.

The *maître d'hôtel* hurried over once the prince walked away from them. "I will show you to your table now," he said in a thick French accent and then proceeded to lead them to a spot in the north end of the café.

Osbourne, the rascal, stepped ahead of James and assisted Lady Anna with her chair. Once they were all seated—and it wasn't at all surprising that Osbourne had commandeered the chair closest to Lady Anna—Osbourne sipped from his goblet and then turned toward her. "Lady Anna," he said, "I must agree with Schwarzenberg's observation that you gather flocks of admirers wherever you go. Our acquaintance is but a few hours, and I must say, I am already an admirer—as, I suspect, is the happily married prince." He smiled. "Not to mention my associate, here."

"You are overstating the truth, Mr. Osbourne," Lady Anna said. "I daresay I've seen no flocks of admirers."

The waiters arrived with their first course, and conversation stopped while they were served.

Once the waiters left, Osbourne returned his attention to Lady Anna. "In fact, I am not at all convinced, Lady Anna, that there is not a bevy of admirers you left behind in England, missing you and ardently awaiting your return."

She looked at Osbourne with a serious expression on her beautiful face. "I can assure you, Mr. Osbourne, that at the present time, my mind is less taken with how many admirers I do or do not have than with finding my brother before his rightful inheritance falls into the hands of a villain."

She then turned to look at James, and her eyes, in the low restaurant light, glowed like hot sapphires.

She was exquisite.

The waiters soon arrived to remove the first course and serve the next.

"Best eat quickly, Lady Anna," Osbourne said in a low tone once the waiters left. "It appears your latest admirer, whatever you may say, is looking to steal you away so that you may witness the finer points of chess."

Lady Anna responded with but a smile.

And James intended to use a portion of the time she was with the prince to speak more frankly with Osbourne about his reasons for dining specifically at Café de la Régence this evening.

"Mr. Osbourne, I strongly suspect that you set me up to be prey at our dinner this evening," Anna said as they rode in the carriage back to their lodgings. "The prince of Schwarzenberg is charming, but watching a chess match for nearly two hours while he explained the strategy behind each move was a bit much. And based on a few comments he made, he has dined regularly at Café de la Régence since arriving in Paris. That would have been, at least, since the beginning of April. As it is now the second week of May, it is knowledge I'm certain you already had."

Mr. Osbourne shrugged. "You have found me out, Lady Anna," he said. "I admit I took advantage of your beauty in the hopes that Schwarzenberg would enjoy meeting you." He paused in his justification for what he'd done. Mr. Jennings looked as though he might challenge his friend to a duel, his face was so red and his mouth so set.

"Why?" she asked.

"To be frank, being included in Schwarzenberg's inner circle when neither Aylesham nor Castlereagh is present is something the prince is less likely to consider when it comes to Jennings and myself. I hoped that having a rare beauty like our new acquaintance"—he gestured toward her with his hand—"might appeal to his gallant, masculine nature."

"Well, you are indeed fortunate, then," she said, feigning indifference when she felt more inclined to slap Mr. Osbourne for his presumptuousness. "He invited me to a soiree being held at his residence tomorrow evening, which you undoubtedly knew all about, and was generous enough to allow me to invite the two of you to attend with me."

Mr. Jennings made a growling sound deep in his throat—yes, it was definitely a growl. It sounded like something Sparks would do.

Mr. Osbourne shrugged again. "Guilty as charged," he said. "You are not only a rare beauty, Lady Anna, but a new face in Paris and, as a result, have given us admittance to the prince's soiree, which was what I had hoped. But before judging me too harshly, allow me to state my reasons: his guests will be those with whom we must further our acquaintance. Napoleon may be in exile, but there is much to be done in the way of unifying all parties in a peaceful manner."

"It isn't right to use people without their knowledge in such a way," Mr. Jennings said.

"I didn't do anything other than take a calculated risk," Mr. Osbourne said. "Lady Anna, I assure you that had Schwarzenberg shown no interest, I would not have pushed the matter. The Café is an excellent place to dine, as is obvious by the fact that the prince was there at all. The cuisine was delicious, wouldn't you agree? But the fact that he *did* delight in making your acquaintance—as we all have, I might add—works to our advantage, for the Coalition and, therefore, for England."

"Ah, I see. The peace of the Continent falls into the hands of one simple female, it would seem," Anna said with great irony. "Thank you for your explanation."

Mr. Osbourne actually laughed, which Anna supposed was an appropriate response, especially from someone who was used to using his charms to draw people to his way of thinking. "Lady Anna," he said, "trust me when I tell you there is nothing simple about you in any sense of the word. You're a rare jewel, and your arrival couldn't have been more timely." He turned to Mr. Jennings. "She's a true find, Jennings. I'd keep her close, if I were you."

Anna only shook her head. Mr. Osbourne was a likable gentleman, but his words held little veracity with her.

"Indeed, Osbourne, I believe you're correct," Mr. Jennings replied.

Unlike Mr. Osbourne's words, Mr. Jennings's made Anna's heart swell within her.

Anna found herself faced with a dilemma, which grew in size and anxiety the farther they got from the Café de la Régence and the closer they got to their lodgings. The dilemma, along with Mr. Jennings's words, overwhelmed her thoughts. She stared out the carriage window at the passing scenes of Paris at night, wondering what she should do and trying to determine her feelings about it.

"Are you troubled, Lady Anna?" Mr. Jennings asked, interrupting her thoughts. "If you are angry at Osbourne here, which I consider justified, you may vent at him to your heart's content."

"Truly, Lady Anna," Mr. Osbourne said, "I should think it an honor that such a luminary—a war hero, no less—would wish to meet you and be inclined to include you in his party. But you may do as Jennings here suggests, if it will make you feel better."

She shook her head. "I am resigned to attending the soiree, if your being in attendance will further peaceful negotiations. I confess to not knowing much about any of that. My concerns are of a more personal nature." She sighed and turned to look at the two gentlemen seated across from her. "The prince wishes for me to put off my mourning attire in order to attend. My eldest brother has been gone but four months, my father barely six weeks. How am I to justify this? How do I honor my father and brother by donning a cheerful color? Is it not enough that I attend?" She turned to stare out the window again, but now, instead of seeing the landmarks of Paris at night, she saw only her own darkened reflection.

"What precisely did the prince say?" Mr. Jennings asked softly.

"He said that his soiree is in celebration of the victory over Napoleon, that everyone has lost loved ones in this horrific war, and that black would be a damper on the spirits of the others in attendance. He encouraged me to be a source of joy for those who were there. How am I, who am only here in France in the hopes of finding the last member of my immediate family alive, supposed to be a source of joy for others? And yet I told the prince I would attend. I feel as though I am being unfaithful to the memory of Papa and John and, perhaps, though I dare not think it, to Avery."

"Don't you think your father and brothers would wish you to celebrate the end of decades of battle and loss?" Mr. Osbourne asked her.

His words didn't help. "I'm sure that, to you, mourning is little more than an armband or a cravat, Mr. Osbourne. But everything I have is black. And yet, to please a prince I didn't even know until this evening, I am to appear out of mourning so as not to dampen the spirits of his guests. It would be better simply not to attend, yet I have given my word. I do not converse with princes on a regular basis, you understand. I should have little trouble saying no to *you*, Mr. Osbourne, were you to request something of me I feel I cannot do, but I have less confidence when it comes to dealing with royalty."

Mr. Jennings leaned forward in the carriage seat and laid his hand atop hers. "Lady Anna, we can send our regrets to Schwarzenberg, if you prefer. There undoubtedly will be other soirees and balls in the near future—probably more than we would care to attend."

Anna saw Mr. Osbourne shoot an unhappy look at Mr. Jennings.

"Lady Anna, if it is a lack of suitable attire you are concerned about, there are shops aplenty in Paris that can provide you with a gown for tomorrow," Mr. Osbourne said. "Jennings and I are happy to escort you to any—or many—of these shops to procure a gown and anything else you may need. I am also certain the talented French modistes in Paris, of all cities, will be able to find something in a half-mourning color that will meet your sensibilities and also suit Schwarzenberg's request." He nodded encouragingly at her. "What say you, Jennings? Do you not agree? We have met many fine ladies while here in Paris whose style of dress would not only fit the decorum of one who has lost family but would also lighten the spirits of those who have endured so much."

The man excelled at presenting his case, Anna thought begrudgingly. "I thought it was Mr. Jennings who was the lawyer, not you, Mr. Osbourne."

He chuckled. "I studied the law, Lady Anna, although I have never practiced it, as my esteemed friend here has."

"But the decision is entirely up to you, Lady Anna," Mr. Jennings interjected. "Despite Osbourne's words of persuasion here, it is you who must be at peace with your decision. I, for one, will support you in whatever you decide." He shot another glare at Mr. Osbourne.

"He speaks true, Lady Anna," Osbourne said. "I may wish to persuade, but I most certainly would not use force."

Anna stared out the carriage window again. They were nearing their lodgings, she could tell. *What would you have me do, Papa?* she thought to herself.

She waited, truly hoping that, somehow, he would provide her with an answer.

No answer came.

Was she intending to dress in a manner to draw attention to herself? No. Was she trying to further her cause in finding Avery? Always, yes. Would lifting the spirits of those here in Paris from all over the Continent be deemed helpful or frivolous?

She sighed deeply. "Very well. I am willing to consider finding a gown that is not black to wear tomorrow evening— but only if I feel it is also respectful to Papa and John."

"Excellent!" Mr. Osbourne said.

"But *only* if I feel the gown is respectful to my father and my brother," Anna repeated.

"Understood," Mr. Osbourne said. "We shall fully explain the situation to the modistes when we begin our search tomorrow. Ah, here we are."

The carriage came to a halt, and the footman opened the door. Mr. Osbourne hopped down first, followed by Mr. Jennings, who then turned to assist Anna from the carriage.

"Do not feel unduly pressured, even if the request did come from Schwarzenberg," he said softly to her as she descended from the carriage with her hand in his. "You must do as you see fit, and I will support you in your decision."

He continued holding her hand a bit longer, which was comforting and reassuring. "Thank you, Mr. Jennings," she replied.

"Come along," Mr. Osbourne called. "Tomorrow is going to be a busy day and an even busier evening."

Mr. Jennings gave Anna a long look and then brought her hand to his lips—and Anna wondered how it was possible to feel breathless and worried and eager and calm all at the same time.

Oh, Mr. Jennings!

CHAPTER 8

Anna blinked and raised a gloved hand to shield her eyes while they adjusted to her surroundings once she entered the prince of Schwarzenberg's residence in Paris. The hall was large and spacious, with marble floors and arched ceilings that seemed to rise to the heavens. It seemed appropriate to Anna, as they were painted to look like the sky, with golden clouds and birds winging upward and large chandeliers that shone brightly and made the room feel as though it were noonday rather than evening.

It was the most elegant dwelling in which Anna had ever set foot. Clifton Hall, while lovely, didn't compare, and what few stately homes Anna had visited previously had been lovely, of course, but not like Prince Karl Philipp's residence. *Exquisite, fashionable, grand, luxurious* were all words that had sprung instantly into Anna's thoughts upon stepping inside.

Mr. Osbourne and Mr. Jennings had taken her to a well-respected dress shop and had spoken to the modiste in rapid French, who had then barked instructions to her seamstresses and shop girls in more rapid French, while Anna and Mary had stood by in awe, watching the commotion that had spun around them. After a final flurry of French words that had ended with Mr. Jennings handing the modiste a packet of money—which Anna was determined to address at a later time—the two gentleman had returned to Anna's side and informed her that they would be back to collect her and her packages in precisely three hours. Fortunately, that three hours—during which a few French words, a few English words, and a lot of gesturing had taken place until all parties had seemed satisfied with the results and the purchases had been boxed up—had flown by.

The jewelry Anna had chosen to wear this evening was the strand of pearls she'd inherited from Mama, along with the earrings that accompanied them. She had wanted at least one keepsake from the people she had loved most in the world with her this evening.

A footman assisted her with her cloak while she gazed about and marveled. The hall itself was breathtaking enough, but the guests . . .

Anna had never seen so many gentlemen in colorful military uniforms covered in ribbons and sashes and medals, nor ladies in such ornate gowns and feathers and jewels. Footmen wove through the throng, bearing trays of champagne and somehow managing not to spill a drop. Couples waltzed to the music soaring from the orchestra on the dais at the end of the room. And even with all this whirling about, the hall itself had room to spare for the additional guests entering behind Anna and the others.

"It is because of you that we are able to be in attendance this evening," Osbourne said quietly to her while they waited in the queue to greet their host. "There are people here who need a gentle touch, as they say, to smooth their entrance into the Coalition. You have proven to be pivotal in that and will no doubt prove it further."

"Enough, Osbourne," James whispered.

"Ah, Lady Anna," Prince Karl Philipp said with a bow over her gloved hand. "I am so glad you were able to join us this evening—you and your excellent companions. And I am pleased that you would choose to set aside your mourning attire for this evening—your lavender gown is stunning, and you are even more beautiful than I recalled."

"Thank you, Your Serene Highness," Anna said with a deep curtsy.

"I'm confident your father would agree that the end of the war is a good thing and worthy of celebration," he replied.

Anna simply smiled in response.

Then the prince turned to Mr. Jennings and Mr. Osbourne. "Gentlemen," he said.

That was all he said to her "excellent companions," who each bowed to the prince in return.

"Come, I will introduce you to some of my guests, Lady Anna," Prince Karl Philipp said and took her by the elbow— not forcefully but certainly in a manner that suggested he got his way most of the time. He then proceeded to introduce Anna to several of the people in the colorful uniforms and gowns and with titles such as *count* and *duke* and *countess*. When names such as Auguste, Wilhelm, Frederick, Leopold, Gertrude, and Sophia began flying about Anna in a conversational mix of German, French, and English—the latter spoken with such heavy accents that Anna could barely tell that it *was* English—she felt certain she would succumb to her confusion. Thankfully, Mr. Jennings had followed behind her and the prince and had assisted her with translation.

She smiled and curtsied and offered her hand to be bowed over and to receive indulgent kisses as the prince introduced her as "his special friend," which was rather generous of him, considering they'd met only the evening before.

Mr. Osbourne had deserted them and was currently off chatting with an older gentleman with impressive sideburns who was wearing a grand, red uniform covered in medals.

"Ah, Mr. Jennings, I'm pleased to see that you are in Paris once again."

Anna and James both turned their attention to the gentleman who'd spoken—a rather tall, blond gentleman wearing formal evening attire rather than a uniform.

"Herr von Oberhausen," Mr. Jennings said with a polite bow in greeting, although Anna noted that his tone wasn't overly welcoming.

"As you see," the gentleman replied. He immediately turned his attention to Anna and smiled beguilingly at her, which made Anna shift a bit uncomfortably, although she couldn't say precisely why. Herr von Oberhausen was an attractive gentleman with a pleasant disposition, so her reaction confused her other than having noted Mr. Jennings's slightly cool tone. "And what a lovely lady you have with you," he said to Mr. Jennings, nodding in her direction. "We haven't had the pleasure of an introduction. Do we understand correctly that she is Schwarzenberg's particular friend?"

"Allow me to introduce Lady Anna Clifton," Mr. Jennings replied rather unenthusiastically. "Lady Anna, Herr Gunter von Oberhausen."

That the prince had referred to her as his "special" friend when introducing her had already taken her by surprise. "Particular friend" had a rather indecent ring to it, and she didn't want any gossip following her. She could barely imagine anyone here referring to her in such a manner, so absurd it was. "I only had the pleasure of meeting the prince yesterday. He was very kind to offer invitations to me and my friends for this evening despite our recent acquaintance."

"Ah, yes, so I see," Herr von Oberhausen said, although he didn't act convinced by her explanation. "I imagine he was as charmed by your beauty as any gentleman would be, myself included." He extended his hand toward her. "Will you permit me to invite you to dance, especially as Mr. Jennings here has failed to do so? The waltzes this evening are delightful, and I do not think they allow such a dance so frequently in London as they do here in Paris."

Mr. Jennings made a noise in his throat but said nothing. Anna doubted Herr von Oberhausen heard it, but she was exceedingly aware of the nuances of Mr. Jennings's utterances by now.

She was at a loss as to what to do. Dancing wasn't something she had expected at the soiree, and it certainly wasn't something she'd considered doing while in mourning, although it wasn't quite as frowned upon during half-mourning, which was conveyed by the color of her gown. Besides, she wasn't entirely sure she wished to dance with someone who was so obviously flirting with her; it felt oddly dangerous.

And yet Mr. Osbourne had impressed upon her the fact that there would be people here this evening whose position within the Sixth Coalition needed smoothing. Was Herr von Oberhausen one of those people?

She straightened her spine and inhaled deeply. "Thank you, Herr von Oberhausen," she said, hoping the smile on her face looked genuine. "I would be honored."

Mr. Jennings made another small sound in his throat.

She smiled the same smile at Mr. Jennings that she'd just given Herr von Oberhausen.

"Excellent," Herr von Oberhausen purred. "And you must call me Gunter." He offered her his arm and led her out onto the floor, where others were dancing.

Anna couldn't help but glance back at Mr. Jennings as Herr von Oberhausen—she would *not* refer to him as Gunter—took her in his arms . . . and then pulled her in far too closely for her liking.

⁓⟊⁓

James turned on his heel and stalked to a side of the hall where there were fewer people with whom to engage in conversation but where it still allowed him to keep an eye on Lady Anna and von Oberhausen. James tried not to appear to be pacing, and he did manage brief conversations with a few people. He also tried not to be too obvious in following Lady Anna's actions, despite himself.

He already distrusted von Oberhausen from their previous encounters, few though they had been, and his instincts were telling him that the man was up to something. That von Oberhausen would also refer to Lady Anna as Schwarzenberg's "particular friend," as in the prince's mistress, was extremely unsettling.

Herr Gunter von Oberhausen was from the Grand Duchy of Berg, which had been poorly ruled for the past decade: first passed as a concession from the kingdom of Prussia to the French Empire and impoverished for the past decade due to Bonaparte's failed economic plans. The kingdom of Prussia had just reclaimed the duchy, and James wondered if von Oberhausen might be planning to use Lady Anna as a pawn somehow, especially if he truly thought Lady Anna was a "particular friend" of the powerful prince, who, besides being *generalissimo*, was also ambassador to France and highly regarded among the Coalition members.

If this was von Oberhausen's plan, it would be of no use to him, since Lady Anna was *definitely not* Schwarzenberg's "particular friend," so to speak. And while James recognized several highly regarded mistresses of some of the elite in attendance this evening—along with countesses and duchesses and wives—he was unsure whether Schwarzenberg indulged in such abhorrent but socially acceptable behavior.

Lady Anna finished the waltz with von Oberhausen, but then another gentleman, one of von Oberhausen's associates, claimed her for the next dance. James doubted Lady Anna would have preferred to dance at all this evening and had only agreed in order to comply with the prince's wishes that she relax her state of mourning for the evening.

If von Oberhausen thought to apply pressure to Schwarzenberg by seducing the prince's supposed "particular friend" . . .

James would not allow it.

Thus resolved, he made his way through the crowds and stood near where Lady Anna was dancing. He had met her dance partner only once and couldn't recall his name at present. James hadn't exerted himself when it had come to von Oberhausen's friends.

The music drew to a conclusion, and James immediately walked out onto the dance floor toward Lady Anna, but unfortunately, von Oberhausen must have noticed James's movements and arrived at Anna's side right before James did.

"It is a pleasure indeed to watch you dance, Lady Anna—nearly as much as actually dancing with you," von Oberhausen said.

"Lady Anna," James interjected.

Lady Anna turned and looked at him, her eyes large. He wished he could discern what her eyes were telling him, but no matter. He was on a mission now.

"And yet I dare not invite you to dance again," von Oberhausen continued, his voice low and inviting, "for I know we must maintain appearances, no? But a stroll around the room would not be forbidden, surely. And I will enjoy introducing you to so many of the prince's esteemed guests."

"The prince took care of that himself," James said, trying to maintain his composure. "Come, Lady Anna, I believe I see—"

"Surely you cannot begrudge me a stroll with such a beautiful woman as Lady Anna," von Oberhausen interrupted with a smug smile that James wanted to wipe from the man's face. "I only wish to have *my* turn to enjoy Lady Anna's charms before Schwarzenberg takes his opportunity to spend time with her. And *you*, of course, have undoubtedly enjoyed *much* of Lady Anna's attention and time already; is this not fair to say?"

Von Oberhausen's last statement held enough innuendo that James felt his muscles tense.

"I believe you are under a misapprehension, Herr von Oberhausen," James said, stepping closer to the couple. He glanced at Lady Anna, at her beautiful, anxious face and her large, worried—yes, worried—eyes. "I cannot speak for Lady Anna as to whether I have taken too much of her time." He stared at her, hoping she would read his thoughts, somehow, and politely decline von Oberhausen's invitation. "And it is certainly Lady Anna's choice with whom she wishes to stroll or dance or engage in conversation."

"Lady Anna?" von Oberhausen asked with just a hint of challenge in his tone.

She smiled brightly—too brightly for James's liking—at von Oberhausen. "I should be delighted to stroll with you and meet more of the prince's guests. Thank you," she said.

Von Oberhausen offered Lady Anna his arm. "Excellent. I am the most fortunate of gentlemen, my lady." He shot a triumphant glance at James.

Lady Anna looked at James with those dazzling blue eyes of hers, still smiling, yet her smile didn't reach her eyes.

James needed to assure her of his protection from von Oberhausen, whom James mistrusted completely now. "I should enjoy taking a turn with you around the room myself, Lady Anna, and perhaps even sharing a dance, if that pleases you, after your stroll with this gentleman."

"Thank you, Mr. Jennings," Anna said in return, and James thought he caught the merest sign of relief in her expression.

"I shall ardently await your return to my side," he added. He spoke to Lady Anna, but the words were directed at von Oberhausen.

Von Oberhausen merely nodded, and the two of them strolled away from James and disappeared into the crowd.

"Here you are!" Osbourne's too-cheery voice exclaimed behind James. "I've been looking for you and Lady Anna."

"I'm sure you have been," James growled.

"Someone is in a foul mood," Osbourne said, stating the obvious.

"In a word, von Oberhausen," James replied.

"Ah," Osbourne said.

"The man implied that Anna was Schwarzenberg's mistress, and I believe he wishes to ingratiate himself with her to get in the prince's good graces—or, at least, to manipulate the prince in some way. I doubt she is enjoying herself."

"Hmm," was all Osbourne said in return.

Osbourne's reply confirmed at least part of James's suspicions: his friend was involved with this particular scheme in some fashion.

And James intended to get to the bottom of it.

How dare he!

First, Mr. Jennings did nothing while Herr von Oberhausen took her onto the floor to dance and whisper unseemly things to her while holding her too closely for propriety's sake.

And *then* he simply stood aside and let *her* decide whether to stroll with Herr von Oberhausen—*she*, who only knew that being amiable was important for diplomatic reasons but nothing else. Surely, Mr. Jennings should have realized that she was ill-equipped to deal with the likes of Herr von Oberhausen. This stranger was no fool, and despite his handsome outward appearance and smooth charm, it had only taken an introduction to him for her to realize that he was a rogue and not to be trusted.

She wished she'd had a decent response to keep him in his place, but while her upbringing had taught her how to behave in polite society, it hadn't precisely taught her how to deal with rakes or rogues. And the circumstances this evening were far removed from London gatherings and especially distant from simple life at Clifton Cross.

She chided herself as she strolled next to Herr von Oberhausen and smiled and nodded greetings at the people—mostly gentlemen—to whom she was being introduced. She should be grateful to Mr. Jennings for crossing the dance floor to check on her at all, she supposed.

"May I introduce Herr Schreiber . . . Herr Franck . . . Herr Schmidt and Fraulein Vogel . . . Baron Eric von Klein . . . Herr Müller . . . Monsieur Fontaine . . ." The names he said seemed to drone on endlessly.

She did her best to act normally, smile, curtsy, offer her hand to be bowed over and respond properly as Herr von Oberhausen introduced her to the people with whom it was obvious he was most acquainted. It was also obvious that those people had heard a rumor about her being the prince's "particular friend," if their hidden smirks and the wanton glances from the gentlemen were anything to go by.

Because she'd been urged by Mr. Osbourne to be cordial for diplomacy's sake, she did her best, but inside, she was seething.

It had only gotten worse when Herr von Oberhausen had leaned close to her ear as they'd finally strolled back toward Mr. Jennings. "You are a tempting morsel, my dear," he whispered, making her shudder. "The prince is the most fortunate of men; I envy him. Perhaps you will tell him of my restraint. It was most difficult, I assure you."

By the time he returned her to Mr. Jennings's side, Anna had had enough. She was being used as a pawn; she could feel it. She wanted to leave, and the sooner the better.

"Thank you for the stroll, Herr von Oberhausen, and for introducing me to so many fascinating people," she said flatly, even while doing her best to appear truthful.

He bowed to Anna but not without shooting a victorious glance at Mr. Jennings. "My dear Lady Anna, our time together draws to a conclusion. *Auf wiedersehen*, lovely lady. It has been a pleasure—a brief, perhaps *unfulfilled* pleasure, but a pleasure, nonetheless. Perhaps we shall see each other again soon. That is my hope."

She responded with a slight curtsy and then watched with relief as he sauntered off.

Mr. Jennings offered her his arm, which she chose to ignore.

"You're upset," he whispered.

"Upset does not even begin to cover what I am feeling at present," she replied, glancing at a footman standing nearby, pretending not to listen. She could only pray the man didn't speak much English.

"We are in unusual circumstances here, even more so than I realized," he said softly, also glancing at the footman. "Come, dance with me. Most of these people will ignore us if we're dancing, but they will surely remember a contretemps they witnessed at Schwarzenberg's soiree."

He made a good argument, Anna thought begrudgingly. Of course he had; he was a lawyer. "Very well," she said.

Once again, Mr. Jennings offered Anna his arm, which she took this time. He led the way back to the area set aside for dancing, deliberately adjusting their steps so they appeared to be strolling in a leisurely manner. When they were among the other dancers, he turned and offered her his arms for the slow waltz currently in progress.

Anna held up her arms and allowed him to take her in his . . . and the moment he did, she felt as though she were on fire, and her reaction to him only made her angrier.

"What's the matter now?" he whispered against her ear.

"It's rather hot in here," she said. She wasn't about to confess her attraction to him when she was so upset.

He had the good sense to remain silent.

And then he pulled her in more closely, and she thought she truly might burst into flames. It was the complete opposite of how she'd felt when Herr von Oberhausen had done the same thing.

"Then, why has your heart sped up so?" he asked. "We are not dancing so quickly that you should be . . . breathless . . ." He had the masculine audacity to whisper that last word near her ear.

She shivered—entirely against her will.

He gracefully spun her, and they danced, now in silence, thank goodness, while she continued to fight the urge to touch his face and breathe in his masculine scent and draw him closer to her and relish the strength of his shoulders.

She was in trouble.

"Ah! Here you both are," someone said behind them. "I've been trying to find you."

It was Mr. Osbourne, and the smirk on his face said much more than his words did.

Anna told herself to stop blushing even as she felt her cheeks heating up.

"I invited Lady Anna to enjoy a waltz with me," Mr. Jennings said smoothly. *He* wasn't blushing in the least, which was *entirely* unfair.

"I thought von Oberhausen had claimed her . . ." Mr. Osbourne let his words linger in the air.

"So he had," Mr. Jennings said. "And yet, here we are, Lady Anna and I, dancing together until we were unfortunately interrupted."

Mr. Osbourne glanced at Anna. She couldn't tell what he was thinking, and she dearly wished she could—or maybe not—and then he smiled what seemed to her a knowing smile at Mr. Jennings. This was becoming unbearable. Perhaps she'd been in safer hands with Herr von Oberhausen; at least with him, she'd had some clarity about his actions and intentions.

"My apologies for the interruption," Mr. Osbourne said. "I shall leave you to your waltz." He chuckled and sauntered off.

"Mr. Osbourne seems pleased with himself," Anna said as they began dancing again.

"Indeed," Mr. Jennings said.

"I couldn't bear the way Herr von Oberhausen and his friends were looking at me," Anna said candidly to him. "A man may do as he pleases, but a lady . . . Even the smallest hint of scandal can follow her for years. You and Mr. Osbourne needn't worry about such things; being gentlemen and sons of noblemen, you are allowed certain indiscretions. But I cannot bear to let these circumstances bring dishonor to my family. My honor may be all I have left in the world if I don't find Avery."

"I understand better than you may think," he replied. "But for now, we must play the part, so to speak, so we shall smile and dance and be congenial toward anyone with whom we converse while we remain. We shall sort everything else tomorrow. And I promise you, all will be well."

And then he twirled her, bringing her even closer to him, their bodies nearly touching, and she felt unable to push him away, even though she was confused and embarrassed and . . . and her soul dearly wished she could believe what he had just promised her.

The waltz was drawing to a close, and James reluctantly adjusted his hold on Lady Anna to allow more space between them. Oh, but she felt soft and warm and smelled of jasmine and vanilla, the commingled scents both strong and light, just as Lady Anna herself was.

He looked at her face, directly into her sapphire eyes, unable to let go of her hand or draw his other hand from her slender waist. They danced this way until the waltz ended . . . and then her gaze went to something or someone behind him, and he immediately felt a tap on his shoulder. He broke his dance hold with Lady Anna and turned.

"Mr. Jennings," a footman, who'd apparently been the person to tap his shoulder, said. "Prince Karl Philipp requests the company of you and your dance partner. Please, follow me."

James offered Lady Anna his arm, and they followed the footman to an area arranged with chairs for people who wished to sit and take refreshments. James spied Schwarzenberg in conversation with men whose lands had been part of the Confederation of the Rhine under Napoleon. James didn't know everyone gathered around the prince, but he recognized a few: Prince Johann, the prince regent of Liechtenstein, and envoys from Luxembourg, Belgium, and the Netherlands, who represented only a few of the sovereignties scrambling to find their footing now that Napoleon had abdicated.

"Ah, Mr. Jennings and Lady Anna," Schwarzenberg said in a cheerful tone after he and the others rose to their feet in greeting. "Have you met the other members of my group here?" He then proceeded to make all the introductions. "There! Now we are all acquainted. My friends, Mr. Jennings, along with Mr. Osbourne, whom you met earlier, serve with Lord Castlereagh and, therefore, deserve not only your acquaintance but your respect, for we are indebted to our English friends, are we not?"

"Yes," a couple of them said. "*Ja*" and "*Oui*" were also commingled with the English, as were "*Merci*" and "*Danke*." But James also noticed a few raised eyebrows among those to whom they'd been introduced. Rumors appeared to have spread even here, it seemed.

"And while I would enjoy nothing more than to have you become further acquainted with Mr. Jennings and the lovely Lady Anna, I'm afraid I must take them from you for a few minutes so I may converse with them. Please excuse us."

The others nodded politely in farewell as the prince gestured toward a nearby corridor. "Shall we?" he said, addressing James and Lady Anna, and then he led the way down the corridor until they were at a door, which a footman opened.

"Please," the prince said, gesturing for them to enter the room first.

It was an elegant study, James noticed, decorated in deep velvet and dark woods, but he was more concerned about the private conversation that was about to occur. Lady Anna's eyes couldn't get any larger. He laid his free hand reassuringly atop her hand, which was gripping his arm now rather than resting on it.

"You may not be able to tell," the prince began once they had all seated themselves, "but I am exceedingly angry at present. Only years of serving diplomatically and militarily and the self-discipline I have developed as a result have kept my other guests from seeing my displeasure."

James glanced sideways at Lady Anna, who sat next to him on a settee. She had visibly paled.

"I enjoyed our time together yesterday evening, Lady Anna, over the finer points of chess and thought you an honorable English lady with whom I could share a congenial friendship. I even bestowed a distinct honor upon you by personally inviting you here this evening, extending the invitation to your two friends as well. I confess I would have felt more comfortable had their associate Lord Castlereagh been in Paris. And now my intuition tells me I was correct to have concerns."

"Your Serene Highness—" James began to interject.

The prince held up his hand to silence him without so much as looking his way.

"I am grieved, Lady Anna," Schwarzenberg said, shaking his head in feigned sorrow.

James remained quiet since he'd been silenced once already by the prince. He was rarely at a loss, but this occasion required delicate maneuvering, for it was easy now to see just how angry Schwarzenberg was.

No one spoke. Anna sat rigidly next to James, her full lips quivering. James wanted to take her hand in his own but didn't dare move.

It dawned on him then that they were very much in their own chess match at the moment, he and Lady Anna, facing down the prince. James felt like a pawn. He imagined Lady Anna did too. Whose move was it?

"What have you to say for yourself?" the prince asked after a tense pause.

Lady Anna straightened her back and took a deep breath. "I accepted your invitation to attend this celebration in good faith," she said. "My only intent on traveling to Paris was to locate my brother, the last of my immediate family, who was wounded in battle and is missing. What is it I'm supposed to have done?" she asked. "I have but danced two dances and was invited to stroll briefly."

Well done, Lady Anna, James thought. She was acting with dignity and had not recoiled under the prince's surprising anger.

"And apparently thought it to your benefit to suggest to your partners that you had a, shall we say, *intimate* relationship with a certain prince," the prince said. "Me, in fact."

Anna shook her head in denial. "I would *never* presume such a thing on our brief acquaintance and your kindness in such a manner as I have been accused, Your Highness," she said. "In fact, I would never agree to be someone's mistress at all and am offended at the damage such an implication would make to my family's and my reputation."

"Your Serene Highness," James said again. "Allow me to speak on Lady Anna's behalf. I am of the opinion that Gunter von Oberhausen is the source of the rumor."

"Von Oberhausen?" the prince asked, not replying to Lady Anna.

"Yes, Your Highness," James replied. "While I might be willing to suggest that my colleague Mr. Osbourne hoped that introducing you to our beautiful new friend here would gain us an invitation to tonight's soiree, owing to your generous nature, it was never our intent to do anything rather than further

Lord Castlereagh's diplomatic work. Von Oberhausen, on the other hand, seems willing to dishonor not only Lady Anna but you yourself also by his actions and choice of words."

"Von Oberhausen," the prince repeated. He rose to his feet and assisted Anna to hers. "My deepest apologies, Lady Anna, Mr. Jennings, for putting you through this questioning. But instead, you have succeeded in confirming long-held suspicions regarding von Oberhausen. Please excuse me." He bowed and then left the room abruptly.

"'My apologies for suggesting you are telling people you're my mistress,'" James muttered as he stood, pretending he was Schwarzenberg. "And then he leaves, just like that." He shook his head. "Were he not a prince, I would challenge him to a duel on your behalf. I have half a mind to do so anyway."

"It would accomplish nothing," Anna said, looking heart-breakingly crestfallen. "Prince Karl Philipp is a better chess player than we thought. But thank you, Mr. Jennings. If you'd be so kind, I should like to leave now."

"Yes, we should probably join the other guests," James said.

"You misunderstand," Lady Anna said. "I wish to leave this place."

CHAPTER 9

Anna felt utterly overwhelmed after the conversation she and Mr. Jennings had just had with Prince Karl Philipp. Somehow, she managed to put one foot in front of the other and allowed Mr. Jennings to lead her back to the main floor of the prince's grand Paris mansion.

"We are being watched, so I suggest you smile," Mr. Jennings whispered to her out of the side of his mouth. "Looking adoringly at me wouldn't go amiss, either, in order to further dispel rumors."

"You are tempting fate with your words," Anna whispered back as she smiled up at him and then at the guests they passed as they walked. "We would only be creating a different rumor to take the place of the first, and my reputation would sink even further."

"As much as you would like to leave right now, I fear we must stay and allow events to play out," Mr. Jennings said. "Despite your concerns, leaving now would make you appear even more guilty to others. Be strong, Lady Anna. You are the young lady who is determined to cross France in order to find your brother. You can withstand an unfortunate turn of events at a soiree."

The current dance, a quadrille, was ending, and Mr. Jennings had just taken her hand to lead her in the next dance when she heard those around her begin to murmur. Thankfully, as it turned out, the murmurs weren't about her.

"Lords and ladies, *médames et messieurs*, welcome!" Prince Karl Phillip said in a booming voice one would expect from someone who led military troops. He was standing on the dais alongside the orchestra. "Please allow me to share a few thoughts with you, but I would ask you to allow me to share it three times: in English, in French, out of appreciation for our host city, and in German." He then spoke French and German; Anna presumed it was to repeat what he'd said in English. She glanced briefly at Mr. Jennings; he appeared to be listening attentively to the prince's words.

"I am glad we are able to meet in such joyous circumstances and continue our celebration of the abdication of Napoleon Bonaparte," Prince Karl Philipp said.

The guests applauded enthusiastically, so Mr. Jennings let go of Anna's hand in order to applaud with the others. There were also boos and hisses at the mention of Bonaparte, with ensuing laughter.

"Ah, I see you agree with me," the prince said. "We now begin the task of uniting, setting aside past grievances, and looking toward the future."

The guests reacted with more applause as he repeated his words in French and German.

"It will be difficult, my friends," Prince Karl Philipp continued. "Most of us have suffered losses great and small over the past many years. We have tried to work *with* Bonaparte; we have tried to work *against* Bonaparte. We have had to become enemies with each other at times only to unite as allies later. We have strong ties to our lands and our people and have lost loved ones. These past many years have taken a toll on us all."

Anna felt a knife of pain slice through her heart at his mention of loss. Oh, how she prayed Avery wasn't one of those lives lost!

The prince then repeated his words in French and German. Anna appreciated what he was saying and that he meant to reach everyone in the hall in as personal a way as possible. But his abrupt apology to her and swift dismissal after his accusations, combined with the thought of Avery and the searing emotions it brought with it, were more than she could bear.

"May we leave now?" she whispered to Mr. Jennings.

"Soon," he replied, his attention entirely on the prince.

"We must work together, my friends, to form a new, stronger coalition that will allow us to live in peace," the prince boomed, raising his hand in a gesture of triumph. The guests clapped and cheered. He waited until all was silent. "And yet," he continued in a softer voice, "even tonight, there are those among us who would use deceit to gain a stronger position at the negotiation table."

Anna gasped along with a number of the guests.

"Rumors and innuendo have circulated amongst us this very evening . . ."

Anna studied her slippers while the guests murmured. Mr. Jennings put his arm around her shoulders. "I need to leave," she whispered to him.

"I'm afraid we can't, not yet," he replied. He tightened his arm around her briefly in a reassuring gesture.

Despite his reassurances, Anna felt dread, like a heavy cloud, creeping over her. If the prince's accusations were about

Herr von Oberhausen, they would lead back to her—and she had done nothing! How was this evening to end?

She searched the crowd for Herr von Oberhausen and spied him near the side of the hall, his arms crossed, a smirk on his face. That told her much.

And then by accident, she spied Mr. Osbourne in the crowd. He wasn't far from them, actually, and if her eyes weren't lying to her, he was actually holding back a smirk of his own.

And just like that, she knew. She knew! These horrid men, these so-called diplomats, these politicians, had used her. Against her knowledge and her will, she'd been a puppet in their little games of subterfuge.

"I am leaving *now*," she said in a normal voice—no whispers this time—to Mr. Jennings. "I would welcome your escort from this place. Or you may choose to stay with your clever associate and any of the others who may have had a hand in this duplicity. But I am leaving."

What the devil is going on? James asked himself. He planned on getting to the bottom of things, and quickly, but right now, he had to stop Lady Anna from drawing any attention to them, for her own sake, if nothing else.

He held tightly to her hand as she tried to step forward. His mind scrambling, he drew her back and then leaned in toward her. "Please, *do not* do anything to bring any attention to us," he said. Then he brought her hand to his lips, hoping to soothe her and . . . and he didn't know what else.

Even with the noise and the distractions around them, the touch of her hand to his lips started him shaking internally.

He fought to keep his control when what he wished to do was just as she'd said—escort her from the hall . . . and then take her away from here to a place where they could be alone and he could kiss her again, tasting her lips this time.

But they needed answers, and that meant staying a bit longer.

"I have been used," Lady Anna said.

"I believe you're right. But it will be easier to determine how all of this happened if we remain. Please, trust me, Lady Anna," he said. He'd dealt with the machinations in politics often enough in his work with Lord Castlereagh and the Foreign Office, but never had he had to deal with it in such a personal manner.

"Please, Mr. Jennings," she whispered.

"Trust me," he said and kissed her hand once more.

She heaved a sigh. "Very well," she said.

His heart, which had overflowed with the mere touch of his lips to her hand, nearly broke. "I will find out who is behind this, Lady Anna. I promise you."

"I daresay your friend Mr. Osbourne would be a good source for answers," she said.

She was undoubtedly right, considering Osbourne's enthusiasm in presenting Lady Anna to Schwarzenberg at the café last evening.

Schwarzenberg appeared to be concluding his remarks, so James returned his attention to the prince. "Despite such disappointing news, I do not plan to act on this information this evening. But I encourage us all to be open and forthcoming as we work together going forward. Yes?" There was applause in response. "We *can* work together. I know it! Now, eat, my friends! Dance and drink and enjoy yourselves! It is my greatest wish!" He spoke briefly to the orchestra conductor, stepped down from the dais, and approached *them*, bowing to James and shaking his hand, and then bowing to Lady Anna. "My dear Lady Anna, I must apologize once again," he said in a low voice.

Lady Anna didn't respond, and James felt like a stone as he gripped her hand, needing to embrace her and reassure her but unable to do so with Schwarzenberg standing right next to him and the crowds milling about them. Of course, she couldn't help but feel that the other guests were looking at them—too curiously for her own comfort.

The orchestra began playing a quadrille so loudly that it drowned out the murmurs of the crowd, which James presumed had been intentional on Schwarzenberg's part. "Please, join me once again, if you would be so kind," the prince said.

James and Lady Anna followed the prince away from the guests, who had begun taking their positions for the dance. He slid her hand through the crook of his elbow and placed his hand reassuringly atop hers—not for the first time this evening—as they followed the prince back to the room where they'd been before.

The prince spoke briefly to the footman who still remained at the door and then closed the door behind them.

James felt Lady Anna's hand clench within his.

"Mr. Jennings, Lady Anna, please, be seated," Schwarzenberg said, gesturing toward the chairs they'd sat in before. "We are awaiting the arrival of one more person."

James led her to the chair where she'd sat previously. He then seated himself next to her, all the time keeping her hand in his.

Schwarzenberg gestured to a different footman standing at the side of the room, and the footman brought a tray containing goblets of wine. Anna refused a goblet with a shake of her head. James, however, took one and gulped the contents down rather too hastily before returning it to the tray.

"Lady Anna," Schwarzenberg said once the footman had slipped from the room. "Thank you for trusting me enough to join me here once more. I left you and Mr. Jennings abruptly before, but I needed to let certain individuals know posthaste that I—*we*—were now aware of their deceptions and stop them before too much damage was done. Steps have been taken behind the scenes in this regard. I doubt you realize it, but you have actually helped the Coalition greatly. But to my great sorrow, you were used without your—or my—knowledge."

He turned fully in his own chair so that he was face-to-face with her. "You are owed not only a most sincere apology for all that has occurred this evening but also our sincerest thanks."

She did not reply when Schwarzenberg paused to take a breath, and James wondered if he should interject something himself but opted to let things play out.

The door opened, and Osbourne was shown into the room.

"Ah, here is the final person now," the prince said. "Please, Mr. Osbourne, be seated."

James glanced at Osbourne, who shot him an unreadable look.

"I believe Mr. Osbourne is the key to explaining the circumstances in which you found yourself this evening, Lady Anna. Is this not true, Mr. Osbourne?"

"Yes, sir," Osbourne said.

"Osbourne," James said, looking directly at him. "What the devil were you about? And why didn't you tell me?"

"There were some things it was best to keep to myself, my friend," Osbourne said. "You see, *you* are the honorable lawyer and translator and are highly regarded, and you needed to remain unscathed by these particular matters. I, however . . ."

James shook his head, disgusted.

"There was no guarantee any of this would work," Osbourne continued. "I merely took a calculated risk."

"To continue," Schwarzenberg said. "As you may have gleaned already, we have long suspected von Oberhausen of subterfuge but had no proof. Now we have caught him in the act, and it may put a stop to him at last."

Anna had no words for Prince Karl Philipp. She only knew she was still angry that *she*, an innocent, seemed to hold such little value to these people.

She remained silent.

Prince Karl Philipp looked straight into her eyes. "You do not speak, Lady Anna, and yet your eyes speak volumes. If I had sapphires that rivaled your eyes, I would be a wealthy man."

"You *are* a wealthy man," Anna said, surprising herself that she'd actually said the words aloud.

"Ah, my dear lady," the prince said, "there is wealth, which we think of as property, but then there is *true* wealth. Am I not correct in this, Mr. Jennings?"

Anna looked at Mr. Jennings, who looked intently back at her before returning his attention to the prince. "Indeed, sir," he said.

"And while I am a wealthy man, as you say, Lady Anna," the prince continued, "there are occasions when a man may envy another man and his wealth."

She was utterly confused by his cryptic words.

"Enough," the prince said, seeming to shift topics. "Lady Anna, there are many gathered here in Paris who wish for a peaceful beginning for our lands after so long a time at war with France."

Mr. Jennings and Mr. Osbourne nodded their concurrence to his words.

"It is difficult to remember a time when war has not been waging somewhere. You understand?" the prince continued.

"Yes," Anna replied.

"One might think that all men wish for the same things, but that is not the case," he said. "And some who have come to Paris in anticipation of the Congress in Vienna to occur later this year have less-than-honorable motives. Mr. Osbourne?"

Mr. Osbourne cleared his throat. "You see, Lady Anna, when you arrived in Paris with Mr. Jennings, I immediately recognized your rare beauty. Trust me when I tell you that your beauty is indeed rare, and I doubt any man alive would disagree with me. I thought to introduce you to Schwarzenberg . . . but only with the slimmest of hopes that his gallantry in meeting you would gain us entrée to his soiree. We had no invitation without Castlereagh here with us in Paris. But I also knew von Oberhausen would be in attendance, and we had already concluded that he may be the source of the diplomatic problems we have encountered as of late."

The prince smiled. "Lady Anna, as Osbourne said, I doubt there is a man alive who, upon seeing you, wouldn't be moved by your beauty, including myself."

"I am no one special," Anna said, contradicting the prince and feeling wholly embarrassed by his words. "There are many, *many* with more beauty than I."

"Ah, but you see, there is a difference between many of these so-called beauties you mention and yourself," the prince countered. "For they know of their beauty and flaunt it, and there is no prize to be had. But the beauty who shines with a goodness and a vulnerability and also has a fire burning within her—ah, now *she* is a prize to be won."

"A pearl," Mr. Jennings said softly to himself, but Anna heard him.

So, apparently, did the prince. "Precisely, Mr. Jennings. And if I may wax religious for a moment, a pearl of great price." He chuckled. "The nuns at the priory of St. Judith would be pleased to know I have retained some ecclesiastical knowledge after all my years in battle. And so, Mr. Osbourne was correct in his assumption: that it would be my pleasure to learn more about the rare young beauty who is friends with Castlereagh's agents. But back to what Mr. Osbourne was saying—while some, like myself, will recognize the pearl's true value, others will see it only as a fine bauble to be won."

"Which brings us to von Oberhausen," Mr. Osbourne said. "He has long felt that the Grand Duchy of Berg, his homeland, was especially mistreated. But he also saw this as an opportunity to enrich *himself* rather than work for the good of his people. Others began to see a pattern in the ways he manipulates others, including using women."

"And so you decided to manipulate Lady Anna into playing a role in all this?" Mr. Jennings asked.

"Had you arrived in Paris with me and read Castlereagh's letter then, you would have known he had asked us to attempt to ensnare von Oberhausen before the Congress of Vienna was set to commence. We have long suspected von Oberhausen of manipulating various sovereigns by insinuating himself with their courtesans and then using blackmail to gain favors for himself, as well as damaging delicate diplomatic relations. But this is the first time we have caught him at his game."

"But you didn't think to inform me," Mr. Jennings said.

"When I realized the opportunity Lady Anna presented, it was better for you not to know. Nothing might have occurred when we introduced Lady Anna to the prince. And when the prince *did* offer her an invitation, it would have been unfair to ask her to play a part in a charade when she has no experience in such things, and von Oberhausen might have become suspicious if her behavior hadn't seemed genuine.

"I saw a rare opportunity to draw out von Oberhausen, for you are unknown here in Paris, Lady Anna, and von Oberhausen would know nothing about you and might be inclined to believe whatever he thought he'd heard," Mr. Osbourne continued. "But I vow to you now that I only ever said that you were a special guest of the prince. The fact that von Oberhausen presumed you were the prince's 'particular friend' and what that would imply was his own doing, as we had hoped."

"You must have emphasized the words rather heavily for von Oberhausen to infer that Lady Anna was something more than that," Mr. Jennings said.

"I agree," Prince Karl Philipp said. "I, too, was not told of this subterfuge, Lady Anna. We have both been used as pawns in this particular chess match."

"My apologies, truly, sir," Mr. Osbourne said. "And my apologies to you, Lady Anna, for causing you distress. But this is a diplomatic success of huge proportion, as the scoundrel has been caught red-handed. I shouldn't be surprised if Castle-reagh were to award you a medal over this."

"No, thank you," Anna said. "I have no need for such a thing."

"And yet it seems we *are* truly in your debt, Lady Anna," Prince Karl Philipp said.

"If I may speak frankly," she said, "I doubt any of you are remembering that a man's reputation is never tarnished by such a rumor, but my reputation will never be the same, being a woman." She was shaking with anger. "Now, if you will excuse me, I wish to leave. I believe I have had enough intrigue for one evening."

"Certainly," the prince said. "I shall have my own carriage brought around for your use, if you'll allow me."

"Thank you," she replied tersely.

"I shall see that Lady Anna arrives home safely," James said. "I shall leave the rest of the evening's activities in the hands of Osbourne here."

The prince nodded and rang a bell sitting on a side table. A footman entered. "Have my carriage brought around," he said to the footman, then he stood and offered his hand to Anna. "Thank you again, Lady Anna, and my deepest apologies for any wound you have suffered as my guest this evening. And if I can ever be of service, you have only to ask."

She took his outstretched hand and rose to her feet.

"Come, Lady Anna," Mr. Jennings said softly.

She curtsied to the prince, and then she and Mr. Jennings left the room.

James and Lady Anna walked in silence until they reached the large main doors of Schwarzenberg's residence. When they arrived, James realized it would take several minutes for the carriage to be readied, and he'd had an idea while they'd been walking that would be better to act upon now rather than later.

"Will you be all right if I leave you for a few minutes?" he asked Anna. "I promise I will return shortly."

"Yes," she replied in a dull, muted tone.

He beckoned to a nearby footman. "*S'il vous plaît, veillez sur la dame pendant mon absence,*" he said to the man, asking him to take care of the lady while he was gone.

"But of course, sir," the footman replied in English.

James nodded appreciatively and then hurried back to the room he and Anna had just exited. "Is the prince still within?" he asked the footman at the door.

"*Oui,*" the footman replied.

"Will you announce me?" James asked.

The footman was thoughtful for a moment too long for James's liking. "*Oui,*" the footman said at last. He knocked and then opened the door. "Monsieur Jennings," he said.

Feeling impatient, James pushed past him and entered the room.

"Jennings, I didn't expect to see you again so soon," Schwarzenberg said. Osbourne was still with him.

"You said if there were ever a service you could perform, Lady Anna was only to ask," James said, addressing Schwarzenberg and ignoring Osbourne.

"I did."

"There is something you can do for her," James said.

"Tell me," Schwarzenberg said.

James recounted Anna's whole story, from losing her brother and father to setting off on her own to find Avery, resulting in her being in attendance with them tonight.

"Ah," Schwarzenberg said. "I begin to see. I am even more impressed with our Lady Anna than I was before. For her to journey such a long way in search of her brother is extraordinary. Brave." He nodded to himself, looking impressed. "The regiment to which her brother belongs, the 61st Regiment of Foot, campaigned at Toulouse after Orthez. They lost their commanding officer, Lieutenant Colonel Coghlan, during that battle, which may account for a delay in communication. I was informed that they were heading to Bordeaux on their way back to England."

It didn't surprise James that Schwarzenberg, a military general, would have kept abreast of such details. "You have already provided more information than she has gotten thus far," James said. "She will be exceedingly grateful to know this."

"Lieutenant Avery Clifton," Schwarzenberg repeated aloud. "Injured, missing . . . I shall have his situation looked into immediately. Now that we have snared von Oberhausen, we may be able to mend alliances with those whom he turned against us. Let me see what we can do for Lady Anna's personal cause."

"Thank you," James said wholeheartedly. "It will mean the world to her."

"You give yourself away, Jennings," Schwarzenberg said.

James sighed. There was no reason for him to lie if his feelings had become this obvious. "I confess, I have become rather attached to the lady."

"Go now," the prince said. "See your Lady Anna home. Perhaps you will remain in Paris for a few more days while we make inquiries regarding her brother."

"That, I'm afraid, I must leave entirely up to her. After what happened this evening, she seemed ready to depart from not only your soiree but also Paris, full stop." He stared directly at Osbourne as he spoke.

"I promise I will make things right with Lady Anna," Osbourne said apologetically.

"It had better be a promise you are able to keep," James replied. He nodded to both men and departed the room, anxious to return to her side. He wondered whether he should tell Lady Anna about Schwarzenberg's willingness to search for information on Avery. He didn't wish to build up her hopes only for them to be dashed, but he also didn't wish to keep anything from her, especially after what had transpired this evening.

When he returned to the entrance, he found that the carriage had arrived, and a footman was assisting Lady Anna inside.

James climbed in after she was seated and decided he was going to sit next to her rather than on the seat across from her. He needed to be where he could touch her, comfort her in any way possible.

She silently stared out the window.

"Anna," he said softly, purposefully refusing to include her title.

"Please, Mr. Jennings," she said. "Not now." She didn't respond to the familiarity with which he'd addressed her.

"I understand," he replied. He laid his hand gently on her shoulder and felt her shudder, but she didn't speak again and merely continued to stare out the window. He honored her wish and remained silent but moved his hand from her shoulder to rest on her clasped hands, hoping she would feel his support—and perhaps even his feelings for her.

As they rode back to the apartments, James reflected on their association, short as it had been. Even during their first meeting aboard *Serenity*, he had felt a spark, an attraction to her, although he'd denied it, thinking her foolish.

And then, as fate would have it, he had become a companion in her journey to find her brother. He had witnessed the depth of her love for her family, something he understood completely, and her strength and commitment and endurance. And his attraction to her had quickly grown—against his wishes, frankly, considering how inconvenient the timing of it all was—until there was truly an affection and respect for her that he couldn't deny.

He would honor her wishes to remain silent tonight. But tomorrow . . .

Tomorrow, he would speak.

The carriage rolled up to their apartments, and the footmen opened the doors for them and then assisted them as they disembarked.

Tomorrow, James would speak to her. He would tell her of Schwarzenberg's commitment to find information about her brother. James might even confess his feelings for her, depending upon . . . upon myriad things.

He would see what tomorrow brought.

CHAPTER 10

The music of the orchestra was lilting and graceful. It was a waltz. She was dancing. They were dancing too closely— she knew they were—and then the music grew louder and faster, and she was being spun around and spun even more, and she felt dizzy and thought she would faint. And the gentleman's arms were binding and cruel, and he forced her face against his chest. She tried to breathe, to call out . . .

"You are nothing," the man—he was no gentleman, although he had seemed to be one at the start—hissed into her ear. "You are a toy, a mere plaything, to be used to win favor or make enemies."

"No!" she cried out, pushing against his chest as hard as she could.

He only laughed.

The music went faster, and she pushed away from him even harder, and yet she clung to him, too, to keep her balance. "I have no wish for this!" she declared. "Let me go!"

She fought even more, and suddenly, she was free, and she collapsed to the floor—except it was the ground, and it was dark outside, and the man who had forced her to dance and had spoken cruelly to her was gone.

She struggled to her feet, still dizzy, and looked around her through the darkness. She pressed her hands to the sides of her head, trying to hold the dizziness at bay. She sobbed. "Help me!" she cried.

And then Papa was beside her. "There now, my child," he said. She looked up at him, and he was smiling at her. "All will be well."

She clutched his knees and pressed her head against him. "Papa," she whispered, and then he was gone.

Her heart hurt. Why? Why, if Papa had said all would be well, did her heart still hurt? Was it because of Avery?

Where was Avery? She called his name, but there was no response. "Where are you?" she cried. "Help me find you!"

She rose to her feet, and there was music again. It was another waltz, and she recognized that she was not outside but instead was in Schwarzenberg's lavish hall, and she was dancing once more but with someone else. Once again, she couldn't see her partner's face.

And then she knew: this time her partner was Mr. Jennings. He was leading her gently, and she felt safe, but she was exhausted and collapsed to the floor, and he sat next to her, placed his hand on her shoulder, and said, "Lady Anna, wake up."

"Lady Anna, wake up."

She opened her eyes. Mary was sitting on the bed next to her, looking concerned. Mr. Jennings stood just outside the doorway, and Anna could see Sparks and Mr. Osbourne behind him.

"Are you ill, my lady?" Mary asked. She rested her hand on Anna's forehead for a moment. "It doesn't appear that you're feverish, thank goodness."

"Why—" Anna started to say. *"Why are you all here, staring at me?"* was what she wanted to ask, but she wasn't ready to speak.

"I was concerned," Mr. Jennings said. "We all were, actually. You have been asleep for several hours. It's near midafternoon now. And when we heard you calling out in your sleep, I felt it was time to act."

"Against me will," Sparks muttered. "But I were overruled."

"Well, *I*, for one, were *glad* Mr. Jennings asked me to wake 'er," Mary said, sounding a bit defiant to Anna.

"Enough of that for now," Mr. Jennings said, his eyes still on Anna's. "There is tea and breakfast for you when you feel ready."

"Thank you?" she said. It felt like more of a question than a reply for some reason. Her thoughts were a jumble; it had been such an odd, upsetting dream. Usually her dreams were merely curiosities to be forgotten when she awoke. But this dream . . .

"We shall leave you now that we know you are well," Mr. Jennings said.

She still couldn't speak, so she nodded at him.

He gazed at her, making her feel breathless, and then closed the door, leaving only Mary in the room with her.

Anna placed her hand over her eyes, still trying to make sense of the images in her dream. There had been a message in her dream, she was sure of it. She didn't understand it all, but one thing she knew for sure: she needed to concentrate on finding Avery. *That* was why she was in France; *that* was what was most important to her, for her and her family's sake.

She rose from her bed and washed and dressed with Mary's assistance. It was going to be a difficult day, and she would need to be stronger than she had ever been.

"I told you I would apologize to her again, and I will," Osbourne said grumpily. He was slouched in an upholstered chair in the corner of the parlor with his arms crossed over his chest.

"I wouldn't have believed it of you to use an innocent in such a way," James shot back. He paced the room, unable to sit for any length of time, as he hadn't been able to sit for the entire day. If he hadn't wished to be here when Lady Anna awoke, he would have gone on a brisk walk around Paris. Who knew, he might have walked all the way to Calais and back, he was so agitated.

Sparks simply stood next to a wall, his hands shoved deep in his pockets, glaring at them, not speaking a word but saying volumes.

"Look, Jennings, I've said it a dozen times or more now. You know the Foreign Office has been watching von Oberhausen and others. Only recently it became apparent that von Oberhausen was a main instigator. The Duchy of Berg is so near France and many of the states of Germany who joined the Confederation of the Rhine in the past—"

"I don't require a history or geography lesson," James said, cutting him off.

"I know that," Osbourne replied, "but we were exceedingly fortunate that just before you arrived in Paris, von Oberhausen not only showed his hand for once but also one of his weaknesses."

"That being beautiful women," James said. "It is a weakness for most of us, Osbourne, so it doesn't excuse—"

"Yes, beautiful women," Osbourne said. "And you're right, drawing Lady Anna into my plan was—"

"Ungentlemanly? Callous?" James asked sarcastically.

"Necessary," Osbourne snapped. "Do you think I went into this lightly? There was no guarantee von Oberhausen would assume Lady Anna was Schwarzenberg's mistress and fall into the trap. We were fortunate."

"Fortunate," James said. *He* didn't feel fortunate. He felt bereft, as though part of his heart had been torn from him. How could Lady Anna ever believe that he truly had not played a part in this? She'd known he had tasks to perform with Osbourne for the Foreign Office. She wouldn't trust him were he to ask for her hand in marriage after this.

The thought hit him like a lightning strike: her hand in marriage. Blast it all, he wanted to marry her! And yet he'd barely known her a week; such a thought seemed contradictory to his reasoned mind.

"Yes, fortunate," Osbourne said, "for the Coalition and for Britain, Jennings. Come, man! You're not seeing things clearly."

"*I* am," Sparks said, speaking for the first time. "I see that it's time fer Lady Anna to leave Paris."

Sparks didn't know how right he was.

They all turned at a noise in the hallway. Lady Anna must have opened the door to her room; it could only be that. Shortly thereafter, she appeared in the doorway of the parlor, gripping the doorframe, dressed in black once again, her beautiful, pale countenance and blonde hair creating a striking contrast. James's heart leaped into his throat.

He and Osbourne both rose to their feet. Sparks strode to her and offered her his hand as Mary slipped into the room behind her.

"Please, Lady Anna, come and sit down," Sparks said. "I'll bring ye tea and somethin' to eat from the kitchen."

"Thank you, Sparks," Lady Anna said softly.

"I'll fetch the tea, Sparks," Mary said quietly. "Since I made the tea already, as ye know."

Lady Anna sat in the chair where Sparks led her, looking entirely uncomfortable, and then Sparks followed Mary from the parlor.

"Lady Anna—" Osbourne began.

She held up her hand and shook her head. "Before you say anything, I would like to inform you both that today I intend to pack my things and leave. I have traveled this far with only one goal: to find my missing brother. It is time I continue my search. I believe after I have eaten, Sparks and Mary and I shall pack our belongings and hire a coach in order to—"

"Lady Anna, there truly is no need," James said.

She looked at him with hollow eyes that clearly showed him the hurt and betrayal she felt.

Mary quickly returned with a tray bearing tea and a plate of pastries and set it on the table next to Anna's chair, then poured a cup of tea for her. Sparks had followed Mary back into the room and stood in the corner.

"Thank you, Mary," Lady Anna said. She sipped her tea and then sighed deeply.

"I am—we are—truly grateful that your arrival in Paris created the opportunity for which we have been striving," Osbourne said. "Perhaps you may understand Schwarzenberg's and my relief and gratitude at finally catching von Oberhausen in the act. The fact that you were known only to Jennings and the prince and myself was the key: it was easy for von

Oberhausen to believe you had arrived in Paris for the reason that had been implied. You were truly a godsend."

"I suppose you're welcome, then," Lady Anna said unenthusiastically. She took another sip of tea.

"Would you be willing to take a stroll with me?" James said, needing to do something, *anything*, to help relieve the hurt she was feeling. "There is something I feel I should tell you."

She gazed at him and sighed again, looking for all the world as if she wanted to go back to her room and sleep forever. It broke his heart to see her appear so beaten—the young lady who'd been brave and determined enough to embark on this journey in the first place.

"Not until she's had somethin' to eat," Sparks said.

She reached for a pastry and then stopped. "I shall go straightaway and get my bonnet and shawl." Then she placed her teacup on a side table, stood, and went to her room.

Sparks and Mary looked at each other and left the room together.

"You are in deep trouble, my friend," Osbourne said. "You have found your woman, and she might not have you. Poor devil."

"If such a thing turns out to be so, I will lay the reason entirely at your feet," James replied.

Anna stood in front of the mirror in her room and tied the bow on her bonnet. She barely recognized the face that looked back at her.

What a hopeful little fool she'd been to think that she could cross France on her own! She had known it was going to be an arduous undertaking. But she couldn't have imagined just how arduous and painful it would be—and she'd barely begun.

She grabbed her shawl and draped it around her shoulders and tugged on her gloves. She felt so alone. She hadn't made sense of her troubling dream. All that would have to wait, however. She was to have a conversation with Mr. Jennings now, and whatever it was, he wished to tell her in private, which didn't bode well.

She took one more look at the ashen face in the mirror and left the room.

The scene in the parlor hadn't changed much since she'd left the room. Mr. Osbourne was still slouched in his chair, and Sparks stood nearby, looking as though he'd like to punch something, with Mary standing next to him, holding a small basket. Mr. Jennings was by the door, holding his jacket and hat.

"I still think ye should eat before ye go," Sparks muttered. "Me and Mary packed some food for ye, just in case." He sent a sour look to Mr. Jennings.

"Thank you, both," Anna said.

Sparks nodded, and Mary handed the basket to Mr. Jennings, who had donned his jacket and hat while Sparks had spoken.

Mr. Jennings took the basket from Mary, then opened the door. "Shall we?" he said.

"Yes," Anna replied.

He offered her his arm when they reached the street, but she clasped her hands behind her back. She didn't think she could bear his touch right now. It might set off fireworks inside her and tear her limb from limb.

He dropped his arm.

"There's a little garden not far from here, according to Osbourne," Mr. Jennings said. "He has walked quite a bit while here in Paris—more than I. Would you care to go there?"

"Very well," Anna said.

As it was midafternoon, there were several people out and about, and Anna thought it oddly funny to think that other people were going about their lives normally when hers felt as if it were all a shambles.

"May I ask what you are thinking?" Mr. Jennings said.

She told him.

"Ah," he replied. "Of course. I'm sorry."

Anna said nothing.

They walked in silence down the street, nodding to the people they passed along the way. Anna gazed about her, taking in the architecture and the flowers and breathing in the fresh air, trying but failing to lift her spirits.

Soon they arrived at a small square surrounded by an elegant wrought-iron fence. The trees were green, and flowers of all kinds bloomed along a pathway that seemed to meander through the plantings.

"I would presume we have found the place Osbourne mentioned," Mr. Jennings said. He gestured for her to enter first.

As soon as she did, she was surrounded by sweet fragrances, and leaves and petals fluttered in a gentle breeze she hadn't noticed before. She breathed in deeply—and suddenly had a deep longing for home. For Papa and Mama and John and Sarah and Betty. For Avery.

She brushed away a tear.

"Are you unwell?" Mr. Jennings asked, looking concerned.

"No, I'm . . ." What to say? "I'm feeling nostalgic, I suppose. This garden is lovely."

"Yes," he said. He offered her his arm again, and this time, she placed her hand in the crook of his elbow. Thankfully, there were no fireworks, and she didn't find herself torn from limb to limb. Instead, she felt a warmth that gradually filled her with a sort of peace. She brushed away another tear.

"Truly, Anna, I wish to help," Mr. Jennings said.

She noticed he hadn't used her title when addressing her. He'd done it once last evening too. After all they'd been through the past few days, especially the last twenty-four hours, it probably felt natural to him to do so, she supposed. She decided to allow it.

They passed an amorous-looking couple; their arms were wrapped around each other as they walked, and they were trading kisses along the way. Anna felt her face bloom with color.

"Ah, the French," Mr. Jennings remarked when they were sufficiently past them.

She said nothing in reply. How could she possibly have responded?

She spied a gardener working in a corner of the little square, the only other person here, thank goodness.

They eventually approached a bench made of the same wrought iron as the fence. "Would you care to sit?" Mr. Jennings asked her. "Perhaps you'd like to eat whatever it is Sparks and Mary packed for us—you," he amended.

"I suppose I would, thank you," she said.

They sat.

Mr. Jennings opened the basket. "Nothing to drink, sadly," he said. "I hope you're not thirsty. But there are some pastries here." He handed her a napkin, she chose a pastry, and then he took one from the basket for himself and set the basket on the ground at his side. "Mmm," he said. "The French do know how to bake, do they not?"

"Yes," Anna replied.

"And the hospitality of the people," he said. "They seem more open, whereas we English tend to keep our emotions to ourselves."

"Mr. Jennings," Anna said. "Stop avoiding things and tell me what it is you wished to say."

He looked off into the distance for a moment. "Anna," he said. "I'm not avoiding things, as you claim. Our walk has been quiet and peaceful, and I'm reluctant to change that. I should like nothing better than to sit here with you all afternoon, if it were possible." He paused before continuing. "And after all we've been through together, I wish to ask if you would call me James."

Anna waited anxiously, unsure what to think about what he'd just said and what it might imply about his feelings for her. Was some sort of declaration of his feelings what he'd wished to share?

Finally, he turned toward her. "I don't wish to get your hopes up," he began, "but Schwarzenberg was indeed grateful for what happened last evening. I could tell that he truly wished to compensate you in some fashion for your role in the charade, especially as it was done without your knowledge and you were injured as a result. That is why I left you briefly last evening. I returned to speak with the prince. I told him of your search for Avery"—Anna's hands began to shake— "and he ordered an immediate investigation into your brother's whereabouts with his regiment."

"He's searching for information about Avery?" Anna said in a whisper, her entire body shaking now.

"He is," Mr. Jennings said.

"Oh, James!" she exclaimed, impulsively using his given name, and then despite herself and their public surroundings, she threw herself into his arms and began to cry.

James closed his eyes and held her. He could feel her sobs against his chest, and he savored the emotions, her life filling his heart, and hoped beyond hope it wouldn't be the last time he held her thus. He untied her bonnet and slipped it from her head, setting it down he knew not where, and then moved his hand to rest against the back of her head. He pressed his cheek to hers. "Anna," he said softly.

He allowed her to cry, grateful that this little garden was as private as it was. Grateful the other couple had left and that no one else had entered. And grateful that he'd noticed the gardener—who must be a true romantic—look at them, scratch his head, pick up his weeding tools, and leave.

"Schwarzenberg is a *generalissimo*, you know," James murmured as he reached into his pocket for his handkerchief and placed it in her hands. "When he speaks, others listen. He is having his subordinates look for documents regarding Avery's regiment to determine those who were wounded in battle—or killed." He added those last two words reluctantly but felt he must include them so that her hope held a degree of reality.

He felt her nod as he continued to hold her.

"What do you say we rest for a day or two and await his response?" James added. He'd been careful to choose words that gave her the choice rather than presume what it would be. As a lawyer—and not only a lawyer but a lawyer with *outspoken sisters* too—he knew it was important to let her voice her opinion, especially after last night.

"I can scarcely believe the prince is looking into Avery and his regiment," she murmured as she pressed the handkerchief to her eyes.

He let go of a breath he didn't realize he'd been holding. "It is a grand opportunity neither of us could have imagined when we left Calais," he said.

They grew silent again, and Anna, against James's wishes, moved out of his arms. She stayed close to him, however, at least closer than she'd started out when they'd seated themselves on the bench, which James took as a hopeful sign.

He looked at her. She was gazing out at the park, so he turned his gaze too. The leaves on the trees fluttered in the light filtering through their branches, the shrubs and flowers were in bloom, and James could hear birdsong. He returned his gaze to Anna. A few strands of her hair had come loose from her coiffure and fluttered in the breeze, the blonde strands glinting in the occasional bit of sunlight that peeked through the shade.

The prince had been correct last evening: she needed no expensive gowns or sparkling gems to appear entirely beautiful.

"Would you care for another pastry?" James asked her, simply searching for something to say.

"No," she replied with a smile.

"Shall we take advantage of a beautiful afternoon to stroll?" he asked. "The garden is lovely, but parts of Paris are equally enchanting."

She nodded, dabbing at her eyes once more.

He stood and picked up the basket resting on the bench, then offered his hand to her while she stood. She slipped her hand once again into the crook of his arm.

"What are you thinking?" James said as they strolled toward the entrance of the little park. "You seem far away."

She blushed charmingly. "If you must know, I was listing some of the qualities I have come to admire about you."

"I can't say I'm displeased about that," he replied with a chuckle. "I have recently created a similar list of my own regarding *your* qualities."

She looked at him incredulously. "How can you be the same James Jennings I met on the pier by the Duke of Aylesham's yacht?" she asked.

"I was not at my best then, I confess," he replied. "I could see only a naive young lady who was setting off on what I perceived to be a foolish journey. I understand your brave intentions much better now."

"Thank you," she said.

As they left the garden, they spied a too-familiar person approaching them at a quickened pace.

"I thought I might find you here," Osbourne said when he reached them. He pulled a handkerchief from his pocket and dabbed at his forehead. He'd obviously been in a hurry to reach them.

"What is it?" James asked, suddenly turning serious.

"Lady Anna, you received a letter from Schwarzenberg, and the footman who delivered it asked that we—as in, the three of us—meet with the prince at four o'clock. When you didn't return directly, I thought it prudent to look for you. Thankfully, you are here."

"Did you get any impression whether the news was good or ill?" Anna asked.

"No," Osbourne said. "But I brought the letter with me." He reached into his breast pocket and retrieved the letter and handed it to her. It bore the seal of the prince of Schwarzenberg. She broke the seal and unfolded the missive, then read it aloud.

> *Dear Lady Anna,*
>
> *Fortune is indeed your friend, for I have been able to locate documents related to the 61st Regiment of Foot, under the general leadership of my esteemed friend the Duke of Wellington. It is rare that such documents would come so easily into my hands. If you would grant me the privilege of your presence this afternoon, I shall explain further.*
>
> *Yours,*
>
> *Prince Karl Philipp*
> *of Schwarzenberg*

She gasped. "News so soon! Oh, but I dare not hope too much! Oh, James!"

"It is not long until it is four o'clock," Osbourne said. "We must return with haste so that we may prepare to leave for his residence."

"Indeed," James said. "Come, Anna."

"Yes," she said, looking dazed.

James was rather surprised. The prince already had documents relating to Avery's regiment. It had taken him less than a day. But he hadn't revealed what those documents held, and that was troubling. Did he wish to give Anna bad news in person in order to be at hand to offer consolation? Or did he wish to give her good news in person so he could be the bearer of such news?

He wished he knew. He prayed it was the latter.

CHAPTER 11

They arrived at Schwarzenberg's residence at precisely four o'clock. A footman greeted them, then ushered them into a different room from where they'd met during the soiree last evening. This room, while still sumptuous, was arranged in a manner that suggested it was Schwarzenberg's study. Three chairs had been placed close together, and an additional two chairs were facing the other three.

"The others will join you shortly," the footman said. "Please, be seated." He then left and closed the door.

James led Anna to the middle chair in the group of three. "Others?" she asked him softly as she seated herself.

"I haven't any idea," James answered quietly. He glanced at Osbourne, who only shrugged at him and remained silent.

Anna clasped her hands in her lap, but they didn't remain still, so James reached for her nearest fidgeting hand and held it to offer her comfort.

Anna looked up at him, her eyes huge and blue and, he thought, grateful. Relief flooded him; the last thing he wished to do, after the fiasco of the evening before, was to make her feel uncomfortable once again in the presence of others, even if Osbourne had already guessed at James's attachment to her.

The door opened at that precise moment, and Schwarzenberg and another man entered the room. Osbourne, James, and Anna all rose to their feet and greeted the duo with courteous bows and curtsies while the prince introduced them to Captain David Manning.

They all sat.

"As we were making inquiries into the disappearance of your brother, Lady Anna," Schwarzenberg began after they all were seated, "we quickly discovered that General Wellesley had sent his aide-de-camp Captain Manning here to Paris. Captain Manning is Wellesley's aide-de-camp assigned to record keeping."

"When the armistice was signed," Captain Manning said, "the regiments were instructed to travel to Bordeaux for crossing by sea to Cork, Ireland, and from thence home to England—Bristol, to be precise. They are in the process of doing so at the present time.

"I, however, was instructed to travel from Toulouse to Paris and from thence to London," Captain Manning continued. "While Bordeaux to Ireland is a considerably quicker route back to England for the regiments, it was deemed that travel to Paris and Calais and then on to London would get the documents to the Foreign Office sooner." He reached for a leather case that he'd set on the floor next to his feet. "At General Schwarzenberg's request, I have brought the lists of casualties for the 61st Gloucester Regiment of Foot. We both perused the lists but were unable to find your brother listed amongst the dead."

Anna gasped, and James squeezed her hand.

"That being said, Lady Anna," Captain Manning added, "we were writing these lists on a battlefield, which is not the most ideal of locations, you must understand. Therefore, we thought it prudent for you to read the lists and assure yourself that your brother is not amongst those named."

"You didn't find his name among the dead," Anna whispered. "But the last word we received said he'd been injured in battle and was missing. To have been notified in such a manner led us to believe that surely the worst must have occurred."

"There are various types of wounds a soldier may encounter on the battlefield," the captain said. "They range, of course, from the minor to the deadly. If you received notice of his wounds, there is a likelihood that he may have succumbed after the letter was sent to your family. Or he may have needed to remain behind in order for his wounds to be treated and, therefore, may not have made the lists, as the regiment would not have known of his subsequent death. There is also a chance that he was able to recover. Where was he wounded? Did I understand correctly that it was at Orthez?"

"Yes," Anna said.

Captain Manning looked thoughtful for a moment. "The battle there was in February. It is likely that if your brother were well enough to travel, he would have gone with his regiment to Toulouse. There were terrible losses there, including your brother's commanding officer, Lieutenant Colonel John Coghlan. Good man." The captain solemnly looked down, as though offering a moment of silence to honor the fallen officer. "But the battle ended when word arrived of Napoleon's abdication, so the French general agreed to a cessation of fighting. Had word come but two days earlier, there would have been no battle at all, more's the pity, but such is the nature of war and the communications during war."

"Which is why it is best that you check the lists yourself, Lady Anna," Schwarzenberg added. "We shall leave you in peace. I have asked my servants to bring tea to you so you may spend your time comfortably."

"There is one more thing," Captain Manning said. "If your brother is alive, it is highly likely he has already crossed the Atlantic to Ireland or may yet be in Bordeaux with other soldiers awaiting their turn for transport." And then he retrieved a separate sheet of paper folded neatly to fit in his pocket and handed it to Anna. "Should you need a contact in Bordeaux, here is the name of one of my fellow aides-de-camp. I am certain he will assist you in any way he can."

Then Schwarzenberg and Captain Manning rose to their feet, so the rest of them followed suit once again. The prince bowed over Anna's hand, as did the captain.

"There is much loss in war, and the effects are felt for generations," the captain said to her. "I pray you will be spared that loss when you arrive at the end of your journey."

"Thank you, Captain Manning," she said.

He nodded, and then he and Schwarzenberg left.

"Well," Osbourne said. "Good fortune, indeed, Lady Anna. There appears to be some hope after all."

"Perhaps," Anna said.

"There is more we must discuss, Jennings," Osbourne continued. "I received word from Castlereagh just before you arrived. It was addressed to us both, saying he wishes us to further our service with the Foreign Office through the congress to be held in Vienna." He pulled a letter from his coat pocket. "Here's the letter. I had intended to tell you sooner, but there were unexpected distractions upon your arrival, I'm afraid." He glanced at Anna.

James read the missive, which was indeed from Castlereagh. "Well," James said. It was all he could think to say.

"And now the task turns toward holding together an alliance of jealous, selfish, and weak states and princes by a singleness of purpose when all convene in Vienna later in the year," Osbourne said. "But if any of you claim I said anything so disparaging about the figureheads of Europe, I shall deny it."

James swallowed the lump that had formed in his throat. Osbourne was trying to lighten the mood, and James couldn't fault him for that. But a different task was preying upon James's conscience even more than that of peaceful terms among the Coalition.

The footman brought in a tea tray, and another footman followed with a tray of pastries, cheeses, and meats, and once they'd situated the trays, they retreated from the room.

"I shall prepare cups of tea for everyone so Anna may begin reading the lists," James said.

"Anna, eh?" Osbourne said. "Here, let me do that, Jennings," he added, moving to the table where the tea service was. "You may assist *Lady* Anna."

"Thank you, *Mister* Osbourne," James said. He sat and picked up one of the lists. "Hmm, Lieutenant Avery Clifton," he said to himself.

"Avery Humphrey Clifton," Anna said, seeming to ignore the repartee between James and Osbourne regarding her title.

He nodded and began carefully reading the names on the list he'd taken, cognizant of the fact that each one represented someone who had given his life for king and country.

He was also keenly aware of all that Anna might have lost.

To whom did he owe his loyalty at this precise moment? Anna or Castlereagh? The question, especially after reading the letter from Castlereagh, was like a knife tearing him asunder. His heart was with Anna. Where did his duty lie?

Anna felt as though she were holding her breath with every name she read. She needed to focus on Avery right now, not on the news that the foreign secretary had asked James to extend his service in Paris and Vienna.

James. She had begun to think of him as James rather than Mr. Jennings. When had that happened?

She returned her attention to the casualty lists, which dealt specifically with the battle fought in Orthez and the battle at Toulouse, so they were the best sources imaginable for finding any further word of Avery. She couldn't believe the miracle that had arrived in the form of Captain Manning and his lists.

Mr. Osbourne had brought her tea and a small plate with cheese and meat, but Anna had only nibbled on them and had barely sipped the tea, as anxious as she was. Now the three of them were nearly done reviewing all the lists, and they hadn't come across Avery's name yet. Dared she hope?

James placed his final sheet on the stack of papers they'd already reviewed. "No Avery Clifton, Lieutenant Clifton, A. H. Clifton, or otherwise on this page," he said.

"None that I've found either," Mr. Osbourne said. "Lady Anna, I suggest you write to that other aide-de-camp Captain Manning mentioned. If your brother recovered from his wounds, you might intercept him before he sails with his regiment for Cork, assuming he hasn't already done so."

"Not finding Avery's name on the lists *is* encouraging," Anna said. "At the very least, he isn't a known casualty." She rested her elbows on the table and buried her head in her hands. Not finding Avery's name among the lists was reassuring, but learning that the regiments were, at this very moment, traveling back to England created an unexpected complication she hadn't considered. "How ironic it is that after a war that has lasted decades, the time my brother goes missing is the time Napoleon Bonaparte is exiled, bringing the war to an end," she said to herself.

A warm hand settled on her shoulder. "Anna," James said softly. "It is *good* news, not finding Avery's name on the lists. This is a reason to hope, is it not?"

She heaved a sigh. She couldn't help herself. Between the arduous Channel crossing, the long coach journey to Paris, and becoming a pawn in a political scheme, she was utterly spent.

"What do you wish to do?" James asked her, his hand still resting on her shoulder. "Do you wish to send a letter to the aide-de-camp in Bordeaux?"

She raised her head and looked at James and then glanced at Mr. Osbourne while James's hand remained on her back, warm and reassuring. "It is true that we have found vital information regarding my brother," she began slowly. "Or more precisely, we have found nothing specific about my brother, and yet this information is strangely vital. But I cannot presume that Avery is with his regiment on his way back to England either."

Mr. Osbourne rose from his chair and moved to a far corner of the room and crossed his arms over his chest. James, by contrast, squeezed her shoulder gently and reassuringly.

"I need time to think," Anna said.

"I wouldn't take too much time doing that," Mr. Osbourne said. "You may lose your chance to communicate with the other aide-de-camp and your brother if you do. And if you are considering traipsing all over the French countryside on what still appears to be rather poor odds, I would counsel you to think otherwise."

Anna turned to look Mr. Osbourne fully in the eyes. "Mr. Osbourne, I cannot have traveled as far as I have to make the presumption that Avery is safely returning home with his regiment. I cannot simply turn around and return to London. There is too much at stake. Do *you* have a brother, Mr. Osbourne?"

He pursed his lips in what appeared to be irritation. "I do have a brother, Lady Anna," he said.

"If there were any chance of finding your brother alive when you received word that he was wounded and was not accounted for on the lists, would you simply shrug and say, 'Oh well, I pray he recovers from his wounds and returns home someday'?"

"It is not the same thing," Mr. Osbourne said. "You have been given good indication that your brother returned to active service and the communication has simply not arrived yet."

"It is *precisely* the same thing," Anna replied. "And I have been given *none* of the assurances you suggest. There is nothing to indicate he returned to his regiment. Additionally, when we communicated with Avery's regimental headquarters before I undertook this journey, their description of field hospitals and what usually happens to a soldier when he is wounded was horrifying, to say the least. While a few of the more fortunate ones may be helped by local citizens, pain, infection, and death were but a few of the things they described to our steward—things they would not tell a lady but that I insisted our steward tell me."

"Which is why it is unwise for you to attempt this ill-fated rescue mission you seem determined to undertake," Mr. Osbourne countered.

"I could not then and cannot now leave Avery to endure such terrible circumstances on his own," Anna declared forcefully, her mind made up. "If there is *anything* I can do for my brother, *I will do it*, despite the hardships, whether others consider it foolish or not."

"That is a brave choice," James said at length. "Tomorrow we shall undertake preparations to leave for Toulouse—and I shall accompany you, if you will give me your permission."

"Oh, James, thank you!" she whispered.

"You've both lost your senses!" Mr. Osbourne exclaimed, throwing his hands in the air. "And what of Castlereagh, Jennings? What of his request for your continued service? Are you going to defy your country's need for your legal and diplomatic skills at the very hour that England and the Coalition are working to unite the Continent after twenty-odd years of war? What of that?"

James was silent, and Anna waited for him to speak, fully expecting that he would realize he'd erred in agreeing to accompany her into southern France and would change his mind.

"Well, Jennings?" Mr. Osbourne said.

James heaved a great sigh. "The peace of the Continent has many in whose hands these negotiations lie. My absence will have little effect on the overall outcome of the peace treaties to follow. Lady Anna, however, has but her manservant and maid to help her find her brother and save her family from desolation. By going with them, I can help assure their safety as well as provide translation services, for we both know that few of the local French will be able to understand much

English and may distrust strangers. I ask you, Osbourne, Why have we been fighting all these years if not to secure our families and loved ones? Castlereagh will get along fine enough without me. Lady Anna may not."

Anna was certain her heart had stopped beating when James had begun to speak. Now it fairly burst from her bosom with love for him. *Loved ones*, he had said.

Loved ones.

It was late when James and the others arrived back at the apartment after leaving Schwarzenberg's residence since the prince had also graciously invited them to remain and dine with him. It had been a long day, and James was tired and wished to retire. He watched as Anna excused herself and went to her room, Sparks and Mary following behind her.

The moment they were out of sight, however, Osbourne turned abruptly to James.

"What the devil are you thinking, Jennings?" he hissed quietly. "This is about as foolish an endeavor as I could ever begin to imagine. You intend to follow Lady Anna all over the French countryside in what will undoubtedly see no results. At what point will she concede that this futile search for her brother needs to end? Will you search every cottage and barn between Toulouse and Orthez and the coast of France until she is finally satisfied that there is no brother to be found, either dead or alive? And what if her brother arrives home at the family estate—miracle that it would be—and his sister is not there, and he has no idea where *she* is? You are making decisions based on your obvious infatuation with her and not thinking practically."

James said nothing.

"Have you no response? The esteemed lawyer and diplomat has no defense he cares to make? The man who is never at a loss for words is speechless?" Osbourne's words were sharp as arrows.

"What would you have me do, Osbourne?" James said at last. Sometimes it was better to reply to a question with a question of one's own. "What would you do in my place?"

"What I would have you do is come to your senses," Osbourne replied.

"That is what you wish *I* would do. I asked what *you* would do," James replied. "If *you* were in love with a lady—not an infatuation, mind you, and not just any lady but one who is honorable, faithful to her family, and fearless in her defense of them, who will undertake any means to protect them, even at the risk of her own safety—if *you* were in love with such a lady, what would *you* do?"

Osbourne's face contorted. "That your best defense is simply to redirect the hypothetical situation back at myself only proves my point! Yes, I have a brother, and I imagine I would do what I could to find him. Thankfully, I have never had to do that for Kit. And I imagine if I loved a woman enough, I might be inclined to help her search for her brother. But both of those come with a caveat: I would do what I could *within reason*."

"So you say," James said. "And had I never met Anna, I might have responded as you just did. But I *did* meet her, and I *am* moved by her. And heaven help me, I will do what I can to stay at her side in this cause of hers. And after the harshness I directed toward her when we first met, it is my dearest hope that she not only forgive me but that I also prove myself worthy to her and earn her favor in return."

Osbourne merely shook his head in apparent disgust.

"One day you will understand, my friend," James said.

"I understand some things better than you think, Jennings," Osbourne said. "Kit and I lost our parents to pneumonia. I was but twenty and two, and Kit just two years older. There was nothing we could do to arrive before their deaths and save them, though I doubt we could have saved them even if given the time and opportunity. *Nothing we could do*." He spoke the last sentence slowly and with emphasis. "I learned there are times when one must let go and accept things one cannot change."

It broke James's heart to hear Osbourne speak of his loss. He remembered learning about the death of his friend's parents while they'd both been attending Oxford. It had been nearly ten years since. "I see," James replied softly. "I understand better, and I am truly sorry, my friend. But *had* there been any way to arrive in time to do *something, anything,* would you have done it, even if it had proved futile?"

Osbourne turned to stare out the window. He was silent for several long minutes, and James wondered if he would ever speak. Eventually, he turned back to look at James. "Go," he said with a wave of his hand.

James stood, feeling hurt. "Very well," he said and turned to leave.

"No," Osbourne said. "I mean *go*. Go with your newly found love. Earn her favor. Do what you must to help her find her brother—or at the very least, find the answer. I will deal with Castlereagh. But I still think you're on a fool's errand, and

I won't be at all surprised if I see you back in Paris within a day or two or three."

James strode across the room and grabbed Osbourne's hand and shook it vigorously. "Thank you, Osbourne. I am in your debt," James said. Then he let go of his poor friend's hand and threw his arms around him in a great hug before letting go. "Truly."

"Don't thank me too soon," Osbourne said. He sighed. "I shall miss you, my friend. Where am I to turn now for a rational thought in the midst of all the petulant peacocks who refer to themselves as sovereigns—oh, never mind, you have shown yourself to be somewhat less rational than I always have given you credit for."

James chuckled, and Osbourne slapped him on the arm and laughed with him.

"Good evening, then," James said. "I expect we will be off to an early start—or at the very least, *I* shall. I have a coach to hire for the journey ahead."

He was nearly out of the room when Osbourne quietly called after him. "I lost a colleague in the Duke of Aylesham to a woman. And now I am losing you for the same reason. You know, Jennings, as a betting man, these odds are beginning to frighten me."

"I daresay your day will come, Osbourne," James said with a smile.

Before retiring to his room, James knocked quietly on Anna's door. Mary answered.

"Please inform Lady Anna that I intend to arrange for a coach tomorrow so that we may begin the journey to Toulouse as soon as she is ready," he said.

"I hear you," Anna called softly from behind the door. "I just gave Sparks instructions to do that very thing."

"He is welcome to join me," James replied, wishing he could see her. "But I believe we may get a coach of a better quality if someone who actually speaks French negotiates the terms."

"That makes sense. Thank you so much, James," Anna replied.

Once again, she had called him James. Oh, how he wanted to place his hands on either side of her face and press a long kiss to her enticing lips! "Sleep well, Anna," he said, and then he nodded at Mary when she looked at him, tacitly asking for his permission to shut the door, which she did.

Being a gentleman was blasted difficult at times.

Anna awoke early the next morning to find Mary nearly finished packing her belongings.

"Oh, you're awake, Lady Anna! I hope I didn't—"

"You didn't wake me, Mary," Anna said. She stretched her arms out to the side and yawned before quickly covering her mouth with her hand.

"When Mr. Jennings said we be leaving first thing in the morning, I figured I best get us ready to leave *before* the first thing in the morning," Mary said.

Anna groggily wondered how something could come before "first thing in the morning" and then decided not to contemplate it.

Mary set about finishing the packing while Anna saw to her personal needs and washed and dressed, with Mary helping her with her hair afterward.

"There now," Mary said. "You look right fine, and we're ready to face the day and the travel that comes with it. Sparks said he were going to fetch breakfast for us, and then we'd be off." She tucked the brush into the last bag, closed it, and gave it a nod of finality.

When Anna and Mary left the bedroom and entered the main room of the apartment, Anna realized there was a strange gentleman seated with James and Mr. Osbourne. The three men stood at Mary's and her entrance.

"Anna," James said, "allow me to present Monsieur Étienne le Touffe, who has agreed to be our coachman for our journey south. He is the coachman we rely upon whenever the Duke of Aylesham or Lord Castlereagh are in France, and Osbourne suggested we try to make arrangements with him first. Fortunately, he agreed. Monsieur le Touffe, *permettez-moi de présenter* Lady Anna Clifton."

The gentleman bowed. "*Enchantée*," he said.

"A pleasure, Monsieur le Touffe," she replied.

A knock at the main door heralded the arrival of Sparks, followed by a serving girl from the dining room downstairs bearing a tray of tea, eggs, toast, and the like. She set it on a table before curtsying and leaving.

"Ah, perfect timing," Mr. Osbourne said. "Lady Anna?" he added, gesturing to an empty chair near the gentlemen. Once Sparks had closed the door behind the serving girl, he took a chair in the corner after directing Mary to sit in the chair next to his.

James then spent a great deal of the time speaking in French, with Mr. Osbourne and Monsieur le Touffe nodding in acknowledgment. Occasionally, Monsieur le Touffe made a comment in French or Mr. Osbourne replied to James in

English, but it didn't nearly explain what details they were talking about. Anna only understood a smattering of the French words, and Osbourne's comments in English didn't divulge much.

Anna listened intently while drinking her tea and nibbling a croissant, but by the time she'd finished the croissant, her patience had grown thin. She cleared her throat rather loudly to draw their attention.

All three gentlemen turned their heads to look at her, all with raised eyebrows.

"Perhaps," Anna began, deciding to err on the side of tact, even though she wished to be blunt, "as it is *my* brother we are seeking, you might think to translate what plans are being made on my behalf while said plans are being discussed."

"But, *ma dame*, eef you weel excuse me, " Monsieur le Touffe replied in broken English, "but eet eez my experience zat zee lady does not care about such details, only zat she travel safely."

"Thank you for your honesty, monsieur," Anna replied. "But I have had my fill of gentlemen making choices for me without consulting me first"—she waited as a guilty-looking James translated that much of her statement to the coachman—"and so I would prefer to understand those choices while they are being made."

James finished translating her words, and the coachman chuckled and nodded. *"Ce que femme veut, Dieu le veut,"* he said.

Anna looked to James to translate, his expression changing from serious to amused by Monsieur le Touffe's words. "What women want, God wants," James said.

Anna smiled at the coachman and nodded. "*Précisément, et merci,*" she said to him with a smile, glad she remembered enough French to say that much.

He nodded in return.

"Now, may we get back to business?" Mr. Osbourne asked in English.

"I don't know why *you're* so concerned," James replied. "You're not going with us."

"As I must report to Castlereagh, hat in hand, with unpleasant news regarding my colleague's unwillingness to be here to assist, I would like to be able to give the foreign secretary any and all details he may wish to know," Mr. Osbourne said.

"Five days but most likely a week or more? In a *coach*?" Mary suddenly exclaimed from the corner of the room.

Anna and the gentlemen all turned to look. A clearly worried Mary had thrown her hand over her mouth, while a chagrined-looking Sparks patted her free hand, which was clenched in a ball on her lap.

Anna turned to look questioningly at James. "Come, Anna," he said, "you must have known the journey south would be long and arduous. Why do you think I insisted on accompanying you? You must have looked at maps and realized the distance from Paris to Toulouse—and even onward to Orthez."

"Yes, I did, but—" Her words ground to a halt. She'd been so intent on finding Avery that she knew she'd avoided acknowledging the details in preference to focusing on the goal at hand.

"You don't have to continue," Mr. Osbourne said. "It's not too late to change your mind." He looked at Monsieur le Touffe, who merely shrugged.

"What he says is true, Anna," James said. "Now is the time to clearly understand all the details, which you yourself just adamantly claimed you wished to know. And now is the time to decide whether or not to proceed."

Anna looked at Sparks and Mary, who were clearly waiting for her answer. She wished she could read their expressions. Sparks's face was inscrutable, and Mary looked worried. But Mary often looked worried . . .

They had willingly joined her on this journey without fully realizing what it would entail, just as she had not realized. And the next part of the journey would be much longer and more difficult.

"It's yer decision, me lady," Sparks said. "We come this far. We can go on, can't we, Mary?" He looked deep into Mary's eyes, as though sharing his strength with her.

"Yes," Mary whispered after a brief pause.

Sparks nodded his approval.

"But go with faith, Anna, or go not at all," James said.

Go with faith or go not at all.

It was an illuminating thought for Anna.

She took a deep breath. "I would very much like to continue the search for my brother," she said.

"Very well," James said, giving her a look that she would swear was similar to the encouraging one she'd just witnessed Sparks give to Mary.

And that look gave her hope.

CHAPTER 12

Travel across the country in a coach was uncomfortable under the best of circumstances. But more than six days of continuous travel was going to test the mettle of all four of them, James was certain. Were he back in England, he would have spent a great deal of the journey on horseback, free of the confinement of the coach. A saddle might not be the most comfortable, but it was more comfortable than wooden benches—even these that had been furnished with padded upholstery.

He would also not have felt obliged to ride facing backward for those six days. But poor, nervous Mary, who had spent her time on a yacht being ill from the motion of the ship and had endured in silence the coach ride from Calais to Paris, needed to be in a seat in which she could face forward. Not only was it the gentlemanly thing to do, but it was the safest option as well. James wasn't of a mind to have to stop the coach frequently were Mary to cast up her accounts while enclosed in tight quarters.

So, he sat facing Anna, while Sparks sat facing Mary, and he watched Paris vanish from sight, unable to see what towns or inns they were approaching. It was frustrating at best. He also watched coaches and the occasional travelers on horse-back pass them and disappear in the dust. It wasn't much to break up the tedium, but it was something, he supposed.

Additionally, conversation between two members of the upper class and two of the working class, especially after already having traveled by coach from Calais to Paris in each other's company, was stilted—at least on the initial leg of their travel south thus far.

James was of the opinion that no one was looking forward to spending at least a week traveling to the southernmost part of France despite their willingness to do so, which might also explain the lack of conversation. He pulled out his pocket watch to check the time. They'd been on the road for only two hours on their first day, heading south from Paris—and the journey had already become tedious.

He subtly studied Anna's face as she gazed at the countryside through the window next to her. She was a study of contrasts: the stark black of her traveling dress and bonnet, the blonde sheen of her hair, and the brilliant blue of her eyes. Her beautiful face was drawn into a frown, however, and he wondered what she might be thinking.

"A penny for your thoughts," he said softly, but not so softly that he couldn't be heard over the rumbling of the wheels of the coach.

She turned her face to look at him and attempted to smile. "Oh, I don't know," she said.

"I think you can do better than that," James replied, hoping he sounded reassuring.

Sparks and Mary both turned their attention toward her.

Anna sighed deeply. "Very well," she said. "What if—" She stopped speaking abruptly.

"What if what?" James asked. "What if we arrive and learn Avery has returned to England? What if no one has any information to provide? What if we arrive and we learn the worst—"

"Stop," Anna said, holding up her hand. "Don't speak those last words aloud. I couldn't bear it."

"But it is a truth that may have to be faced," James said.

Anna acknowledged his words but with the barest of nods. She turned to stare out the window again.

"What if your vile cousin has already ensconced himself in your family estate, your brother has died, and you are homeless?" James asked.

"I say, sir, that's cruel!" Sparks exclaimed, as Mary's hands flew to her mouth, which, James noted, they did frequently. Anna continued to look out the window.

"Truth can ofttimes be cruel," James said softly. He knew his words were blunt, but they needed saying. While travel into Paris had felt relatively safe, they were now to travel through areas of France dealing with the aftermath of war. He wouldn't tell her this, but he'd tucked his revolvers and ammunition into his bag before leaving Paris, in case they were needed. He prayed they wouldn't be. James had discovered that he would go to the ends of the earth for her. But based on her gloomy countenance, he would rather ask the difficult questions again than continue onward if she were having any doubts.

Before he could say anything further, however, the coach rolled into the courtyard of the inn that was their first change of horses.

Once they'd come to a halt, the footman opened the door, and James stepped out and offered Anna his hand so she could descend from the carriage. Sparks glared at him the entire time, and then followed behind and assisted Mary from the coach.

"I would still like a truthful answer from you," James said to Anna after Sparks and Mary had walked a few paces away from them.

"I realize that," Anna said. "And you deserve as truthful an answer as I can give."

"Perhaps we may speak privately," he suggested. "I will see if Monsieur le Touffe is amenable to the idea of waiting an extra half an hour or so to give us the time we need."

"Yes," was all she said.

It would have to be enough for now, he thought as he offered her his arm and she slipped her hand inside his elbow.

After only having been in the coach for an hour, Anna had begun to realize once again just what endurance everyone would need, and her guilt mounted with each mile. They had all agreed to continue on, but at what sacrifice?

And yet, how could she give up on finding Avery?

James took her hand in his and tucked it securely into the crook of his elbow. She wondered if he could feel it tremble.

"Come, let us stroll a bit and see if we may find a quiet spot to converse more privately," James said.

She nodded her consent.

They walked toward a side of the inn where they discovered a well-tended garden full of a variety of blooming shrubs and flowers along with some vegetable plants.

"Ah, this is nice," James said. "Much like the little garden we found in Paris." He looked at her for her approval, which she gave once again with a nod of her head. She knew a difficult conversation was yet to come, and she was trying to prepare herself for it.

"The questions I asked you in the coach were blunt and cruel, yet I cannot regret asking them; you must face the truth of the situation," he said in a kind tone.

"I know," she murmured. "I have asked myself those same questions many times, lest you think me some sort of idealistic fool."

He patted her hand with his free hand and then let it rest upon hers. "I don't think that. I understand the love and devotion you have for your family. And I have promised I shall go with you wherever it takes us."

Anna stared at her hand under his and then at his handsome face. "Oh, James," she said. "You have already done more to help me find my brother than I could have ever hoped."

"I have four brothers," James said. "That may seem like more than enough, and indeed, at times while we were growing up, it was, but I cannot imagine the pain I would feel were I to lose any one of them. I have a youngest brother who is of a rebellious nature, and his actions already make him feel as if he is lost to us. To actually lose a brother to death, as you have, and then suffer the additional burden of not knowing the whereabouts of your only remaining brother, I cannot imagine."

Anna remained silent and pondered his words. They were the most personal he'd ever shared with her—and were highly insightful.

"And your sisters?" she asked at length.

"Three, and I would do anything in my power to protect them too. Hence, the reason I remained in London and

Osbourne continued on to Paris without me. I had to be there for my sister, you see, when she married the Duke of Aylesham."

"I gathered the situation was unusual," Anna said.

"Highly suspect, you mean," James said. "But I am not so afraid of this particular duke that I cannot settle a score should he treat my sister poorly. I am assured that he will not."

"That is good, I suppose," Anna replied.

"Yes," James said. "For I would not have any lady mistreated or left feeling abandoned." He locked eyes with her.

Her pulse sped at the intensity of his look. She swallowed. "And that, I suppose, is the reason you have chosen to assist me."

"It is one of the reasons," he replied.

His answer was cryptic, but she wasn't inclined to ask for further explanation at the moment out of fear of what he might say.

"I was presumptuous to refer to you simply as Anna," he said, "and yet I cannot regret it either. I was rather pleased when you began calling me James."

She said nothing, could say nothing in reply.

"I hope you will continue to call me James and that I am afforded permission to refer to you as Anna," he murmured.

"I think that after all we've been through together, we have gone beyond the formalities of titles and surnames," she said a little too breathlessly.

"Thank you. Anna." He said her Christian name deliberately, as though testing it upon his tongue this time.

"James," she said, "I *must* continue to search for Avery. I cannot stop."

"I understand," he replied. "And so, we shall continue. Now, I think we must join the others before they begin to search for *us*," he said softly.

"Yes, James," she replied.

He smiled, looking pleased, and then raised her gloved hand to his lips and pressed a long kiss on it that nearly made Anna swoon.

"Oh, but I wish to remain in this garden with you," he whispered, his lips barely removed from her hand.

She could only nod, so overcome she felt.

They turned to stroll back.

It was just as well, for they had barely arrived back at the front of the inn when Sparks and Mary came out the door.

"There ye are!" Mary called to them. "We have refreshments inside for ye but wondered where ye got off to."

"Le Touffe is still inside takin' his refreshment, so ye have time," Sparks added, but Anna thought he looked at her and James a bit suspiciously. "I invited Mary to go on a short walk so we can stretch our legs before le Touffe is ready to shoo us back into the coach."

"There is a nice garden down the side of the inn, just there—" Anna bit off the rest of her statement.

Sparks looked at James with a raised eyebrow, which told Anna she had probably said too much.

"As Lady Anna says, it's a nice garden. Flowers. Quite peaceful," James added with a smile.

"It sounds lovely!" Mary gushed.

"Then, we must go an' see," Sparks said to her.

As they headed off in the direction from which James and Anna had just come, Sparks gave the two of them another suspicious look right before they disappeared around the corner of the building.

"Let's go find those refreshments Mary said were waiting for us," James said.

As they walked through the entrance of the inn, she noticed Monsieur le Touffe at the bar, dipping a pastry into a cup of tea, and then a serving girl approached them and said something in French, to which James responded. The girl nodded and then gestured for them to follow her to a table, where there was a hot pot of tea and a large plate of pastries filled with ham or cheese or both and some filled with fruit.

Anna did her best to eat, despite the flurry of butterflies in her stomach from James's words—and his unexpected kiss.

Soon enough, they were back in the coach and on their way to Orleans, their final destination for this first day of travel. James noticed that for the first few miles after their interlude in the inn's garden, Anna seemed determined to gaze out the window at the countryside.

Eventually, Sparks began softly humming, and the sound seemed to soothe the general mood within the coach; indeed, James felt himself relax.

Sparks had an excellent voice, and his humming gradually turned to singing, albeit quietly. James listened, grateful that Sparks's singing was sparing them from conversation for a while, and he even recognized some of the melodies as hymns from his youth. And Mary, timid Mary, listened to each hymn and then harmonized with Sparks, which was delightful to hear.

After a while, the music Sparks chose changed from hymns to folk songs.

James glanced at Anna. She appeared to be enjoying the singing, just as he was, for her countenance seemed lighter, and she was smiling.

"My love is like a red red rose, / That's newly sprung in June, / O my Love's like the melodie / That's sweetly play'd in tune," Sparks sang with Mary.

James suddenly thought it striking that neither he nor Anna had joined in the singing. Why was that? Blast, it was time for that to change! As Sparks and Mary began the second verse of this particular folk song, James decided to join them. "As fair art thou, my bonnie lass," he sang, adding his voice to theirs, "So deep in love am I, / And I will love thee still, my dear, / Till a' the seas gang dry."

When he got to the end of the verse, he realized that Sparks and Mary had ceased singing and were staring at him. He didn't much care. Singing had felt blasted good!

But the look on Anna's face captured him: her brilliant eyes were wide, her mouth slightly open, as if in surprise— and yet also *not* in surprise. That didn't make sense, but that was the only way James could think to describe it. He realized the words he had just sung were words declaring an undying love, and he had been looking directly at Anna.

And then Sparks and Mary faded entirely from his view, and he could see only Anna. *His* Anna. Softly, by himself, he sang the couplet from the final verse, which they had not yet sung: "And I will come again, my Love, / Tho' it were ten thousand mile."

He stopped singing and simply gazed at her.

Silence.

He smiled at her and nodded his head—only once—at her. It was merely a song, and he hoped the words wouldn't frighten her away. But he realized the words he'd sung were essentially true; he would do whatever he could to win her favor . . . and her love. *Even tho' it were ten thousand mile.*

Her eyes filled with unshed tears, and her delicious lips turned up in the most beautiful smile. He could live happily in that gaze of hers, he was sure.

The coach began to slow, which broke the spell under which James had fallen. He quickly glanced out the window and saw that they had arrived at the inn where their last change of horses would occur before reaching Orleans.

The coach eventually ground to a halt, and le Touffe opened the door and assisted Anna and Mary from the coach. James followed, with Sparks behind him, and le Touffe shut the door after them.

James quickened his pace in order to be with Anna, but when he reached her side, he could see that she was speaking in a low voice to Mary.

"Mary and I need to refresh ourselves once we're inside the inn," Anna said softly to him when she noticed his presence next to her.

"I shall order refreshment for you both, then, if that pleases you," James replied.

"Thank you, James," Anna said. She glanced at Mary, who nodded slightly. "Thank you for both of us." And then they hurried into the inn.

"Well, Sparks, my man, it appears we have been temporarily abandoned by our fair companions," James said with a slight shrug of his shoulders. "I suspect they will join us sooner rather than later. In the meantime, let's be about our own needs and arrange some refreshment."

"Right about that, Mr. Jennings," Sparks said. "I'm thinking some sandwiches an' tea an' ale will put everyone to rights."

"You're on to something there, Sparks," James replied. "I believe we English males have had our fill of dainty pastries and are in need of heartier sustenance."

The inn was surprisingly busy, but within a short amount of time, James was at a table with Sparks along with a nice platter of rolls, cheeses, and cured meats. "Tuck in, sir," Sparks said. "I doubt the ladies will mind if we start without 'em, don't ye? Especially when who knows how long they'll be? Ladies be a mighty mystery to me, but these two are nice 'uns, at least."

"Indeed. By the way, well done with the singing, Sparks. You've a fine voice," James said before taking a sip of ale from the mug a serving girl placed in front of him.

"It's not a solo voice I have, sir," Sparks said. "But I thank ye all the same. Ye know I sing in the church choir. Mary is in the choir too."

"Mary is a nice 'un, as you say," James said.

Sparks turned solemn for a moment. "I had me heart broke a while back. I vowed never again. Was betrothed to be married, we was, but she wouldn't stick by me when Lady Clifton died and poor Lord Westbury were so badly injured. On death's door, he was." He nodded to himself. "'Never again,' I tells meself. 'Sparks,' I says, 'if a woman can't stick by ye through the hard times, she ain't the right woman for ye.'" Then his face lit up. "But then, lately, I says to meself, 'Not all women is the same, and maybe I'll think of taking a wife sometime.' But now is not the time, I reckon, what with being in France and all."

"Wise man," James said, reflecting on his own recent thoughts on the matter. He raised his mug. "In the meantime, here's to the two nice 'uns."

Sparks grinned and raised his own mug. "I 'spect ye've yer eye on our Lady Anna, if I'm not mistaken."

James leaned forward. "I'll let you in on a little secret, Sparks. You are *not* mistaken. But as a gentleman, I will use restraint and refrain for any untoward advances, for her sake and reputation." Especially after what had happened in Paris. He sipped his ale and then began to assemble a sandwich from the fare in front of him, as did Sparks. It might actually kill him to keep his distance from Anna. But needs must.

The "two nice 'uns" arrived shortly thereafter, and they all ate in mutual silence.

CHAPTER 13

The next morning, after having arrived in Orleans safely and securing lodgings for the night, Anna awoke, washed, dressed, and headed down to the dining area to look for her fellow travelers. Mary must have awoken early, for she was not in their shared room.

When Anna arrived in the dining hall, she found Mary in a corner of the room near a window, looking out onto the courtyard and crying. Sparks, looking frustrated and outraged, was trying to comfort her.

What could have happened? And where was James?

Anna had barely formed the questions in her mind when her eyes were drawn to what Sparks and Mary appeared to be looking at through the window.

James and le Touffe were speaking—arguing, more like, if their expressions were anything to go by—and both men were gesturing wildly with their hands. It also appeared that the horses were already hitched to the coach. So what could possibly be the matter?

Rather than join Mary and Sparks at the window, Anna snatched up her skirts and hurried out into the courtyard toward the two men arguing loudly in French.

"What is going on?" Anna asked.

James swung around to face her as though he might strike whoever it was before realizing it was her. "This blasted French fool has informed me—*now* and not at any time along our journey—that it has always been his intention to return to Paris once he deposited us in Orleans. So, here we are in Orleans without transportation going forward." He then turned back to le Touffe and began berating the coachman in French again.

They were being abandoned by their coachman?

"What do you mean, you are returning to Paris?" Anna exclaimed, her voice sounding more like a shriek in her ears. It hadn't been a ladylike sound, but really, being abandoned in the middle of France wasn't what she'd expected to encounter first thing this morning. Obviously, none of them had.

Le Touffe didn't even glance her way.

James, however, did. "Unbeknownst to us, Osbourne was so certain that we would realize the folly of our decision and return to Paris once we began our first leg of the journey that he assured le Touffe here that he would only be bringing us to Orleans and then would be returning to Paris, either with or without us. When next I see Osbourne . . ." His words trailed off, but the scowl on his face told Anna precisely what he was thinking.

She found herself gasping for breath. Why had she presumed the coach and le Touffe would be with them the entire journey? The truth was that it was just another example of her inability to anticipate what they would encounter. Her eyes welled with tears, but she fought them back. She was *not* going to behave as a simpering, dependent woman. Not after all they'd already endured.

James had turned to continue arguing with le Touffe, but it was obvious the coachman had made up his mind.

Anna laid a hand on James's shoulder. "James," she said. "Tell me his reasoning, beyond the fact the Mr. Osbourne told him this would be as far as he'd need to go."

James continued to glare at le Touffe, and his breaths came hard and fast from the intense emotions it was obvious he was experiencing. "He said he must be at hand when Castlereagh arrives, and he only agreed to do this because it was good money and he'd also be back home with his wife and children within a few days. He assumed we knew."

Wife and children. The foreign secretary.

Anna understood that as far as le Touffe was concerned, *her* needs were a distant third. "James," she began.

"I know!" he spat. "I *know*. But I am *furious* with Osbourne! He fully expected us to rethink our plans and return to Paris when le Touffe told us he was returning. It is *beyond the pale* for him to make that decision against our knowledge."

Anna glanced over at the coach, where its horses were pawing the ground with impatience while a stableboy controlled the harness.

Le Touffe said something more to James and then turned to Anna. "My apologies, *ma dame*," he said in his broken English, "but I must return to Paris."

"I think I understand, monsieur," she said. "Have you spoken to the innkeeper here about coaches?" she then asked James.

"I wasn't about to let le Touffe leave without talking to him first," James said. "Be off then, man," he said to le Touffe with a dismissive gesture of his hand, apparently forgetting for that brief moment that the man spoke little English.

Le Touffe understood his words well enough, for after bowing to Anna, he turned, strode to his coach, jumped into the driver's box, and took up the reins. And then he and his coach sped off, leaving a cloud of dust in their wake.

Anna quickly retrieved her handkerchief from her pocket and held it in front of her nose to keep the dust at bay, while James watched the coach until it disappeared from sight.

"I'm sorry," Anna said at last, guilt eating away at her empty stomach. "We wouldn't be in this predicament if it weren't for me."

"This is not your fault. I should have seen it coming." He brushed accumulated dust from the sleeves of his coat and then offered Anna his arm. "Come," he said, his voice lacking the intensity he had just used. "Let's return inside. I will speak to the innkeeper to see what our options are, and a good, hearty breakfast wouldn't go amiss for either of us, now, would it?" He offered her a weak but encouraging smile.

She allowed him to lead her back inside the inn. But this morning's unexpected turn of events had drained her of strength. They had barely set off through France after leaving Paris, and they'd just gotten their first taste of trouble.

She dearly hoped it wasn't an omen for the rest of the journey to come.

James needed all the discipline he could muster to control his anger and frustration. He could see Sparks and Mary looking at him through the window of the inn—Mary's hands clasped over her mouth, the utter horror on Spark's face. They'd seen the coach leave the yard and were undoubtedly shocked and dismayed at what they'd witnessed.

And Anna? Her steps were slow, and he could only think that he'd failed her.

He'd failed her, for he knew Phillip Osbourne as well as anybody. Osbourne was a fine gentleman, someone who saw to matters and ensured decisions were made. He was a man of action and loyal to his country. James should have realized that Osbourne would not understand the need for James to assist Anna in her quest—not when Castlereagh would be arriving in Paris and from there on to Vienna for the negotiations between countries to proceed.

James should have anticipated this.

Sparks hurried over to them when they entered the inn, but Mary stayed back by the window, looking frozen with fear.

"We have a duty to perform, Sparks," James said. "Unbeknownst to us, our coachman only planned to bring us as far as Orleans. If you will arrange breakfast for Anna and Mary, I shall speak to our host to see what coach services are available to take us onward."

"Yes, sir," Sparks said, sounding as though *he* were frozen in fear too. "Right away, sir."

"Come, Anna," James said in as gentle a tone as he could muster when he was still in the mood to yell at someone, anyone. He led her to the table in the corner near where Mary stood. "Please be seated," he said. "Sparks is arranging for breakfast for you. I am going to find transportation to take us to our next stop . . . and hopefully beyond this time."

"Chateauroux," Anna said softly.

"Yes, Chateauroux," James replied. "Now, please excuse me while I find the innkeeper."

He bowed and strode off, dearly wishing he could throw back a brandy—or throw his fist at a hard object, such as the wall. Instead, he gritted his teeth. The others were relying on him.

Fortunately, he found the innkeeper's wife near an entry to the kitchen. She must have seen the rage on his face, for she immediately curtsied and left after James asked where her husband was, and the man himself arrived in short order.

"My fine fellow," James said in French to Monsieur Tessier, the innkeeper, "you may have observed that our coachman left and is currently on his way back to Paris. We are now beholden to you to help us find transportation to Chateauroux and beyond. Our final destination is Toulouse."

"Toulouse?" Tessier repeated. He then clucked his tongue and shook his head, and James's limited patience began to fray even further.

"Monsieur," James said, then he stopped speaking. Monsieur Tessier was a businessman, first and foremost. James pulled his wallet from his pocket and began counting out bills.

That caught the innkeeper's attention. He stopped tsk-tsking and shaking his head and began to scratch at his chin thoughtfully.

Soon enough, James and Tessier had come to an agreement with Tessier's son-in-law, Lafitte, who *just happened* to be the coachman who traveled between Orleans and Paris or Orleans and Chateauroux whenever there was a need. James didn't think it occurred routinely, as Lafitte had had to remove his apron when he'd left the kitchen to come meet with them. Apparently, the son-in-law spent more time as a cook than a coachman, but James would take what he could find at this point.

Lafitte eventually agreed to take them as far as Limoges, which was to be their stop after Chateauroux, *but only* after an extra monetary incentive for him and his father-in-law had been agreed upon and hands shaken.

After that, James was through negotiating for the day, and Lafitte left to inform his wife and prepare the coach and horses for their departure.

James returned to the dining hall to inform the others of the arrangement. When he approached them, he saw three sets of worried eyes turn to look at him.

He wondered if he should instruct Lafitte to take them all back to Paris instead.

"A coach has been arranged for us to continue our journey and will take us as far as Limoges," he announced when he reached their table and took a seat. "We will have three more travel days after that in order to reach Toulouse and will be subject to whatever travel arrangements can be found when we get there." He didn't ask the question whether they *should* continue—he presumed the question was implied in his statement.

"Excellent news, isn't it, Mary?" Sparks said in a hearty tone that James suspected was intended to boost the spirits of both women. "We should go up and pack our belongings so that we be prepared to leave when the coach is ready." He stood and looked encouragingly at Mary.

"Yes," Mary said with a nod and an attempt at a smile. James thought her very brave in that moment. Here she was in the middle of a strange country—they all were, of course—ready to continue onward despite what fears she must certainly have.

Sparks assisted her from her chair, and then the two of them left to return to the rooms the four of them had used last evening.

James turned back to Anna, who had been watching the two servants leave. He reached for her hand and took it in his own. "I shall be frank, Anna," he said. "Things may get worse—*much* worse—before they get better, whether we find your brother or not. We are heading toward the locations of battlefields, and the aftermath of battles is never pretty. I have spoken bluntly before, and while I resisted saying anything about this situation in particular, I feel it my duty to speak now. Truly, if we are not committed to the task at hand, now is the time to turn back, just as Osbourne had expected we would."

Anna took in a deep breath and then let it out on a slow, mournful sigh that nearly broke James's heart.

"How are you bearing up?" he asked softly.

"I pray I am not on a fool's errand," Anna said. "I have searched the face of every man we have passed along the way, to no avail. And more and more, I realize that I had no idea what the personal cost would be to those who were willing to travel with me. That includes you, James. But I have to continue. I'm sorry."

"There is no reason to be sorry, my dear," he said. And he wondered how he was going to survive this journey without pulling her onto his lap, protectively wrapping his arms tightly about her, and pressing kisses to her hands and cheeks and lips.

The coach that now stood in the courtyard of the inn, horses pacing to be on their way, was not the elegant form of transport they had been fortunate enough to enjoy on their journey from Paris, Anna quickly observed. *This* particular coach had seen better days, and those days had happened many years ago.

But it *was* a coach, at least, so she straightened her back, gave a reassuring glance to Sparks and especially to Mary, who looked as though she thought the coach were a form of torture, then stepped toward its door, where James currently stood waiting to be of assistance. The coachman, a Monsieur Lafitte, whom Anna had just met and who was apparently a relative of Monsieur Tessier, loaded their bags into the coach's boot. A boy who appeared to be in his early teens and must be the coachman's son, if the orders the man was barking in French and the boy's reactions were any indication, was acting as groom and was currently trying to hold the horses.

"Oh dear," Anna heard Mary say to Sparks. They were standing behind Anna, waiting to climb inside the coach. Anna turned to look at Mary peering inside the coach.

"I shall return in one moment, Lady Anna," Sparks said, and then he pivoted on his foot and returned swiftly to the inn.

What was that about?

James held out his hand, and Anna climbed inside the coach only to discover threadbare upholstery, its cushioning having taken a severe beating over the years. It was flat and lumpy and looked to have been quickly but not thoroughly dusted. The floorboards showed wear as well.

She sat facing forward and shifted in her seat to try to get the lumpy parts of the cushion into places that didn't offend her backside.

James then handed Mary into the coach, and she sat next to Anna. The seating arrangements had aided her travel sickness thus far, thankfully.

James climbed into the coach next and sat across from Anna. He looked squarely into her eyes and nodded, a sign of support she sorely needed. Then Sparks bounded into the coach and sat next to James. He was holding an old, bent bucket. "The missus of the inn caught on to me gestures well enough," Sparks said to Mary. "And when I pointed to a bucket what was in the kitchen, she understood and fetched this one from the dustbin. Just here in case it's needed, Mary, but don't ye worry. I'm sure everything is going to be fine."

With those unsettling words and the jostling of the coach as Monsieur Lafitte and his boy jumped into the coachman's box, they were finally on their way.

It took little time to realize that the coach's springs were either worn out or nonexistent, for Anna felt every bounce and bump and shake all the way down to her bones as the coach hit every rut in the road.

Mary moaned.

Alarmed, Anna looked over just in time to see Sparks kneel before Mary with the bucket firmly in place should Mary suddenly lose her breakfast.

Anna looked at James, although she wasn't sure why; it wasn't as if James could fix their current situation. No, *Anna* had brought them to this, and now they were suffering again in one form or another.

Mary lost her breakfast.

Sparks held the bucket and patted Mary's shoulder in comfort. "There now, Mary, it can't be helped," Sparks said soothingly. "Ye're a brave lass and all."

Anna and James each pulled their handkerchiefs from their pockets. Anna pressed her handkerchief against her nose after Sparks refused to take it from her, but James was insistent on Sparks taking his should it be needed.

"I still have a bit of that ginger root we got on board the yacht," Sparks said. "Do ye think it would help here too? Or just on the water?"

"It's worth a try, for Mary's sake," James said. "Good man." And then *James* actually held the bucket for Mary while Sparks rummaged around in his pockets until he came up with a fairly shriveled and battered-looking piece of ginger and his penknife. It didn't look particularly appetizing to Anna, and she doubted it did to Mary either, if her grimace were anything to go by.

"Just a bit, Mary, to start," Sparks said, cutting off a tiny piece with his knife and handing it to her.

She dutifully put it in her mouth.

"There now; that's a good girl," Sparks said. He folded his knife and set it and the ginger next to Mary on the seat.

Considering the seat's lack of cleanliness, Anna picked up both items and held them on her lap, even though they had been lurking in Sparks's pockets for days before this. It was something she could do under the circumstances rather than feeling helpless.

Sparks then took the bucket back from James.

"Perhaps, Anna," James said, "it would be easier for Sparks to sit next to Mary so he isn't required to kneel the entire length of our journey today—or at least until Mary feels better, which hopefully will happen sooner rather than later." He shot a kind smile at poor Mary. "But only if you're willing to ride facing backward."

"Willingly," Anna said, relieved that now, at least, she felt as if she were actually being helpful.

She handed Sparks the ginger and carefully slid from her seat to sit next to James. Sparks then handed the bucket to Mary and shifted himself into Anna's place. But just as Anna sat, the coach hit a huge rut, which sent her flying. Somehow James managed to wrap his arms around her before she fell and pulled her back into the seat.

After such a tumultuous beginning to the day, she welcomed the security of his arms and nestled a bit closer to him. She couldn't help herself.

Fortunately, Sparks had managed to brace himself with his foot on the floor of the coach, so he'd been spared the same upheaval Anna had experienced.

"Ye managed that big bump well," Sparks said to Mary, who had wrapped her arms around the bucket but wasn't needing to use it at present. "Here's another bit of ginger, me girl. I think we's on to something." He cut off another bit of ginger, and she slipped it between her lips.

They hit another bump.

And Anna was exceedingly grateful that she was safe in James's arms.

CHAPTER 14

The two days riding in the shabby coach were difficult ones. The vehicle was unable to travel at the same speed as the one le Touffe had driven, and more than one coach passed them on the road. James was certain his back and legs might never recover from his body being tossed to and fro and his bracing himself against each jerk and thump on the road from Orleans to Limoges. Granted, there were brief periods of time when the road had been decent enough, and James knew he wasn't the only one who appreciated that respite, if the shifting and quiet groans from the others, especially the women, were anything to go by.

There were also the brief respites when Lafitte changed the horses. They didn't last nearly long enough though.

Somehow, thanks to Sparks choosing to keep the remaining ginger they'd gotten, Mary had managed to quell her travel sickness for the most part, which James considered something of a miracle after witnessing her distress on the yacht and then again when they'd left Orleans. At least she had reached a point where she seemed able to determine how much she could eat without suffering afterward, although the ugly bucket got rinsed out frequently and stayed close by, just to be safe. James was relieved for poor Mary's sake, certainly, but the seating arrangement they'd decided upon for Mary had allowed Anna to sit beside him, which made everything infinitely more bearable, at least for him, in his estimation.

James had also spent every opportunity he'd had as they'd traveled to Limoges trying to persuade Lafitte to take them onward to at least the next stop in Souillac. Finally, *finally*, when they'd reached Limoges, James had been able to convince Lafitte that the money he was offering for the extra two days Lafitte would be on the road would be worth it for him and his family back home.

It had been a large sum, thanks to the generosity of Schwarzenberg. Even so, there was no way to anticipate what still lay before them, and he needed to err on the side of caution. He *would not* ask Anna for money. No gentleman would.

When they entered the inn at Limoges, James asked about available transportation—just in case Lafitte changed his mind, heaven forbid.

"Oh, monsieur," the innkeeper said after he'd called for a porter to take their bags to their rooms and had handed over the keys. "But no, do you not know?" The man was speaking in broken English, probably because he'd observed them speaking in English and was trying to be a helpful host. "Zee horses, zay are gone. Pfft! Taken by zee cavalry of Bonaparte." He spit at the floor in disgust.

Apparently, the man was not an admirer of the exiled French leader.

"And my inn? Zee leaders, zay force me to let zem stay here, but do zay pay? No, monsieur! I am a businessman, but zay do not care. And zee horses? Gone. Commandeered, is zat zee vord? *Oui.* Or maybe *maurade* eez zee better vord. Zay leave only zee old nags and mules." He shook his head and then pointed at the horses Lafitte was carefully overseeing being unhitched from the coach. "Ve take good care of zem, don't you vorry."

"*Merci*, monsieur," James said, although the innkeeper's words *did* make him worry. If there were no horses here in Limoges, he feared there would be even fewer as they continued their journey south.

Thankfully, Lafitte was good to his word, and in the morning, they were once again on their way south. No one spoke at breakfast, although the innkeeper had had his cook provide them with a nourishing meal to send them on their way. And once again, they bounced to and fro inside the coach, even though James was certain Lafitte was doing his best to avoid the ruts in the road.

Then it began to rain.

It started out slowly but increased in strength, so Lafitte pulled the coach to the side of the road. James wiped away the steam building on the windows of the coach and saw Lafitte and his boy jump down from the box to don hooded cloaks and then climb back into the box.

They proceeded slowly onward.

Unfortunately, the rain became a downpour, and now they not only felt the ruts in the road, but the wheels also slipped in the mud, making Mary shriek and cling to Sparks and a pale Anna bravely hold on to the windowsill of the coach to support herself.

James slid closer to her and placed his arm behind her, grabbing the frame of the coach with his hand as he did so, and then he took her nearest hand in his free hand and braced his feet on the floor of the coach.

It wasn't particularly romantic, owing to the women's fear, but James relished Anna's closeness just the same.

When they reached their first stop, instead of changing out the horses—since there weren't any to be had—they stayed longer and rested their horses. They huddled near the fireplace of the coaching inn, drinking tea and trying to warm themselves while poor Lafitte and his boy tended to the horses. Every time the door to the inn opened, Anna turned to see who it was only to sigh and continue sipping her tea, as each wet and weary traveler entering the inn was a stranger and not her brother. It broke James's heart to watch her.

Somehow, miraculously, the rain abated enough that Lafitte grudgingly decided the horses had rested enough to continue. They all piled back into the coach and set off, proceeding slowly due to the muddy, slippery roads, Lafitte and his son still wearing their cloaks and hoods in case the rain started again.

"The clouds appear to be breaking to the south of us," Anna observed quietly.

"Yes," James said. "That means the worst of the storm should be behind us." He offered her the most encouraging smile he could give her.

"We're not going to make it to our next planned stop in time, though, are we?" she asked, still keeping her voice low.

James glanced at Sparks and Mary, who seemed to be in their own quiet conversation, which was just as well. "No," James replied. "But the innkeeper told me that with what daylight we have remaining, we should be able to make it to the town of Brive."

"And we are losing our coach and coachman when we reach Brive, aren't we?"

"I'm afraid so. I doubt he will be willing to take us farther."

"Because of the delay due to the weather," Anna said with a nod of understanding. "You haven't told me why we rested these horses instead of changing them, only that we did."

James sighed. "There are few horses remaining in the south of France that weren't seized by the French cavalry," he said at last.

"What?" Anna exclaimed, which drew the attention of Sparks and Mary. When she realized she'd alarmed the others, she took a deep breath and smiled at them. "Pardon me for my outburst," Anna said with a feigned smile, although she gave no further explanation.

Mary and Sparks looked suspiciously at her—and at James—and then resumed their conversation after receiving reassuring nods from both James and Anna.

"We will have to be enterprising when we reach our next stop," James whispered, "so, if you believe in prayer, now might be a good time to do so."

"I do, and I have been this entire time," she whispered with solemn conviction.

His vicar of a brother would be proud of her. "As have I," he replied.

At Brive, James discovered that there were indeed no coaches for hire and few if any horses to be had. What horses James had seen on the streets appeared to be jealously guarded by their owners, who looked at him with suspicion. He had spent the entire evening after their arrival in town asking every innkeeper and merchant he could find—who were few, as it was the Sabbath—for suggestions on how they could continue on to Toulouse, as Lafitte had insisted on returning home.

Lafitte had left that morning before James and the others had even risen from their beds—undoubtedly to avoid encountering James's continual requests that he take them to Toulouse—and James had been unable to sleep, so he'd actually arisen early.

James began walking up and down the main streets of Brive, hoping to encounter shopkeepers beginning their day or farmers bringing their fares into town to be sold.

"*Non,*" he heard over and over. "*Non, monsieur. Je suis désolé, mais non.*"

I'm sorry, but no. James sat on a bench outside a small shop, disheartened, wondering how he was going to face Anna and the others.

A bearded older man in ragged clothes shuffled down the street and tipped his cap at James as he passed, drawing James out of his downcast thoughts. "*Bonjour,*" the man said in a gravelly voice.

"*Bonjour,*" James replied. The old man was the first person to speak to James before James had spoken to them this morning. Despite doubting that this ragged man could help, James decided there was no harm in asking for a moment of his time. "*Pardon, un moment de votre temps, s'il vous plaît?*" he asked.

"*Oui?*" the man asked.

James laid out their situation to the old man and how they must still make their way to Toulouse, and the man clucked and shook his head at the details James shared. The man, who had introduced himself as a Monsieur Durand, scratched at his scruffy chin in thought but said nothing.

"Perhaps you would like to meet the others?" James asked the man in French. "Perhaps you will join us for breakfast?" He had no idea why that specific invitation had occurred to him; it hadn't come to mind with any of the other citizens of Brive he'd encountered, either last evening or this morning. Perhaps it was the man's poor clothing or the fact that he'd greeted James when the others hadn't. James wasn't sure.

"*Ah! Merci!*" Durand replied with a smile that brightened his whole face.

James truly hadn't expected the man to accept the invitation, and belatedly, James realized it would keep him from continuing his search for some sort of transport for them.

Ah well.

They eventually arrived back at the inn, James matching his pace to the older man's shuffling walk, and they found Anna and the others already breaking their fast. He also noted that none of them seemed particularly happy; they must certainly be aware that Lafitte was gone.

They all looked as one at James when he entered with Monsieur Durand, and he could see the glimmer of hope in their eyes until they took in Durand's appearance and undoubtedly realized he wasn't the sort of individual who had a coach in his possession.

"My friends, allow me to present Monsieur Durand," James said to the others, pasting a genial smile on his face as they rose from their seats to greet James and his guest. "Monsieur Durand, *puis-je vous présenter* Lady Anna Clifton, Monsieur Thomas Sparks, *et* Mademoiselle Mary—" And then he realized he didn't know Mary's last name.

"Jones," Sparks piped up, obviously listening carefully despite not understanding the language. "Mary Jones."

Mary curtsied at Monsieur Durand.

"*Enchantée*," Monsieur Durand replied.

Sparks retrieved a chair from one of the other tables so Durand could be seated with them, and Durand smiled and nodded at the others as he sat with a murmured "*merci*." The serving girl eyed him suspiciously but left and returned with utensils and hot tea for the new arrivals.

"I was explaining to Monsieur Durand that we are in need of conveyance to Toulouse," James said. "Although I doubt he can help us, as no one else I have encountered thus far has been able or willing to do so, I invited him to join us; I'm glad to see that the invitation was well received by all of you, despite our current hardship."

"'Tis a difficult situation, to be sure," Sparks said. "But one can always help a person in need."

Durand choked a bit on the tea he was sipping. When James glanced at him, he shrugged. "*Chaud*," he muttered.

James nodded in understanding. "Hot," he replied so the others would understand Durand's reaction.

Food for James and Durand arrived in short order, and soon everyone was too busy eating to say much, but the mood was gloomy, despite attempts to make Durand feel welcome.

When they finished breakfast, James felt the weight of finding transportation for them heavy on his shoulders. He stood to excuse himself from the others, disheartened that he hadn't even had an opportunity to reassure Anna.

Durand stood when James did. "*Merci de m'avoir permis de me joindre à vous ce matin*," he said, offering his hand to Anna.

Anna took the old fellow's hand, apparently picking up on the word *merci*. "You are entirely welcome, Monsieur Durand," she said, and even if Durand hadn't understood a word she'd said, the sentiment must have translated well enough if the smile on his face was anything to go by.

"Toulouse, *non*?" Durand asked Anna, gesturing with his head in the direction of the street.

"Yes, to find my brother. He was reported wounded and missing in action, and no one knows if he's dead or alive. He's my only remaining family, you see. I have traveled to France because I *must* do all that I can to find him or to find out what happened to him."

James was about to remind her that she was speaking English to Monsieur Durand and that he wouldn't understand what she was saying when Durand raised his hand and silenced James.

"I understand, Lady Anna, only too well," Monsieur Durand said in perfectly intelligible English.

Anna's mouth dropped open. She looked at James only to see that he looked as stunned as she felt.

Monsieur Durand shrugged.

What is it about the French and shrugging their shoulders? Anna thought briefly.

Why *that* had been the first thought to cross her mind, she couldn't explain, for obviously, her first thought should have been *Durand speaks English?* immediately followed by *And how is it that in a small town in southern France, we have the good fortune to encounter someone who appears to speak fluent English?*

"You have been keeping a rather large secret from me, monsieur, even if we have only just met," James said—in English, naturally.

Monsieur Durand shrugged again. "There is a right time and a wrong time to share information, is there not, Monsieur Jennings?" he said. "I think perhaps you know this as well as anyone."

Anna watched James's brow furrow.

This time, rather than shrugging, however, Monsieur Durand took another sip of tea. "I am known in Brive," he said. "We protect each other here, and we do not share information readily. We have reason for this, you see, after we suffered so much from *La Maraude*. When strangers come to our door, we ask the questions, and then we share what we learn with each other."

"*La Maraude*," James repeated.

"*Oui*," Monsieur Durand said. "And so you see, your search for a way to travel to Toulouse swiftly reached my ears."

"Because you are . . . ?" James asked.

Anna wondered what *La Maraude* meant.

"I am a simple man who has dedicated his life to France and to the people here. They trust me, and I trust them," Monsieur Durand said.

"I don't understand," Anna said, finally deciding she must speak up and ask her questions herself. "What is *La Maraude*? And where did you learn such excellent English?"

"*Merci*, Lady Anna," Monsieur Durand said with a nod of thanks. "As a young man and owing to my education, I was privileged to travel with French diplomats during times of great struggle with Britain, when we were allies of the Americans. It enabled me to learn English. But I fear I do not speak English as well as I used to, so your words are kind.

"This all occurred many years ago, and I returned to my village with the intent of living out my years in peace. But then came our *hero, Napoleon*"—he nearly spat the emperor's name—"who thought to take Spain, so he demands our grain for his troops. But that is not enough for Napoleon—no, he must take our young men, our old men, our women and girls, in the *Levée en masse*. And our young men die too young, and our old men see too much, and our women and daughters work too hard and suffer in foul ways for someone else's victories."

Anna tore her eyes from Monsieur Durand and briefly looked at James. His face was racked with pain, obviously moved by Monsieur Durand's words.

"But I say too much," Monsieur Durand said.

"Not at all, monsieur," James replied. "I am a diplomat, and the struggle to find peace among the countries involved is not for the faint of heart. I, too, have seen more than I wish to remember."

"And I have suffered my own losses at the hands of Bonaparte and those who would follow him," Anna said. She didn't understand the politics involved, but she knew what it was to lose her family and possibly her home, owing to the selfish desires of others.

"I see that you understand, Lady Anna," Monsieur Durand said. "And with the recent battles to our south and the retreat to the north, we suffer again from *La Maraude*. The armies who pass through take what they want. Our grain goes again, our remaining horses are stolen. And so now we fight back in our own little way, *non*? We have learned, you see, to hide our grain, to hide what few horses we still have. It is not an easy task, and we cannot protect it all, but we keep some, and for us, it is a victory.

"And so, my friends see you arrive in our little Brive needing horses, needing a coach, needing our food and shelter, and we wonder and worry. Ah, but you are English, and the English helped defeat Bonaparte, so what are we to think? We watch, and I am asked to speak to you as a broken, old man who has nothing. And what do you do? You invite me to eat. You make no demands."

James's head dropped to his chest.

"Monsieur?" Monsieur Durand asked.

"You spoke to me first," James said, his voice breaking. "You were the only person to have done so, and so I felt moved to invite you to join us."

Monsieur Durand crossed himself and kissed the crucifix hanging around his neck. "Ah, but this is Providence, *non?*" he said.

"Oh, James!" Anna exclaimed, clasping her hands at her breast as she smiled at him. She turned back to Monsieur Durand. "Yesterday, when our coachman left us to return home, James—Monsieur Jennings—suggested we pray, although I have been praying since I received word that my brother was missing. And while I'm not sure what we will yet face or what we will discover at the end of all this, you have shown us that we are in God's care. And for that, I am truly grateful!"

"Now," Monsieur Durand said, "let us see what we can do to get you to Toulouse, *oui?*"

"Oh, yes!" Anna exclaimed before unceremoniously throwing her arms around Monsieur Durand's shoulders and hugging him tightly.

James very nearly threw his own arms around Monsieur Durand at the same time Anna did hers, but he managed, just barely, to hold on to a small bit of restraint. After James had searched for transportation all last evening and then again this morning, Monsieur Durand's offer to assist was a godsend; Anna was entirely correct about that. How else could one explain meeting a man in such a small French village who spoke fluent English, who was keenly aware of the politics in the world in which they now lived, and who understood the grief Anna was feeling?

It was nothing short of a miracle.

That wasn't to say the miracle didn't have its set of drawbacks, James soon discovered.

He and Monsieur Durand left the others at the inn, but not before Sparks and Mary returned to their rooms to set about packing and Anna pledged to lend them a hand, which was another aspect of Anna that only made James love her more. She didn't stand on ceremony or status, and the farther they traveled into France, the more she seemed to adopt the French republican spirit of class equality.

The way she'd openly hugged Monsieur Durand . . .

They walked the few blocks Monsieur Durand indicated to a large building that looked to house a blacksmith's shop in at least part of it—although James doubted the blacksmith needed that large of a space.

When they passed through the shop's open doors, open to allow fresh air inside so the bellows could keep the fire blazing in the forge, James quickly glanced about while Monsieur Durand walked over to the smith, who set his tools aside and wiped his brow with the sleeve of his shirt. Durand spoke quietly to the smith, who glanced at James periodically.

In addition to the forge and its equipment and tools, the building housed a wagon. James let out a sigh of resignation, for this, he was sure, was to be their conveyance going forward, and he didn't relish the idea a single jot. All the same, he walked over to it to give it a better look.

It was a supply wagon; the sort Napoleon's troops used to carry baggage and supplies along the route from battle to battle. The soldiers would also have used it—as Monsieur Durand had said—to hold items taken from the French citizens since the soldiers relied upon Napoleon's directive of *La Maraude* to supply troops with food, clothing, or whatever else they might need.

The wagon appeared to have needed repairs, which would undoubtedly explain why it had been left in Brive. The repairs to it, however, appeared to be only enough to make it useful and not necessarily to get it back to its original form. And while supply wagons usually had a canvas cover to keep munitions and supplies dry, this particular wagon didn't appear to have a cover or even the spines required to keep a cover in place.

James closed his eyes and pinched the bridge of his nose, reminding himself that at least it was a form of transport. It was wholly inelegant, even when compared to their last conveyance, but it was *something*, and he didn't feel they had the right to press Monsieur Durand for something better—if indeed this was the vehicle Durand was intending to offer.

If this was the miracle, James would try to be grateful for it.

Monsieur Durand stepped next to James, drawing him out of his morose thoughts. The blacksmith was by his side.

"She is not pretty, I know," Monsieur Durand said. "But she is sturdy."

"*Merci*," James replied, not knowing what else to say.

Monsieur Durand began speaking in French to the blacksmith. "See? I told you they would not look down upon the gift but would be grateful." He nodded his head in emphasis.

"But we must pay for the wagon," James answered in French, watching the blacksmith's eyes widen at his use of the local language. "And for any horse you may wish to sell along with it. We must insist upon it."

Monsieur Durand's eyebrows rose as if to say, "You see?" to the blacksmith once again.

"We have a few horses," Monsieur Durand said. "Not the finest stock after *La Maraude*, but if you will allow my friend here to travel with you to Toulouse, with your money, he will be able to buy a better wagon and possibly better horses to bring back to Brive."

"You are certain of this?" James couldn't help but ask.

"*Oui*, for there are horses that were injured in battle, and we are confident the people did what they could to heal the ones that could be saved. We hear things about Toulouse, you see, and it is a much bigger place than our little Brive. We are quite certain, monsieur."

"Then, I am most grateful, Monsieur Durand and Monsieur . . ."

"Villard," the blacksmith replied.

"Villard," James repeated with a courteous smile. "I shall go and inform the others that we will leave soon. As we are traveling with two women, I would ask your assistance in finding ways to make the wagon more comfortable during the journey. After I give them the good news, I shall bring my fellow traveler, Sparks, back with me to assist."

He shook hands with Monsieurs Durand and Villard and turned to leave, but Monsieur Durand grabbed his elbow and stopped him. "Monsieur," the older man whispered, "I hope you have weapons, for the way into Toulouse may hold brigands and ne'er-do-wells. There are those passing through our little Brive both north and south whom we do not trust."

"I have not told my fellow travelers," James replied just as quietly, "but I would not have considered undertaking this journey without my pistols. I am a diplomat by trade, and I am also not a fool."

Durand and Villard nodded to each other in approval.

James then set off for the inn, hoping he would be able to convince the others that their best travel solution for the remainder of the journey was going to be a rather shabby supply wagon.

He honestly couldn't believe he was going to be informing the titled daughter of an earl that they would be traveling without even the comfort of an actual seat. He wondered if he should try to ask more of the town's citizens . . . but then decided against it. The fact that Villard hadn't even questioned Durand's offer of the wagon added to Durand's standing in the town, and his easy use of English in such a remote place assured James that the people here were truly doing what they could to help.

Even so, he didn't relish the conversation—or the journey—that was to come.

CHAPTER 15

"What have you learned? Where is Monsieur Durand?" Anna asked the moment James returned to the inn and rejoined them. Mary had just finished packing Anna's bags, and Sparks had brought his and James's bags into the room. They were all together.

James sank into a chair in the corner of her room, and Anna's heart sank with him.

She went to his side and crouched down to be face-to-face with him. "What is it? What has happened? Was Monsieur Durand able to help us?"

"He has done what he could for us, yes," James replied.

It was a rather enigmatic statement, Anna thought.

"What does that mean?" Sparks asked as he took the bag Mary had just packed and placed it with the others.

James heaved a sigh.

"What is it, James?" she asked. "What are you not telling us?"

"My dearest Anna," he said softly, which worried her at the same time it filled her heart. He'd never spoken so affectionately to her before, and yet his tone was grave. "I have done all in my power to be of service to you and—" He stopped speaking and heaved another sigh. "And yet I am a mere man who has failed, I fear."

Mary gasped loudly behind Anna, and Anna heard Sparks move toward Mary and shush her.

Anna, however, kept her eyes on James. "What do you mean, failed?" she asked. "We have no coach? We have no conveyance, then?"

He looked up, and their gazes locked. James looked more tired and defeated than she'd seen him during their entire acquaintance, however brief—although it felt as though she'd known him for ages now. Instead of the arrogant lawyer she'd met on the Duke of Aylesham's yacht, here was the James she'd come to know: an earnest, caring, and vigilant gentleman with new wrinkles at his eyes, undoubtedly caused by worry over the role he'd assumed in escorting her on her determined quest.

"A supply wagon," he said softly.

"A what?" she asked, wondering what he meant.

"We have a supply wagon. That is the best we can do."

Anna heard Mary gasp again, and Sparks said, "Now, now," or something like that, she supposed—she was still trying to grasp exactly what James had said and if she'd even heard him correctly.

"A supply wagon?" she repeated, just to be certain.

"The answer to our prayers is a supply wagon left behind by Napoleon's troops."

"Left behind?" Anna asked.

"Yes, owing to its condition at the time. It has been adequately repaired."

"But it's a wagon!" Mary exclaimed.

James shrugged, making him look rather French for a moment, Anna thought abstractedly.

"The war has been difficult for the people of Brive, and we were blessed to have encountered Monsieur Durand," James said. "The local blacksmith, Monsieur Villard, will escort us on our journey, if you are willing to agree to the plans. It is their hope that he can return from Toulouse with a better wagon and, more especially, horses."

James looked at her in inquiry, waiting for her to respond.

"A wagon," she repeated.

"Yes," he replied.

"A wagon it is, then," Anna said, resolving to be positive in this unexpected situation. "What must we do to make this wagon as agreeable as possible? I confess I've never ridden in a wagon before—except for a time or two when I was a girl and we held fetes at Clifton Hall . . ." She paused as a wave of melancholy washed over her. "During happier times."

"Oh, my dear Anna," James said softly.

Anna shook her melancholy away. "But you have *not* failed us, James," she said, laying her hand atop his and hoping her voice sounded more resolute than she actually felt. "It was you and your diligence that brought us Monsieur Durand, was it not? And we are seeing more and more that the war has been hard on so many. Not just on me and my family."

"I'll leave Mary here wi' ye, me lady, if that pleases ye, and Mr. Jennings and meself will set about to see what we can do to make this . . . wagon . . . a bit more comfortable for ye ladies—beggin' yer pardon, me lady, for referring to Mary as a lady when ye're a real one . . ." His voice trailed off.

"I understood your meaning, Sparks," Anna said with a smile, relinquishing James's hand and rising to her feet.

"Come, Sparks," James said. He inhaled deeply, then rose to his feet. "We have work to do before we can be on our way. Let's go find Durand and Villard, shall we?"

"Oh, me lady!" Mary exclaimed when they were gone. "I don't know how I'm going to last riding in a wagon. Between the tossing and bouncing and me weak stomach and me bruised bones . . ."

Anna's heart broke. "Mary, I'm so sorry I have put you and Sparks through all this. I didn't know what else to do, but I truly had no idea of the suffering it would bring to us."

And then, despite herself, she collapsed into the chair in which James had just been sitting and broke into tears.

By the time James and Sparks arrived back at the black-smith's shop, the two French men had moved the wagon outside, loaded it with a few bales of hay in order to create seating of a sort, and covered the bales as best they could with old quilts. James was glad to see the quilts, as hay was itchy; he'd learned that from antics he and his brothers had gotten into as children.

The poor horses Monsieur Durand had provided were old, undoubtedly the reason the French troops had left them behind. And while the wagon had originally been sturdily constructed for long-distance travel, it had not been built for the comfort of passengers, since there'd been no expectation that there would ever *be* any passengers.

If they had thought they'd felt every bump and jostle in the carriages, they were in for a rude awakening when they left Brive. When they stopped for luncheon and to rest the old horses on the first day, after listening to Anna and Mary stifle moans, James and Sparks set about pulling the bales apart and rearranging the hay to make softer seating than what had been formed using the firm bales.

They were all grateful to finally reach their destination of Souillac on their first day riding in the wagon. James, for one, had discovered more bruises on his body than he'd thought possible, and his back was sore from being tossed from side to side. He hated to think what it meant Anna and Mary had endured.

The second day was much like the first, adding more bruises to James's personal collection. Additionally, it had broken his heart to watch Anna's disappointed reaction to every soldier who passed them on the road. During one of their rest stops, he assisted Anna from the wagon, her hand gripping the crook of his arm, and its presence there was like a fire in a hearth—warm and delicious despite his bruised body but dangerous if he allowed himself to get too close. He'd resisted the temptation to pull her into his arms and bury his face in her neck, but only just. In truth, all he wished to do was take her into his arms, declare his undying passion for her, and kiss her until she swooned.

On the third day, even though the inn they had stayed at that night had been welcoming, and the supper and breakfast served had been delicious and filling, a gloom settled over James as the day and their travel in the wagon progressed. Clouds had blown in overhead, gray and ominous.

A day of rain threatened them.

When raindrops started to fall, Anna retrieved a small umbrella from her bag. It worked well enough for her and Mary at first until the winds began to blow and the rain poured down on them in sheets. Sparks groaned and pulled his jacket over his head.

There was no respite to be had. Visibility was poor due to low clouds, and the roads turned to pools of mud, yet Villard kept the wagon going, albeit at a much slower speed.

"I suppose we should be glad that it's a rain shower in slightly warmer climes than the one we experienced a few days back," Anna said right after her umbrella blew inside out and was of no further use. "Although I *had* hoped my next warm bath would occur once we reached our last stop for the evening, not while we were still en route."

James couldn't help himself. He laughed outright. And then Sparks laughed, and even Mary chuckled a bit.

"You see up there? That cloud there?" James said to Anna after he stopped laughing, pointing to the cloud right above them.

"Yes, what about it?" Anna said, peering up through the rain and shielding her eyes with her hand.

"I believe it has a silver lining, if you look very carefully."

Anna turned to him then and slapped his arm playfully. "Oh, James!" she exclaimed. And then she laughed. This wonderful, valiant lady, her hair sticking to her cheeks, her bonnet sagging, her black traveling clothes sodden and covered with straw and mud, *laughed*. James had thought her beautiful in adverse conditions before, but at that moment—

"I love you," he said.

Anna gasped.

Blast.

James had always considered himself to be of a disciplined nature. He'd prided himself on his intellect: his skills with languages, his understanding of law, foreign and domestic, and a strict adherence to his life goals. He was a diplomat—he prided himself on choosing his words wisely. What had he done?

Since this woman had come into his life, it was as though his entire being had lost its senses. But the challenge of balancing one's affections with one's duties was blasted difficult.

He had greatly overstepped the mark with his words.

Anna wasn't entirely sure she'd heard James correctly. She'd been laughing, surprisingly, and the rain and wind had been rushing about, and the squeak of the wagon wheels and the thudding sounds of the horses' hooves had made for a bit of a ruckus. She was soaked to the skin, and despite her witty remark about warm baths, she was chilled, and her teeth were chattering.

It was bad enough that she wasn't certain she'd heard a declaration of love from James—although she dearly prayed it had been the case—but then his expression had turned serious and then pained, and then he'd looked away, all in a matter of a few moments.

What had she done? What had her expression suggested to have his countenance change so dramatically so rapidly?

"James—" she began.

Monsieur Villard shouted something in French right then, and Anna, Sparks, Mary, and James all turned as one to look in the direction Villard was pointing. The town where they were staying for the night—James had said it was called Montauban—loomed before them.

James then preoccupied himself with brushing off his jacket sleeves and shouting questions in French to Villard, to which the blacksmith nodded and yelled replies. The sun was sinking in the west, Anna was chilled, and her mood had chilled along with the rest of her person after James's confusing sequence.

She heaved a sigh of relief when the wagon finally pulled off the main street into the yard of the inn and came to a stop. She stood, attempting to maintain her balance, which had been something of an issue the past two days when stepping on hay and uneven wagon slats, and was even more difficult now that her wet traveling gown weighed substantially more and clung to her legs. James reached out to assist her, but she ignored him.

Although she had initially doubted what she'd heard, now that she'd had a minute to reflect, she was certain she'd heard him say he loved her. And then for him to become completely aloof immediately afterward stung. She simply couldn't bear his touch right now. It would be too painful, too confusing.

She was a fool. And right now, she was a wet, cold, dirty, exhausted, heartbroken fool who had subjected others to her foolishness and, hence, to being as wet, cold, dirty, and exhausted as she was.

Her foot slipped, and her arms flailed like windmills at her sides as she tried to regain her balance unsuccessfully and dropped—

Straight into James's arms.

"Are you all right?" he asked, his lips right next to her ear, his arms securely around her waist.

"Yes." It wasn't entirely a lie. She *was* all right, as she'd avoided falling and injuring herself, but she *wasn't* all right in spirit. And while James's arms felt secure, and she *was* grateful he'd caught her before she'd fallen and injured herself and her pride, the entire debacle was frustrating.

Once she had her feet firmly under her again, she turned her head to politely smile at him and say thank you. But his arms were still around her, steadying her, and by turning her head, their faces were barely an inch apart.

Their eyes caught, and then his gaze dropped to her lips.

How dare he!

Her lips began to quiver, which only made her angrier and even more despondent, if that were possible. She tore herself from his arms without saying a word and tromped off toward the inn, without looking at anyone or anything. But then when she reached the door, she realized that she couldn't ask any of the servants at the inn for help because *she didn't speak French.* She was dependent upon James, or perhaps Villard, though he had mostly kept to himself, and the idea that she was *so dependent on others* at *this particular moment* was the final straw.

She stopped right where she was and buried her face in her hands.

"Come, me lady." Mary's sweet voice sounded like heaven. Her familiar arms wrapped around Anna's shoulders this time rather than James's arms doing the deed. "I'm certain there's a nice room to be had inside, and Mr. Jennings and Sparks is seein' to it that we all get nice, warm baths and a hearty meal, and the clouds look to be not quite so threatening as they was all afternoon, so that's a good thing, isn't it?"

Anna nodded but didn't—couldn't—speak and allowed Mary to guide her into the inn, where aromas from the kitchen tried their best to entice Anna out of her gloom—unsuccessfully.

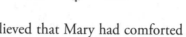

James was relieved that Mary had comforted Anna after she had refused his help. He busied himself with arranging for their rooms, and he and Sparks also needed to have the soaked blankets that covered the hay hung somewhere so they could dry before the four of them continued on their way tomorrow morning.

He went directly to the innkeeper, all the while berating himself. He was wholly embarrassed that blurting out the word *love* was keeping him from speaking to Anna. Yet it was. She'd withdrawn into herself and away from him. Was it his fault? Had his declaration shocked her?

And then James had a dreadful thought: What if she felt some sort of obligation to him? Were he to ask her to marry him, might she agree only because of his service to her these past few weeks?

That would be utterly unbearable.

After arranging for rooms, he walked over to Anna and said only, "Your rooms are on the second floor. I hope they'll be suitable." *Heady stuff, that,* he thought morosely as he left to find the stablemaster and arrange for the care of their horses. But gratefully, he found Villard already seeing to the task.

James went to his room and soaked in a warm bath, then sorted through his clothes to find something that was the least dirty before setting out to ask the innkeeper's wife if he could have a few of his things laundered. When she agreed, he asked—as an afterthought—if she would include a few items from his fellow travelers. "I'm sure Lady Anna, in particular, will appreciate freshly laundered clothing," he explained in French.

The innkeeper's wife was willing to oblige, especially when she realized she had a member of British nobility staying at the inn, and even more so after James offered her a rather generous sum of money. With that done, he set off to find one of the others to pass the word along.

Sparks and Villard had been assigned the small room off James's own, where James knew Sparks was cleaning up, so he knocked on the door and told Sparks he could take some clothes to be laundered. Next, he left to inform Anna and Mary.

He went to their room and rapped softly on the door. Mary answered. It was obvious she hadn't had a chance to clean up yet.

"The innkeeper's wife has offered to launder a few of our clothing items," he said in a low voice so as not to disturb Anna. "If you wish to take some of your and Lady Anna's things down to her, she's expecting them."

"Thank you, sir," Mary said with a small curtsy. "I shall inform her."

He nodded politely, and she shut the door.

Time to arrange for supper, he thought. Then his work would be done for the night.

He wasn't the slightest bit surprised when Sparks joined him downstairs after a while and told him the women had decided to take their supper in their room. Of course they had.

It was probably just as well, he thought as he and Sparks ate their supper in the dining hall, which was fairly busy, mostly with men who appeared to be soldiers. They'd passed such men along their travels, and they had experienced more frequent encounters the closer they'd gotten to Toulouse.

Villard chose to dine with the inn's staff despite James's invitation, saying he might be able to learn something about Lady Anna's brother from the locals, which made sense, and which James appreciated. In fact, James appreciated that Sparks, Mary, Villard, and others had been agreeable and helpful and, blast it all, good company, and he especially appreciated them after so many weeks of bowing and scraping to the elite of the Continent.

James swallowed the last of his ale. "I'm heading up to the rooms," he said as he stood from their table. "You?"

"Not quite, guv," Sparks said.

"Very well," James said. "Good night."

He made his way to his room, fatigue finally hitting him, ready for the void that accompanied sleep.

CHAPTER 16

Anna slept fitfully and awoke in the morning feeling both energized and weary, if such a thing were possible.

Today was the day. Today they would reach Toulouse, the last known place where Avery's regiment had fought before the treaty was signed. She could not and would not think that he might have died in Orthez or remained there without his regiment if he'd lived. She *had* to believe that Toulouse would hold the answer.

She thought she might be sick.

Ever since they had left Paris, Anna had looked at every man—soldier or commoner, it hadn't mattered—they'd passed along the way or shared a dining room with or encountered on their way to their rooms. Every time, she'd looked to see if it was Avery. Each time, she had been disappointed.

The closer they'd gotten to Toulouse, the more men they'd passed along the way, and Anna's emotions had been thrust back and forth from anxiety to despair with each encounter.

Breathe, she told herself firmly. *You must breathe.*

Mary had laid out clothes for her to wear today. The innkeeper's wife had outdone herself, Anna thought as she fingered the fabric of the chemise and traveling gown that were freshly washed and pressed. The black dye of her traveling gown had faded, turning it a dismal shade of gray, but at least it was clean and not covered in mud and hay and who knew what else.

"Let me help ye with yer coiffure, Lady Anna," Mary said once Anna had pulled on the clean clothing.

"Thank you, Mary," Anna said, trying to quell her anxiety and sound cheerful.

A light rap at the door meant Sparks was there to collect their bags.

Mary opened the door. "Just in time, Sparks; the bags is ready." She opened the door wide for Sparks to enter.

He tipped his cap to Anna. "Mornin', me lady," Sparks said.

"Good morning, Sparks," Anna replied.

"Mr. Jennings says as soon as we break our fast, we can be on our way, if that be pleasin' to ye."

"It is, thank you," Anna said. Breaking her fast wasn't something she relished doing this morning, but needs must. She marched determinedly out the door, leaving Mary and Sparks to follow with the bags.

Her stomach was doing summersaults, her heart was pounding, she felt dizzy . . .

Today was the day.

Today *might be* the day, she corrected herself as she headed to the dining hall, which was surprisingly busy this morning. She glanced around the room before all the male eyes that had begun looking at her made her even more uncomfortable than she already felt. One man in particular caught her eye. He was blond, like her . . . *Was it Avery?* Her heart leaped into her throat.

No.

The man smirked at her and looked her up and down.

Disappointed, despondent, she turned away and continued on through the dining hall.

James stood when she approached the table where he was eating. "Good morning, Lady Anna," he said.

Lady Anna. For him to be back to addressing her with such formality was another knife to the heart.

It was too much.

"Good morning, Mr. Jennings," she replied as formally as he had. She wasn't about to bring up the subject of his declaration to her, especially now. She sat and gestured to the serving girl, then ordered tea and toast. She'd learned *that* much French over the past several days.

The serving girl dashed off and quickly returned.

James finished his breakfast, and Anna nibbled at her toast, wondering if she might need to ask for some of the ginger Sparks probably still had shriveling up in one of his pockets somewhere.

Disgusting thought. She hoped it wouldn't come to that.

After a torturous eternity that was really only about a half hour, they finished breakfast and were on their way to Toulouse. The blankets were mostly dry, thankfully, and Anna watched as Sparks loaded their baggage into a corner while James seemed particularly interested in fluffing up the straw in certain areas and making sure the blankets were tucked securely in place. Once everyone was settled in the wagon, Villard gave the reins a snap, and the poor horses responded.

Anna and James sat across from each other on opposite sides of the wagon, facing each other but not looking at each other—at least, Anna pretended not to be looking at James whenever he looked at her. Despite a few clouds that hovered, the rain they'd suffered through yesterday held off, thankfully.

The wagon wheels made too much noise for conversation, so Anna was left alone with her thoughts while sneaking glances at James's somber expression. He seemed intent on watching the countryside as they rode past, which he hadn't done before. Anna assumed it was so he could appear to be preoccupied.

The morning dragged along, Villard only stopping to rest the poor horses and then seeing to luncheon when they reached the town of Fronton.

As they traveled, Anna began to notice that the fields and even the fences around them increasingly appeared to have been trampled, cottages and buildings showed various levels of damage and destruction, and she realized they had to be nearing Toulouse and witnessing the aftermath of battle. They also passed many more groups of men, much like the ones she'd seen along the road the past few days and in the inn's dining room this morning—two or three together, some on horseback but most walking along the road, their clothes dirty and torn, knapsacks on their backs, rifles in hand. Each group they passed eyed Villard's wagon suspiciously, seeming to size them up, and Anna began to feel even more anxious. For the first time in their travels, she actually feared for their safety.

Villard said something over his shoulder to James, and James replied to him. "Villard says these men are mostly foreign mercenaries no longer necessary for the French to retain as soldiers," James said to Anna in explanation.

Anna squeezed her eyes shut, as if to hide from the sense of danger she couldn't help but feel, and once again, guilt flooded her. How was she to have managed dealing with mercenaries on her own? Thankfully, they continued onward relatively undisturbed, but Anna kept her eyes closed for the most part, trying to block the vision of the mercenaries from her mind. It was foolish, she knew, but she needed a respite from everything—even if only for a few minutes at a time.

Amid her thoughts, Anna heard galloping horses approaching them from behind, not unlike other horses she'd heard and had desperately tried to ignore. But this time, their wagon stopped abruptly, and her eyes shot open in time to see two men on horseback grab Villard's horses' harnesses and a third man—the blond man from the dining room this morning—aim a pistol directly at Villard.

Mary screamed. Anna froze, her heart beating like a frenzied bird within her chest.

"Sparks," James said softly. "Now." Without taking his eye off the third man, James reached under the hay behind him and retrieved a pistol Anna hadn't known was there, vaguely recalling now how intent James had been on tucking the blankets around the hay. Likewise, Sparks carefully retrieved a pistol from the hay next to him. Both men cocked and aimed their pistols at the man who had aimed at Villard, startling him just enough for Villard to grab a musket that, unbeknownst to Anna, he'd stowed under *his* seat.

The two men holding the harnesses pulled out their own pistols.

James barked something in French at the blond man, and the man replied, then turned to aim his pistol directly at James.

James and the man began a rather heated dialogue that Anna wished dearly she could understand, and then Villard and the two men holding their team of horses joined in. It was a loud conversation that went on for what seemed an eternity to Anna, especially when the men sneered and pointed specifically at *her*.

She clutched at her throat, barely breathing, praying that these men would leave them in peace as the other mercenaries who had passed by them had done.

"Vat are zey talking about?" Villard surprisingly snapped in English. "Vat eez zis *chambres hautes*—upper rooms—zey keep mentioning?"

James replied in French to Villard, which frustrated Anna to no end. *Upper rooms?*

James kept talking to the blackguards while Anna sat in terror, waiting for someone to shoot someone and fearing they all would die because of her determination to find her brother.

"What is happening?" she whispered to James. "What upper rooms?"

James didn't reply to her question. The men kept their pistols aimed at James, Sparks, and Villard. The discussion in French continued, and Anna could do nothing but hold her breath and offer up a silent prayer.

Finally, with his pistol still aimed at the first man, James shot a glance at Anna. "It would seem these fine gentlemen were sent specifically to thwart our attempt at arriving in Toulouse," he said.

"Why?" Anna asked. "Who would care enough to do something like that?"

"They only knew the person who contacted them as someone sent from the upper rooms. They were to return to Paris with the, quote, 'lady like a pearl' named Anna. They knew it was you as soon as they spied you in Montauban."

The first man snapped at James, and he turned and spat harsh words in French back at the man.

"Taking you back to the upper rooms will apparently make the man in the upper rooms happy," James said. "They will be paid well if they accomplish their task."

"What upper rooms?" Anna asked.

Her question seemed to suddenly enlighten James. "Upper rooms. *Chambres hautes*. Blast, blast, and blast!" he exclaimed. "One of the difficulties of war, treaties, and the like is the challenge of language. These villains were sent by von Oberhausen! *Ober*—'upper' in German—and, of course, *haus* is 'house.' I doubt these villains know enough German to make the distinction."

"Von Oberhausen?" Anna cried, standing abruptly and losing her balance, which made all the men start toward her.

"Stay back, Anna," James murmured, then he spoke to the men in rapid French.

"How much was von Oberhausen going to pay them?" she asked.

Dialog took place between the man and James. "He says, 'More than you can afford.'"

"You're a negotiator, James!" Anna exclaimed. "Do something!"

James shot Anna a glance that essentially said, "What do you think I'm trying to do?" With guns still pointed, he and the man set about arguing in French again. James would shake his head; the man would shake his head and gesture with his free hand. The other men took closer aim with their pistols, and Sparks and Villard followed suit.

Mary was curled up in a corner of the wagon, weeping, and Anna could do nothing. She had never felt so helpless, even after Papa had died. She shuddered. What if James didn't prevail? What would happen to them?

"Anna," James said quietly after what felt like an eternity. "Come to me, please."

She stared at him in horror. He stared back at her, serious but earnest, as though his eyes were saying, "Trust me."

Could she trust him?

What choice did she have? She had brought them all into this.

She swallowed hard and anxiously managed the few steps inside the wagon to James's side.

He handed her his pistol. "Hold it steady," he said.

She pointed it at the first man and tried not to shake. She knew enough about guns from life in the country to see that the pistol was cocked, ready to be used if necessary. That knowledge only made her shake more.

James said something to the men while raising his hands above his head in a gesture of trust, then reached into his breast pocket and removed his wallet. He took out all the bills inside and handed them to the man, who nodded at James in appreciation.

Anna was still highly anxious though. What if the men decided James's money wasn't enough? What if the mercenaries wanted to search all of them for everything they could find?

After a tense few minutes, during which the man counted the money, he conferred with his two fellows. Then, by some great miracle of Providence, they saluted James, released the team of horses, and turned in the direction from which they'd come and headed back toward Montauban.

James gave direction to Villard to continue onward toward Toulouse. Anna handed the pistol back to James and collapsed to the floor of the wagon as she tried to simply breathe.

Once the wagon had moved safely down the road and was well beyond the three men, James instructed Villard to halt at the side of the road.

Once the wagon had stopped, James rose to his feet and offered Anna his hand. "Come with me," was all he said.

Anna, still in shock from what they'd just been through, obeyed.

———— ⋎ ————

It had been much too close a call for James. Somehow, he'd managed to keep his wits about him while facing those brigands, but just barely. He was used to sitting in fancy rooms and speaking eloquently with diplomats and sovereigns. *This* had been about immediate life or death if one made a misstep.

He grabbed Anna's hand again once he'd lifted her from the wagon and strode into the clump of trees bordering the road, dragging her behind him until they were hidden from the others. Once there, he moved behind the biggest tree and pressed her against it before placing his hands on either side of her face and leaning toward her.

"James!" she gasped.

He couldn't speak. Every instinct within him cried to surround her, protect her. He closed his eyes and pressed his forehead against hers, battling to slow his breathing. His heart raced. "Anna," he murmured. It was all he could think to say. "Anna."

Her arms came around him with tenderness—and he was lost. His lips sought hers, and he took his prize, taking and taking, unable to stop. Her hands gripped his back, and on some primal level, he recognized that she was giving as much as he was taking, so he cradled her face in his hands and softened his kisses, pressing them to her cheeks, her forehead, her chin, and then her full, delicious lips again.

"James," she sighed.

"You're safe, and that's all that matters," he whispered in her ear before nipping at her earlobe. "Whether we are fortunate to find Avery or not, you won't have to return to your awful cousin or a place where you're not welcome. You belong with me now." He wrapped his arms around her now and held her, held her so tightly, wanting time to stop—right here, right now—with her safely in his arms and the feel of her lips upon his.

He didn't know how long they remained thus. It was only the sound of someone tromping through the woods toward them—Sparks, by the sound of the voice calling after them— that he regained his senses.

Anna still held him.

"I will always be here for you, my Anna," he said softly before backing slightly out of their embrace. "You have my heart; my entire being belongs to you. Had I lost you to those brigands—"

"Sir! There ye are!" Sparks said. "Me lady!" The man had the good sense to drop his eyes when he saw the two of them together. "We was worried when ye went off like that."

"We're fine; everything's fine," James said. He looked at Anna to make sure his words were true.

She nodded at him.

"Villard says we must be on our way if we's to make it to Toulouse in time to find lodgings before the other travelers on the road."

"We were about to return to the wagon," James said, still looking at Anna. "Let the others know we will be there shortly."

"Very good, sir," Sparks said. Then he gave Anna a good, hard look to make sure she was truly well before retracing his steps out of the woods.

James reached over to caress her cheek with his hand. "If there is anything our encounter with those men taught me," he said, "it's that I love you completely. Were I in a lovely garden with violin music surrounding us and a bottle of champagne, I would ask you to marry me."

"But we are not," Anna said in a low voice, her eyes not sapphires now but the deep blue of the Channel they'd crossed at the beginning of their journey together.

"No, we are not," he replied. "But I will ask you anyway: Will you be my wife and make me the proudest, most happy of men?"

"You are and always will be my hero," she said. "I will gladly be your wife."

It was several more minutes before James and Anna rejoined the others, for they got lost again in the rejoicing that occurred between them after their dangerous encounter and its joyous aftermath.

For the life of him, James could *not* remove his arm from around Anna once they were on their way again or move away from her. He was relieved that he had heeded the warnings of Monsieurs Durand and Villard before leaving Brive and had prepared Sparks beforehand in the event that they encountered robbers as they approached Toulouse. Relieved that the men they had encountered had been greedy but not malevolent by nature.

James had plenty of practice firing a weapon—most gentlemen did—but he'd never actually pointed a weapon at another human being before, and the thought that something like this *might* happen along the journey was altogether different from actually having it happen. He'd never before experienced how it would feel to look down the barrel of a gun at another man. He was exceedingly glad he had not chosen to serve in His Majesty's army; he hoped he never had to point a gun at another man again. He was also grateful for the diplomacy skills he'd been able to develop the past few years.

Both skills had been necessary today.

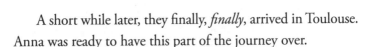

A short while later, they finally, *finally*, arrived in Toulouse. Anna was ready to have this part of the journey over.

"Villard told me earlier that he'd heard there was a decent inn near the middle of the city," James said to her. "I thought the inn, being more centrally located, might work to our advantage in the search for your brother."

Anna nodded.

Their wagon lumbered down the main street of Toulouse toward the center of the city. Anna studied each man they passed along the way. She peered through the windows of the buildings and shops they passed, but her search was in vain.

Finally, Villard pointed to an inn a short way farther down the street. "*Le voilà*," he said.

"*Oui*," James said. "We are almost to the inn," he said to Anna and the others.

Soon enough, Villard steered the horses and wagon into the small courtyard of the inn and brought them to a stop. He jumped down from his seat on the wagon and joined James and Sparks in hoisting Anna and Mary from the wagon. Then James quickly reached into his pocket and pulled out some bills and handed them to Villard, who looked to be planning to take the wagon and stay elsewhere in his own search for finding and buying healthy horses. "*Merci,*" James said.

The man tipped his cap in thanks. "*Merci, et bonne chance,*" he said, and then he returned to his wagon and left.

Bonne chance. Good luck, he'd said. Anna knew that much French.

Another city, another inn. But it was here that, if only they were exceedingly fortunate, they would get answers. Their journey had been more arduous than Anna could have ever imagined, but she now realized that searching a city the size of Toulouse, where thousands of troops had passed through and staged a fierce battle, was going to be their most difficult undertaking.

"Come," James said to her. "Let's settle into our respective rooms, and then we shall begin asking people for any information they might have about your brother."

"Thank you," Anna said softly. *Merci, et bonne chance.*

Good luck to them all.

CHAPTER 17

While still in Clifton Cross, Anna had reached out to Avery's regimental headquarters for information about his whereabouts; in London, Lord Bledsoe had gone directly to Whitehall and the Foreign Office. In Paris, Anna had relied upon James's connections, and they had been fortunate to learn what they had there.

Where were they to go in Toulouse? Were there any government agencies who would have information about the troops who had fought in the city and the surrounding area? Anna doubted it.

But if it meant going house to house, shop to shop to find Avery, she would do it. She must. She owed it to Sparks and Mary and especially to James to do her very upmost to find her brother after all they had sacrificed for her.

James, to whom she was now betrothed! Her heart sang at the thought of his proposal—and his kisses and caresses.

She quickly freshened up once she arrived at her room and hurried back down to the inn's main entrance to wait for James to join her. He was already there when she arrived.

He greeted her by taking her hand and kissing it gently. "I asked the innkeeper for the names of people who might know something of the whereabouts of the soldiers remaining in Toulouse," he said. "He suggested a few places to begin our search. I also described your brother to him, but he was unfamiliar with anyone matching that description. He did confess to keeping to himself when all of this was occurring, however, despite any business it might have brought in."

"Thank you, James," Anna said. "I did wonder where we would go from here."

"Shall we?" he said, offering her his arm.

She nodded and slipped her hand into the crook of his elbow.

They walked south down the main street, considering they had entered the city from the north and she had studied each person she'd seen as they'd ridden toward the center of town, just as she had done along the way to Toulouse. James stopped everyone they passed and asked them in French if they knew of an Avery Clifton. He would gesture at Anna as he did, which, she presumed, was to describe the family resemblance. Anna smiled with each encounter and tried to appear optimistic, but as the afternoon wore on and they received only negative responses, she began to grow weary and disheartened.

"Come," he said at last. "It is getting late, and you are tired and in need of sustenance. I, for one, am famished. I see a small café across the street just there. What do you say we stop and take tea before returning to the inn?"

"Yes," Anna said. The single word was all she could muster.

James turned her toward him. "My dearest Anna," he said in a low voice that was nonetheless firm. "You are the strongest woman I have ever had the privilege of knowing. You braved an encounter with robbers just this morning, and you have heard too many people say no to our inquiries. I don't think I've ever been prouder of anyone in my life than I am of you today. We will sit and take tea and then return to the inn so you may rest. We will begin anew tomorrow."

"Thank you, James," she said.

He ran his thumb under her eye where a single tear had escaped and then placed the thumb to his lips in a kiss. The tenderness of it nearly shattered her. "Come, my dear," he murmured and then gently placed her hand back in the crook of his arm and led her to the café.

The café owner greeted them and showed them to a corner table. The café was not particularly busy and allowed Anna a modicum of privacy in which to gather her emotions. James sat next to her and slid his chair even closer to hers. He quickly ordered for them both.

The café owner snapped his fingers, and a serving girl promptly arrived with a fresh pot of tea and cups and saucers and poured both James and Anna a cup. Then the owner bowed and turned to leave, but he stopped and studied Anna's face rather too closely.

"Mademoiselle?" the man began.

She looked up at him above the cup of tea from which she was about to sip.

James said something to him in reply, to which the café owner rattled off a great deal of French to James, and James's eyes grew big.

Anna's heart began to pound, and her breathing began to race. She set her cup down a bit shakily, which made it rattle.

James took her hand in his own. "I don't wish you to get your hopes up, Anna," he said in a low voice, "but this gentleman was startled by your similarity to . . . his son-in-law, an English soldier they took in and nursed back to health—"

"James," she said, squeezing his hand until she feared she might break his bones, but she needed to cling tightly to him right now. "It can't be Avery. It can't! How could he be this man's son-in-law? He would have written had he intentions to be married. He would have come home. Do you think it's truly possible?"

"Avery? *Oui, il s'appelle* Avery," the café owner said, and then he spoke to the serving girl, who had just walked up to their table with the rest of their order, and she quickly set their food down and hurried off.

"He asked the serving girl to fetch his son-in-law," James said. "He says his name is indeed Avery."

Anna couldn't have been more shocked if James had told her he was Napoleon Bonaparte himself! She began to shake in earnest. Could it truly be that Avery was alive—and he was married?

Avery was married?

"Try to eat something, Anna," James said. "You will need your strength for this moment."

Anna gazed into James's intense brown eyes. She had trusted him to make their arrangements with innkeepers and coachmen. He had handled the conflicts that had occurred at Prince Schwarzenberg's soiree. His presence had kept her and Sparks and Mary safe. She owed him so much.

Oh, how she loved him!

And then a movement caught her eye, and she shifted her gaze to see what it was.

"Avery!" she cried. And then she was on her feet and across the café, wrapped in her brother's solid, familiar arms.

"Anna? What are you doing here? How did you get here?" the new Lord Westbury asked his sister, holding on to her as if his life depended upon it—or perhaps his balance depended upon it. James suspected that Anna had been so focused on her brother's face that she hadn't noticed the walking stick that had fallen to the floor when she had rushed into his arms.

"I came to find you," Anna exclaimed, "and I *have* found you. Oh, it's a *miracle*! *You're alive*! *Oh, Avery*!" She dashed tears from her cheeks as more continued to flow, and James discreetly reached down and retrieved the walking stick, hoping to allow her this private moment with her brother. He also felt he must stay nearby, for there would be questions asked and questions answered, and James would not leave Anna on her own for that.

He knew the thoughts of men well enough to know some of the questions that would follow. Oh yes, he knew how men thought. And he knew how brothers would react. Had he himself not been angry and protective when he'd learned of Susan's betrothal to Aylesham?

Avery's—that is, Lord Westbury's—thoughts would take him there soon enough.

"So much has happened, Avery," Anna sobbed. "John and Papa are both gone."

"Gone? Gone where?" Lord Westbury asked her.

"They're gone! They both died—John of pneumonia this past winter and Papa when he got word that you'd—" She stopped herself from finishing that particular sentence. "That is why I had to find you. I couldn't stand by and let disgusting Cousin Ambrose take claim to Papa's title and lands. *Your* title and lands now. I simply couldn't! They belong to you."

Lord Westbury's body slumped at her words, and his hands slid down her arms to his sides. "*Both* gone?" he asked in a whisper.

"Yes. But you're alive! *You're alive!* I couldn't bear to think the worst—that you'd died in battle after what we'd learned from your regiment. I couldn't even say the words aloud! But you're here! Oh, Avery!" She burst into tears again, and her brother wrapped his arms around her again.

The poor man looked dumbstruck. Then he caught sight of James.

James nodded politely in acknowledgment and greeting but said nothing.

"Who is this?" Lord Westbury asked Anna.

"James!" she exclaimed, her happiness radiating from her like a white light. "We found him! He's alive after all!"

"James?" Lord Westbury asked.

"I wouldn't have found you if it hadn't been for James!" Anna said. "Avery, may I present Mr. James Jennings, Esquire. James, this is my brother Avery—er, the Earl of Westbury."

"It's an honor, Lord Westbury," James said, handing him his walking stick. War had hardened the young earl's face. There were lines at his eyes and a few that bracketed his mouth that James doubted had been there before any battles had been fought. James had seen similar lines in his brother Lucas's face when he'd returned home from the Peninsula.

"Thank you," the earl said, giving James a handshake and a long look. "And thank you for safely reuniting me with my sister."

"Would you care to sit, Lord Westbury?" James asked. It was obvious the earl was still recovering from his wounds and seemed a bit unsteady, which the news he'd just received must surely have intensified. "Anna and I were having tea and a bit of sustenance. Please join us."

"Yes, thank you," Westbury replied. He glanced across the room at the café owner, who nodded. "I think that is a good idea."

Anna grabbed her brother's arm and hugged it to her, then patted it over and over. "I can still scarcely believe it's you," she said, beaming at him. "I am not sure I can ever be happier than I am at this moment!"

James, for his part, hoped that wasn't the case, for having actually found Anna's brother, he had a particular question he wished to ask the earl, and James prayed the earl's answer would be a positive one, as Anna's had been.

"There is obviously much I need to learn about what has transpired. Both John and Papa gone. I can scarce believe it—or that you have traveled such a great distance to find me," Lord Westbury said, shaking his head.

"I *had* to find you, Avery. It's as simple as that," Anna said.

"Truly, nothing would stop her in her determination to learn of your whereabouts, Lord Westbury," James said. "Or even, dare I say, whether you still lived, based on the last word your father received from your regiment."

"Lord Westbury was always my father and was then going to be my brother," the earl said, wincing a bit. "It will take time to get used to hearing myself referred to as such. There is much information I am hopeful you and Anna can provide. Speaking of which," he continued, "how precisely are you acquainted with my sister? You are not from Clifton Cross."

"We met in Dover as she was preparing to cross the Channel," James replied. "She traveled from Clifton Cross to London first to see if there was information to be had regarding your regiment and you, specifically."

"London?" Westbury asked.

"Yes," James replied.

"But they didn't know anything, Avery," Anna said. "And so, I had to go to Paris, where all the leaders were meeting."

When her brother only stared at her incredulously, James decided to continue with his explanation. "When an odd coincidence had us sailing the Channel aboard the same yacht, it became immediately obvious to me that she was ill-equipped to travel to Paris unescorted, as it were, and so I offered my services, as I was heading there myself."

"You were going to Paris?"

"I have done a bit of diplomatic work for the Foreign Office," James said. "When I saw a beautiful young lady of the upper class traveling across France with but two servants, none of whom spoke French, I felt moved to act the gentleman by providing an escort and translation abilities to her, at least as far as Paris. She is an indomitable woman to search for her only surviving family member as she has. I quite admire her."

"Admire her," Westbury repeated.

"Yes," James replied, knowing full well what Westbury was implying. James looked at Anna, which was a mistake, for she utterly glowed with joy, thrilled as she was to have found her brother, and she looked even more beautiful to James, if such a thing were possible. He suspected his feelings would be readily apparent to Lord Westbury, as they were impossible for him to disguise now. "How were you injured, if you don't mind my asking?" James said to Lord Westbury, turning his attention back to the earl.

"Saber wound and a musket ball that thankfully missed anything too important," he replied. "I'm one of the fortunate ones."

"Thank heaven for that!" Anna exclaimed.

Westbury didn't reply.

His lack of reply was telling, James thought. He imagined the earl might feel both blessed and guilty for surviving what many of his brothers-in-arms had not, if Westbury's experience had been anything like Lucas's. James felt for the man.

"But you must tell me more of what transpired at home and your journey here," Westbury said at length.

James was not surprised by the earl's need to change the subject.

Anna had finally begun to believe that it was truly Avery sitting by her in this little café in Toulouse and not some dream she was caught in.

The serving girl brought an additional teacup for Avery and then stared at Anna briefly and glanced back at Avery before leaving them.

Anna poured tea for Avery and added two sugars.

"You remember how I take my tea," he said.

"Of course I do!" Anna replied.

A few customers walked through the door, speaking rather loudly.

"Do you think the café owner has a more private place where we may talk?" Anna asked. "Or we could return to the inn where James and I and the others are staying, if you'd prefer."

"There's a room," Avery said. "I live here. I work here. We have my rooms."

"You work here? At this café?" Anna asked, utterly dumb-founded by his words.

Avery shrugged his shoulders.

He had already picked up the French habit of shrugging!

"Follow me," he said. He then rose to his feet and began leading them toward the back of the inn. He was leaning rather heavily on his walking stick, which Anna noticed now. He was still recovering from his wounds.

The three of them walked through to the back of the café, where there was an attached building that appeared to include Avery's apartments. That he was living *here*, in Toulouse, in what appeared to be permanent apartments, and yet they hadn't received any letters from him was unthinkable to Anna.

Avery opened a door and gestured for James to enter once Anna had passed through. "Please be seated," he said.

Anna perched on the edge of the small sofa in the center of the room, and James sat in a side chair opposite her.

Avery then sat next to her on the sofa and took her hand in his. "Tell me of John and Papa, Anna."

She related the full story of their brother's passing, his wife and daughter choosing to stay with her parents, and the devastation it had brought to their unwell father. "But it was the letter telling us that you'd been injured and were missing in action that took the final toll on Papa," she said. "I was told he'd received a letter, and when I went to find out what it was, I discovered him. But he was already gone, Avery! The physician thought it was too much for his heart to bear, after losing Mama and his health and then John. It was too much."

Avery was silent as he pondered her words. "You received no letters from me?" he asked.

"You mean you *wrote*?" Anna asked.

"More than once, after I was feeling a bit better. I was indisposed for several days, and then it was difficult to find writing materials, but I managed to barter for some."

"Oh, Avery!" Anna said, her eyes welling once again with tears. "I couldn't believe you wouldn't have let us know you were alive! And now I know you tried! But we'd received no word, and so I had to—"

"Look for me yourself, you dear, foolish girl!" Avery exclaimed, chuckling and shaking his head.

"And yet you are healthy enough that you could have returned to England, to your family, but you remained here," James said.

"This is true," Avery said.

"Avery?" a soft, feminine voice behind Anna asked.

Anna turned toward to sound. "Who—" she started.

Avery smiled as he motioned for the young woman to join them. "Anna," Avery said, "allow me to present my wife, Jeanne." He said a few more things to Jeanne in French— his French had greatly improved since his days at university, Anna noted—and he included her name and the words *ma sœur*, which Anna gratefully recalled meant "my sister."

Jeanne's face lit up, and she suddenly grasped Anna's hands and shook them vigorously. Anna didn't know what to do, so she allowed Jeanne to clutch her hands and looked at Avery and James for cues about what to do next. They both shrugged their shoulders.

Anna was so tired of men shrugging their shoulders!

But what was she thinking? This young woman was Avery's wife! That meant she was as much a member of the family as Sarah had been and still was even after John's death, even if Sarah preferred to live with her own family now that John was gone.

Anna pulled her hands free of Jeanne's grasp and stood and wrapped her arms around her to give her a sisterly hug, and then she glanced at Avery.

"And now you know," he said.

She thought if he shrugged after uttering those words, she might hit him, and she hadn't done that since he'd broken one of her dolls when she was six.

Luckily for Avery, he didn't shrug, but then Jeanne said something to him in French and left the room rather than joining them.

"She is making tea," Avery said.

"We just had tea," Anna said.

"She wants her new sister to feel welcome in her home," Avery said. "And since she can't speak much English, she is choosing to do it with food."

"I can't fault her for that," James said with a smile.

Neither could Anna, who realized that while she was filled to the brim with joy, after a long, difficult day and an interrupted tea service, she was utterly famished.

After feasting on Jeanne's excellent culinary wares—it was obvious that she had been well-trained by her café-owner father—James was surprised when Lord Westbury suggested that Jeanne show Anna their garden and get better acquainted while the men did likewise. "I'm sure there will be much pointing and gesturing and smiling," he said to Anna and re-peated to Jeanne in French, "but I suspect you ladies will find a way to communicate just fine."

Jeanne smiled and nodded and offered her hand to Anna, and the two of them strolled off arm in arm as though they were the oldest and dearest of friends.

"That's gratifying to see," Westbury said.

"I imagine so," James replied. "Family is the most impor-tant thing."

Westbury said nothing.

"Jeanne seems a treasure," James continued. "And indeed, her father's keen eye was instrumental in bringing you and Anna back together."

"I should not have lived were it not for Jeanne and her father," Westbury said.

"Will you tell me of Orthez? And Toulouse?" James asked.

The earl sighed. "I should not wish Anna to know the details for the world," he said. "War is an ugly business." He stared out the window for a few minutes before speaking again. James waited patiently.

"We were the victors at Orthez," Westbury said at last. "But it hardly felt like a victory when I saw the fallen. And it was February. It was cold. I'm not surprised that I was reported as missing in the chaos and confusion. I was hit by a bullet, as I said, and while it didn't kill me, the saber wound I received after I fell—to assure, I presume, that I was truly dead—bled a great deal. I don't recall everything that happened after that. I suppose I might have been numbered among the dead when the counts were first made, but luckily, someone saw me after I revived a bit, for I do remember being placed on a board and carried to a tent, where a medic pried the bullet from my side and wrapped my wounds as best he could with what he had at hand."

James shuddered. The pain Westbury must have felt was incomprehensible to him.

"It was decided that my regiment would continue on with others to Toulouse, with a few brigades going to defend the port at Bordeaux. Those of us who were wounded traveled after the rest, when we were able.

"By now it was April. The fighting began on the tenth of April, Easter Sunday. Isn't that ironic? The day of our Lord's Resurrection was the day we began to kill God's children. But I had developed an infection during the march to Toulouse—a fairly bad one. So rather than being someone who might be of use, I was a liability."

"Lord Westbury, I cannot believe—" James began to say.

"Casualties of any kind are expected during battle, I know," Westbury cut James off. "But it was how I felt, nonetheless. My wounds and the infection kept me from fighting, while nine thousand more men were sent to their graves over the course of two days. *Two days!* And would you care to know what made it even worse?" he continued. "Wellington got word from Bordeaux that Napoleon had abdicated on *the fourth of April,* and our battle needn't have occurred at all."

James's head dropped, and he stared at the floor.

"And yet, through all of this," Westbury said, "my salvation has been the French. I was too ill to travel and was left behind. Jeanne and her father saved my life, nursed me back to health. They accepted me. You get to know people rather quickly when your well-being—your *life*—is in their hands. They become family. I love them. I love *her*. So now I have a family here, Mr. Jennings, a new family. Do you understand?"

James thought about the travails he and Anna had gone through together the past few weeks. They were nothing in comparison to what Lord Westbury had experienced, but James knew those experiences had bonded Anna and him together in ways a typical courtship would not have. He knew her soul, and he loved her. "I understand completely, Lord Westbury," James replied.

"You are thinking of my sister, are you not?" Westbury said.

"I am. And as Anna's only living brother and head of her family, I would like to ask your permission—"

Westbury cut him off once again with a raised hand, which took James aback until the earl continued. "You have my permission already, Mr. Jennings, for I recognize only too well the look you have in your eyes when you gaze at my sister and her expression when she looks at you. That you brought her safely to me also says much for your character."

"Thank you," James said, truly grateful.

The ladies returned at that moment, still arm in arm, smiling and laughing. "I am determined to renew my French studies, for I believe Jeanne and I are going to be the best of sisters," Anna announced.

"I have always wished for a sister, and now I have one," Jeanne said in French.

"You have two," James replied to Jeanne.

She looked confused by his words.

Westbury explained briefly to Jeanne that they had a sister-in-law who had been married to his brother, John, and James quickly translated for Anna.

"Sarah," Anna said to Jeanne. "And little Betty."

"You have two families, Westbury," James said quietly. "I hope you find a way to make those two families into one."

He stood. "In the meantime, while there is still much to discuss, I propose that I take Anna back to our lodgings so she may rest, and we can resume our discussions tomorrow. It has been a rather eventful day."

Anna sighed. "It breaks my heart to leave, but I know James is right, although it helps immensely to know I have found you both. What a miracle I have received today!"

Westbury wrapped Anna in his arms once again. "I love you, my beautiful, determined sister. May the best of dreams await you. We shall reunite tomorrow for luncheon, here, at the café. Will that suit?"

"Oh, yes!" Anna said. "Oh dear!" she exclaimed, turning to look at James. "Sparks and Mary must be worried sick about us. We had best return."

"Sparks, eh?" Westbury said. "Good man, Sparks. I'm glad he is with you; he always took such great care of Papa."

"He insisted, Avery. And Mary is my personal maid who was willing to travel with me, even though she's rather timid."

"I think I remember Mary; good for her." Westbury embraced Anna. "Adieu until tomorrow, then, my dear sister," he said. "Mr. Jennings," he added with a nod.

James bowed to Westbury and his wife and offered his arm to Anna.

James's conversation with Anna's brother after meeting him and his wife had raised questions in his mind. But the most important question he had, without a doubt—especially after seeing the obvious bliss of her brother and his wife—was, How soon could he and Anna marry?

CHAPTER 18

When Anna awoke the next morning, she felt more rested and revived than she could remember in the longest time. What a glorious miracle had occurred yesterday! She stretched her arms over her head and yawned in a completely unladylike manner and then slipped out of bed and into her robe.

Her door opened, and Mary came in bearing hot cocoa. "Good morning, me lady," she said. "Mr. Jennings asked that we inform ye that he left to run a few errands this morning, but not to worry; he would be back in time to escort ye back to yer brother. Oh, me lady! I was *that glad* that ye found Mr. Avery—I mean, Lord Westbury! Mr. Sparks and me was over the moon with the news last evening, as ye well know. We still can't quite believe it!"

"My brother was exceedingly glad that you and Sparks were with me," Anna said with a smile to her dear maid. She took a sip of the cocoa, which was delicious and not too hot, so she drank readily. "We are meeting with him and his wife for luncheon."

"Very good, me lady." Mary bustled away to prepare Anna's clothes.

Anna wondered what errands James could possibly have in an unfamiliar city such as Toulouse, but she dressed quickly, eager to be downstairs in the main room of the inn when he returned.

It was just after noon when James returned from his errands. He looked invigorated; his eyes were bright, and he was so handsome that Anna wished she could wrap herself in his arms to feel his masculine warmth and smother him with kisses.

"Good morning—erm, good afternoon," he said, correcting himself. "You look utterly beautiful, my Anna. You glow with happiness." He took her hand in his and placed a sumptuous kiss upon it, which made her heart burst with joy. "Are you ready to stroll to the café?"

"More than ready," she said.

He placed her hand in the crook of his arm.

It could have been raining torrents, there might have been lightning strikes and booms of thunder, but Anna doubted she would have noticed. All she could see was James's profile as they strolled down the street to where Avery was standing with Jeanne outside the café, waving at them in greeting as they approached.

The café owner, Monsieur Remy, showed James and the others to a private nook, which was separated from the rest of the café, and insisted on serving them himself.

"Jeanne's papa insisted on the finest of luncheons," Westbury said once they were seated and Monsieur Remy had returned to the kitchen. "He said, 'Only the best for my new son and his family.'"

"This must all be rather strange for him too," James observed.

"I shall be sure to thank him, Avery," Anna said. "I can never repay him; I owe him the world."

Avery smiled and rested his hand upon Jeanne's and quietly translated Anna's words to her, to which she replied.

"Jeanne says she and her papa have been blessed too," he said, gazing lovingly at his young French wife.

"Before we dine," James said, "there are a few legal items I spent time researching this morning that I think are important to share with all of you."

"Legal items?" Westbury asked. "What can you have learned in only a few hours this morning that could possibly be of such import?"

"My original background," James began, "is in the law. It, along with a modest gift for languages, allowed me to be of service to the Foreign Office and Lord Castlereagh when it came to legal matters, negotiations, and diplomacy amongst the Coalition members and others.

"When we found you and learned you are alive and well, but especially after meeting your lovely Jeanne here, I thought it prudent to research French marriage laws—something I had never thought to do, it having never arisen in my work before. Your marriage raised legal concerns in my mind. After visiting the local magistrate and a couple of local law offices, I learned that a marriage conducted in France for persons who are *not* French citizens is binding while in France . . . but they make no guarantee that the marriage is binding in the person's home country, whatever country that may be."

"Goodness!" Anna exclaimed, turning to look at her brother.

"So," James continued, "while you *are* legally married here in France, there is no assurance that your marriage would be legal were you to return to England. For *you*, Lord Westbury, it means that you are indeed married to Jeanne as long as you choose to remain in France. But should you choose, at any point, to claim your inheritance in England, along with the earldom—or more to the point, should you have any children after having married in France but not in England, there could be complications in determining if those children are indeed legal heirs. I am not in a position to comment on the intricacy of the marriage laws of England at the moment, obviously. There may not be an issue at all. Nonetheless, I personally would advise you, at the very least, to travel to England to marry there in order to assure your progeny of their rightful claim going forward, should they desire it at some point in the future."

Westbury appeared shocked, and James waited as the man swiftly translated this information to his wife. Not unexpectedly, Jeanne gasped.

"My presumption—indeed, the entire direction of my life has always been based on the fact that I was the spare," Westbury said after he finished reciting James's information to her. "Knowing that, I was content to remain here in France with Jeanne and her father. I wrote precisely that in one of my letters shortly before Jeanne and I married. I could not have known what had happened to Papa and John," Westbury added specifically to Anna. "I grieve deeply for them."

"I know that, Avery," Anna said, reaching for his hand.

"What do you plan to do about it now that you *do* know, *Lord* Westbury?" James asked quietly and then translated the question into French for Jeanne's sake. "What of your title as earl?" he added, continuing to speak intentionally in French. "Will you allow your family's heritage to be destroyed by a person who holds the title and estate in such low regard? What of any children you and Jeanne have? What will you tell them about the heritage you allowed to be taken by a usurper?"

Jeanne grabbed Westbury's arm, her eyes even wider, an expression of shock on her face. "Avery! You never said your father was one of those English earls!" she exclaimed.

"It hardly mattered at the time, my dear," Westbury replied, stroking her cheek gently. "I was never intended to inherit. It is why I bought my commission in the army; I needed to make my own way in the world. And it brought me to you, my love."

"It brought you to me, yes, and for that I am glad," she replied. "But we live at a café, where you wash dishes and prepare food. Yet now we find that you are an English earl?"

"None of that mattered to me," Westbury told her gently. "Only that I had finally found my place. With you."

"Sometimes our 'place,' as you called it, changes," James said. "I was a contented solicitor, making excellent money when duty called. My 'place' was an assignment extended to me through connections to Lord Castlereagh. It was not my choice, but I did my duty and changed my 'place' because it was the right thing to do at the time.

"Now that you know all this, I suspect the two of you will need to have a serious conversation about the future of your family, your children, and what to expect going forward, knowing now that you are indeed the Earl of Westbury,"

James said. "At least, for the time being, unless you choose to renounce your title."

———

The luncheon was delicious. Monsieur Remy had outdone himself. Not surprisingly, the discussion ebbed and flowed and alternated between English and French after James's news and what it might mean to everyone involved. Anna had the odd thought that many of James's official meetings and meals must be much like this one—addressing legal issues, formally and informally, with various languages weaving in and out amongst those in attendance. It was a part of his world that she had now been able to glimpse.

Once everyone seemed to have had their fill of food and information, James stood and offered his hand to Anna, which she took and rose to her feet. "With your permission, I should like to take Anna for a stroll."

"It would seem Jeanne and I have a discussion we need to have as well, which will undoubtedly involve her father too."

"I think including him in your conversation is generous and wise," James replied. "Come, Anna."

She nodded her consent and slipped her gloves on.

He tucked her hand securely into the crook of his elbow. They walked along the side of the café, and Anna was half-expecting to find a well-tended garden. It was what had happened in Paris and again on their way to Orleans. It had almost become routine.

They didn't find a garden, but there was a quiet lane just beyond the café. James led her down the lane, and they continued farther until they were by the river that ran through the city. Once there, James led her to a shaded bank that over-looked the water.

"This is nice, don't you think?" James said. He looked at her for her approval, which she gave once again with a nod of her head.

"It's lovely," she replied. "I suppose you found it during those errands you undertook this morning."

"Guilty as charged," he said with a smile.

He removed his jacket and laid it out on the grass and assisted her in sitting on it. He then sat on the grass next to her—near enough to her that she could feel the warmth of his body.

They sat quietly for a while and watched the gently flow-ing river. Anna shielded her eyes and could make out an arched bridge in the far distance.

"Anna," James said at last, breaking the silence and draw-ing even closer to her. "I can but look at you and I am your servant in all things." He took her hand and brought it to his lips. "You cannot know what a challenge it has been for me to remain the gentleman during our travels and not take you into my arms even more than I have. There is nothing I wish more than to know today, now, that I truly have earned your favor and that you will agree to be my wife sooner rather than later, my dearest Anna, my pearl. I would marry you tomorrow if I could."

Once again, Anna could scarcely breathe from the feel of his kiss, even through her gloves. His words struck deep within her, and her heart rejoiced.

He gently peeled off her glove, one finger at a time, and drew her hand—bare and vulnerable as it was now—to his lips.

Anna stared at her hand, at his handsome face, and at those masculine lips as they kissed each of her fingers. And then James turned her hand over and kissed her palm and then her wrist, his eyes nearly shut, and Anna felt her own eyelids flutter from the feelings that coursed through her from her fingers to her toes, making her heart pound. She thought she might swoon.

"Oh, James," she found herself saying with only the faintest of breaths.

She stopped breathing entirely when he reached into his pocket and removed a ring—a pearl ring, the most lustrous pearl she'd ever seen, surrounded by diamonds. She stared at the ring and then looked into his eyes. His handsome brown eyes were darker than she'd ever seen them, and his gaze pierced her very core.

"May I?" James asked.

She nodded, so he slipped the ring onto her finger. "My darling Anna," he murmured. "My beautiful pearl." He brushed a curl from her forehead and captured her lips again. And as they had before, the sensations burst through Anna. His lips were soft, cool, hot, delicious, and all too soon, he'd removed them from her own, but only so he could shift even closer to her. He moved his hand to cradle her face. "You turned my life upside-down, and I cannot regret it for a moment," he whispered, his lips so close to her own that she could feel his breath. And then his lips found hers again, and she could only feel.

Her hand slid up to his shoulder, and she held on for all she was worth. Never could she have believed that the mere touch of his lips would send her spinning. Never had she felt such things before meeting James Jennings.

He began to end the kiss, but she wasn't ready to be released from this newly discovered ecstasy. Her hand quickly slid from his shoulder to the back of his head to hold him close. She felt the quick puffs of breath as he chuckled softly, and then he kissed her again, firmly, possessively, and she thought she might burst into flames.

"My dearest Anna," he whispered at length after ending their delicious kisses and resting his forehead against her own, which made her bonnet slip back on her head a bit. "You are my dearest Anna, aren't you? And I am your James and will be hereafter and always."

Anna laughed and nodded, which was the wrong thing to do when one's forehead was resting against someone else's, for it jostled her bonnet further until it slid down to her neck.

James laughed, too, and helped place it back on her head; she stood absolutely still while he tied the bow. "There now, despite the color in your cheeks and your beautiful, kissable lips, you look as you did before we ventured here."

"James?" she said softly.

"Yes, my Anna?" he replied.

"Be quiet, my dearest love, and kiss me again," she said.

And so he did.

It lasted much longer this time.

And Anna sensed that James's kiss was meant to convey something more than mere passion. The fire was there—oh, indeed it was—but there was much more to it too. A oneness, an unspoken commitment, even a certain possessiveness, although it in no way held her captive but was more of an assurance that truly, she was his as he was hers.

EPILOGUE

On Monday morning, the twentieth of June, James stood near the altar of the small chapel in Clifton Cross, not far from Clifton Hall, residence of the Earl of Westbury. The vicar, the Reverend Reginald Pruitt, currently stood behind the altar. On James's right side stood Avery Clifton, the Right Honorable Earl of Westbury, as he had just been addressed by Reverend Pruitt. And James glanced sideways in time to catch his brother-in-law Avery wince at the title.

Seated in the pews were the few individuals who had been invited to attend—Sarah Clifton, the late John Clifton's widow, and her daughter, Betty, and her parents, who had returned with her when they'd received word from Anna. James could also see Hastings, the loyal steward of Clifton Hall, who had leaped to his feet the moment Avery Clifton had walked through his office door, where Hastings had been meeting with the insistent Ambrose Clifton, and then had proceeded to welcome the true Earl of Westbury with a vigorous handshake. The man had hardly been able to hide his delight in seeing Avery—and in dismissing Ambrose, who had left Clifton Hall the very next day.

Also in attendance was Jeanne Clifton's father, Monsieur Remy, whom Avery had invited to follow his daughter to England to celebrate in her formal marriage to one of Britain's nobility. Remy had left his café in the care of a trusted friend, explaining that he would return in a few months. And last but certainly not least were all the servants of Clifton Hall, including, of course, Sparks and Mary, who were particular guests of honor, there to witness the two weddings, as was only right and proper.

The main chapel doors opened . . .

And Jeanne Clifton walked forward, followed by James's own bride.

James had eyes for only Anna, who looked even more the pearl than she had when he'd first met her. Her gown was cream colored—cream, for Avery, bless him, had insisted the brides not wear the colors of mourning, as this was a grand Clifton family celebration, and he felt his father and brother would wish them all to rejoice. And Anna's hair caught the colors of the stained-glass windows behind the altar and added to her brilliance.

His bride, his Anna.

She reached his side and smiled at him as Jeanne joined Avery at the altar.

"Are you ready?" James whispered softly.

"More than ready," she murmured back.

"Dearly beloved, we are gathered together here in the sight of God and in the face of this congregation, to join together this man and this woman, and this man and this woman, in holy matrimony," Reverend Pruitt began.

James attempted to listen to the words the vicar spoke, but he could barely take his eyes from his bride to focus on anything else. He couldn't have imagined that a mere few weeks ago he would meet the woman for whom he would willingly travel through hardships across an entire country. But he had, and she was gazing at him with those sapphire eyes of hers . . .

There was a pause.

Anna's eyebrows shot up questioningly.

Blast. His mind had wandered too far and for too long. During his own wedding ceremony, no less!

"Wilt thou have this woman to be thy wedded wife, to live together after God's ordinance in the holy estate of matrimony? Wilt thou love her, comfort her, honor, and keep her in sickness and in health; and forsaking all others, keep thee only unto her, so long as ye both shall live?" The vicar's tone suggested he'd already spoken this part.

"I will," James said.

He paid better attention as the vicar continued the service, and he listened intently when Anna also said, "I will."

The rest of the service proceeded, although not speedily enough for James, and finally, they were man and wife.

Man and wife.

After the recessional that included two officially married couples, there were congratulations all around as guests came forward offering handshakes and back slaps to the gentlemen and hugs and kisses to the brides.

"My darling Anna," James said once they had moved off a bit from the celebratory crowd. "There is one other question I wish to ask you. It is not part of the church service, and I don't wish for you to feel that I have tricked you into this by waiting until now to ask."

"Should I be worried?" she asked.

"Possibly," he said, though he couldn't hold back a smile.

"Well," she said. "You certainly have my full attention."

He smiled. "You may recall that while we were in Paris, there were as many ladies present as there were gentlemen."

"Yes," she said, although it sounded more like a question than a response.

"I have always had the impression that you wished to remain here at Clifton Hall, with Avery and Jeanne, after all that you went through to find him. But now I am wondering . . ."

"Yes?" she said, and it definitely was a question this time.

"I am wondering if you are willing to . . ."

"The answer is yes, James," Anna said. "If you are asking whether I would return to France and travel to Vienna with you while you serve the Foreign Office, the answer is yes."

"You would be giving up time with your family," he said.

"*You're* my family, James. Avery is safely home, and Cousin Ambrose has departed—thankfully before he could do too much damage to the Westbury estate. You and I will be together, and that is what matters most to me."

"I cannot tell you how much your words mean to me," he said. "So, now I have another question: Would you be greatly relieved if I told you I had already sent a letter to Castlereagh, informing him that my time in the Foreign Office must come to an end? For I have a greater calling that requires my full attention at present. Here, at home."

"Oh, James!" she cried, throwing her arms around him and then burying her head in his shoulder—no doubt so she could hide from all the curious looks their guests were now giving them. "Truly?" she whispered in his ear. "You will not regret remaining here, when being in Vienna would mean so much to your associates and to Castlereagh?"

"Who knows when the Congress will officially begin? This autumn perhaps? And what if you are with child? I could not bear to leave you if that were the case, and I would not have you travel in such a delicate condition. No, I will not regret it at all."

She heaved a great sigh and pulled back just a bit so she could look him in the eyes.

"My dearest love," he said. "May I kiss the bride?"

"Yes, please," she said with a smile.

And so he did. More than once.

The servants of Clifton Hall had prepared a sumptuous luncheon for the brides and grooms, families, and guests of both weddings. Anna didn't know how they'd managed it, for they had all been in attendance at the wedding ceremony. But everything was ready for them when they arrived back at the manor house.

She looked about her in awe and gratitude. How could it be that a mere few weeks ago, she had been thrown into utter grief and despair over the loss of her brother and her father? That the chance her only other brother was still alive was dubious, at best? That her family home would fall into the hands of someone who cared little for the family and saw it only as a means of satisfying his own desires and greed?

Who could have imagined that she would find the courage to travel across England, across the Channel, and then across France in search of her brother or that, more to the point, she would *find* him? Or that despite the new family he'd created for himself, he would agree to assume his rightful role as earl? Or that his lovely French wife would be agreeable to living in England for his sake?

And who could have imagined that upon their return, the chapel would be filled to overflowing, as all the townspeople had come to witness the simultaneous marriages of an earl to a French girl and his sister to a complete stranger?

Anna could not have imagined any of these things. Yet they had all happened and more. She knew she'd remember them all, especially in the quiet moments, the peaceful moments . . .

And there *would* be peace. And joy.

And so much love.

"You are deep in thought, my dearest," James whispered into her ear as he came up next to her.

"It has been a beautiful day thus far, has it not?" she said.

"It is the best of days, for you are truly and fully mine, by law and by the grace of God," he said.

"Oh, James!" Anna said, smiling.

"You say that a lot, you know," he said, his eyes wrinkling with mirth. "And I find it completely endearing."

"I should like to meet your family, James," she said. "I believe quite fervently in the importance of families, you know—mine, yours, ours. Even the friendships we have feel like family too. It's all quite incredible."

"It shall happen, my love," he said, taking her hand and bringing it to his lips. "And I promise it shall happen sooner rather than later. My family will love you, and undoubtedly, they shall be astonished that such a beautiful, formidable woman as yourself agreed to be my wife."

She laughed, her heart so full that she thought she would truly burst this time. There had been so many times her heart had been full to the brim as of late that she could scarcely count them all.

"In the meantime, I suggest we enjoy the family and friends who are with us today in celebration," he said.

"I agree wholeheartedly," she said, taking her beloved James by the hand to greet each person and bask in the light of love that all who were present could feel that day.

ACKNOWLEDGMENTS

This story was birthed over several months dealing with chronic illness, and I couldn't have done it without the love and support of my husband, Stephen, and my children and grandchildren, who lift me and bring me joy.

Many thanks to my editor, Samantha Millburn, for her patience, encouragement, and grace in seeing this story to fruition. When unexpected life circumstances sent me in the direction of writing fiction, I got the best support I could have ever asked for in Sam Millburn. I will always be grateful for that blessing and her friendship.

DISCUSSION QUESTIONS

1. How does the setting of early-nineteenth-century England and France contribute to the atmosphere and themes of the story?

2. Discuss Lady Anna Clifton's motivations and desires. How do her actions reflect her determination and resilience in the face of adversity?

3. Analyze James Jennings's character and his initial perceptions of Lady Anna. How do these perceptions evolve throughout the story, and what factors contribute to this change?

4. Explore the theme of class and social expectations in the novel. How do Lady Anna and James navigate societal norms and expectations as they work together, in how they deal with both the prince and Lady Anna's servants?

5. Consider the role of family dynamics in the story. How do familial relations influence the characters' decisions and actions?

6. Discuss the significance of the search for Lady Anna's missing brother as a driving force in the plot. How does this quest shape the characters' development and relationships?

7. Explore the themes of trust and loyalty in the novel. How do Lady Anna and James learn to trust each other despite their initial differences and misunderstandings?

8. Analyze the portrayal of gender roles in the story. How do Lady Anna and James challenge or conform to traditional gender expectations of their time?

9. Discuss the romantic tension between Lady Anna and James. How do their conflicting personalities and circumstances contribute to the development of their relationship?

10. Consider the novel's resolution and the main characters' growth. How do Lady Anna and James reconcile their differences, and what lessons do they learn throughout their journey?

ABOUT THE AUTHOR

KAREN TUFT was born with a healthy dose of curiosity about pretty much everything, so as a child she taught herself to read and play the piano. She studied music composition and graduated in music theory, both of which came in surprisingly handy when she began writing fiction. She has written three contemporary romances and several Regency romances, including the popular Jennings series, as well as short stories and articles. Among her varied interests, she likes to figure out what makes people tick, wander through museums, and travel—whether it's by car, plane, or paperback.

Facebook.com/karen tuft
Instagram.com/kktuft
x.com/KarenTuft